NIGHT & CALL

The Walking Shadows series
Book One: Night Call

THE WALKING SHADOWS

NIGHT &CALL

BRENDEN CARLSON

DUNDURN
TORONTO

Publisher: Scott Fraser | Acquiring editor: Rachel Spence | Editor: Allison Hirst
Cover design and illustration: Sophie Paas-Lang

Library and Archives Canada Cataloguing in Publication

Title: Night call / Brenden Carlson.
Names: Carlson, Brenden, author.
Description: Series statement: The walking shadows
Identifiers: Canadiana (print) 20190184353 | Canadiana (ebook) 20190184361 | ISBN 9781459745797 (softcover) | ISBN 9781459745803 (PDF) | ISBN 9781459745810 (EPUB)
Classification: LCC PS8605.A7547 N55 2020 | DDC C813/.6—dc23

We acknowledge the support of the Canada Council for the Arts and the Ontario Arts Council for our publishing program. We also acknowledge the financial support of the Government of Ontario, through the Ontario Book Publishing Tax Credit and Ontario Creates, and the Government of Canada.

Care has been taken to trace the ownership of copyright material used in this book. The author and the publisher welcome any information enabling them to rectify any references or credits in subsequent editions.

The publisher is not responsible for websites or their content unless they are owned by the publisher.

VISIT US AT

 dundurn.com |  @dundurnpress | dundurnpress | dundurnpress

Dundurn
1382 Queen Street East
Toronto, Ontario, Canada
M4L 1C9

For my grandparents,
who made this all possible.

Technological progress has merely provided us with more efficient means for going backwards.

— *Aldous Huxley*

CHAPTER 1

A NOTORIOUS WOMAN with whom I am well acquainted once told me, "Always strike a man when he is down. Give him no reason to think that he may stand and reciprocate."

As I lay on the asphalt, I considered myself lucky that no one was nearby, and luckier still that few people shared that principle.

What should have been a simple drop down a garbage chute had ended badly. I'd been expecting to land in a pile of garbage — I didn't mind what was in the bags, so long as it was soft — but instead, the curved handle of the trash bin had hit the right side of my spine, colliding with my ribs. Momentum had carried me farther, and I'd rolled to the left and tumbled out of the bin onto the asphalt.

The sight of the Plate to the east, beyond the alleyway, indicated to me that I was still alive. There were worse things in this life, I supposed. The drop into the bin might have killed me, had the garbage chute not curved and subsequently slowed my fall.

Something crashed and banged down the chute after me. My Diamondback revolver bounced off the overturned rubbish bin and landed square on my chest, reminding me to breathe as daggers of pain shot through my body.

"Goddamn …"

A few wheezy breaths later, oxygen filled my lungs once more. I forced my aching body to roll away from the building, away from the shouts of the men rushing down to find me. I wished there was time to relax, to look up at the night sky and the cathartic sight of the stars. That was the only good thing about being in Jersey.

"He's down there! Fuckin' get him!"

The screams brought my mind back to the now and my right hand to my revolver. An Automatic landed on the ground a stone's throw from me, its legs screeching from the impact of the three-storey jump. It was a little over six feet in height, with gangly arms stronger than a man's, a smooth humanoid body, and glowing red eyes that told me this wasn't a factory-floor model. It was programmed to search and destroy. The Automatic straightened and ran toward me. Two pulls of my trigger made two fist-sized holes in the machine. Neural-Interface and servos fell out of its seared chassis.

If these boys had one Red-eye, there was no doubt they had plenty more. I needed to get out of there. Fast.

Even with my back in shambles, I found I could still walk. The passing cars didn't quite drown out the sound of leather soles ringing against iron walkways:

the hunters were on the move. I headed away from the sounds, down the alley to a small side street. I hoped it would prove to be a straight shot to the main street, where I'd parked my car. I needed a speedy getaway.

I turned the corner and pressed my back against the wall, inching my way to the corner of the building. I allowed my head to leave the safety of cover for just a moment to scan the street. My senses immediately exploded: a car screeching, men screaming, and a cacophony of gunfire as .45-calibre rounds skipped across the concrete.

"There's the roach, get him!"

I opened the chamber. Four rounds left and only God knew how many targets. I closed it and readied myself, puffing out my chest to try to crack my back. That fall had really affected my breathing. No using garbage chutes anymore.

"You're gunna pay for killin' the boss, roach! Your little lady is next!"

They wouldn't expect me to start running across the road, I thought. They'd figure I would wait patiently for them to fill me with lead, perhaps.

Switching the gun to my left hand and firing perpendicular to my path, I tried to lay down some covering fire for myself. The heated rounds were designed to kill Automatics, so they were overkill for flesh and bone.

The traitorous mobsters were spreading out on the street; I had little time to aim. One round took out a leg, two hit the screeching car behind them, and the final bullet cut through a Tommy gun into an assailant's chest. The others fired after me, unable to get a bead on me after I slipped into a nearby alley that ran between two apartment complexes. It was long enough to be a no man's land between me and my pursuers.

The job had called for only one corpse; the gunmen didn't need to die, too. But neither did I need them following me around after tonight. I cracked the cylinder open and dropped the empties onto the concrete as I slammed myself into the wall for cover. The scattering shells sounded like wind chimes, though it was hard to hear with my deafened ears.

The extra bullets were in my left pocket. Thankfully, I hadn't landed on them during my fall — that would've hurt like hell. The Brunos' footsteps got louder as I fed each round into the revolver. They were advancing slowly, firing into the alley now and then to see where I was, or maybe to intimidate me. But unlike them, I'd been in the War; being surrounded by machine gun fire was my bread and butter.

Looking back over to the street, through the buildings, I caught a glimpse of the Upper City. Its brightness was blinding even from here. Rotorbirds flew all around the mile-high buildings. The fluorescent and neon lights of the Plate glimmered above in contrast to the pitch black of the Lower City beneath. Jersey was a cesspit, but at least its sky hadn't been stolen.

The only illumination in the alleyway came from a lamppost a few yards away from me, directly in front of the building I had my back to. I pushed myself up tighter to the wall, hoping my body would disappear into the darkness and give me some edge in this fight. The single yellow bulb lit the frosted street and splayed light against the wall opposite me, guiding my eyes to where the Brunos would be coming from. A gust of cold wind hit my face and bare arms. I'd left my jacket at home ... or maybe in the car? I wasn't sure where I left things anymore. But adrenalin kept me warm.

I carried my weapon in my right hand now, and I lifted it as I braced myself against the cool brick. All seven .38 rounds were ready to find places to park themselves. I pulled the hammer back, hearing the mechanisms inside switch. Just like a cowboy gun: single-action, built for speed.

The three Brunos were well equipped, but stupid and blinded by rage as they appeared at the mouth of the alleyway. Maybe they were expecting to see me running farther down the alley, making it easy for them. They caught a glimpse of my gleaming steel a moment too late; my finger was faster than their arms. Moments later, they were lying on the bloody street, and another seven rounds were gone from my weapon.

My head was rocking with the blasts, which had been amplified in the enclosed space.

I walked up to the trio of corpses and reached down to grab the leader's Tommy gun. The M1929 was a good advancement on the classic design of the submachine gun. Unfortunately for these boys, weapons had no loyalty. The gunman who'd been spitting out insults earlier was at my feet now. He looked like any Mafia Bruno — pale skin, thick beard, short hair, dark coat. His guts were spilling out, but he was still kicking.

"You should be dead ... asshole. You're a roach, a bug to her. She don't give a ... shit about you. You killed your best chance ... of getting out of this game ..."

"It's Roche, you fuck." I took the magazine out and used the last round to end his story with a period. *Roach.* The bastards were brave to be calling me that.

I headed north to find my car. The sudden silence, calming and eerie, helped me to think as I walked.

My burgundy Talbot was a bit scuffed up from the salt on the roads, but it still looked finer than any other car in this part of town. I opened the trunk, loaded my last seven rounds into my revolver, and threw it inside. I'd felt my trigger finger taking over, and I wanted to leave it to cool for a while.

I got in the car, letting my body melt into the leather upholstery. Laying my head against the steering wheel, I felt the adrenalin pouring out of me, the heat radiating off my face. Pain came soon after, from the pulsing lump on my forehead. I heard a faint knocking on the hood of my car. Two knocks. Twice.

I looked up, but there was no one there. Someone, however, had left me a gift in the form of a small envelope under the windshield wiper. It was unsealed, unsigned, and had some green sticking out of the flap. The street was well lit, but I didn't bother looking around for the boys who'd dropped it; I knew that I wouldn't see them. I reached out my open window and grasped the envelope tightly, then opened it to reveal a wad of cash: three thousand, as promised.

"Damn, you're fast," I said to no one in particular.

The Iron Hands had faith in me; that was why she was willing to pay big rainy day funds like this — or maybe she just didn't mind paying extra to get traitors dealt with fast. Either way, job done, money paid. Since I was in Jersey, I had a friend to visit. Plus, I had to get far away from the Heights, else it wouldn't be just the cops who would make my night hell.

———

The Talbot was humming nicely as I rolled up to a small house on Palisade and parked near the front door. As I got out, I realized my back was still fucked from the fall into the garbage bin. I knocked, and seconds later, Patrick Sinclair cracked open the door, his brow furrowed.

"El. You're late."

"Had work to do. Scotch."

Sinclair opened the door wide and let me in. A couple boys from work were already there, sitting at the kitchen table. Sinclair placed a glass in my hand. Before drinking the amber liquid, I pressed the cool glass against my cheek, feeling the sting from the knuckle I took to the face.

I kept playing the scenes over and over in my head to convince myself I'd gotten the job done: Getting caught and dragged in. Hiding my gun somewhere they wouldn't look. Getting pulled up in front of the boss. Taking a bit of a beating while they pulled teeth for information — Bruno on the left, Red-eye on the right. Breaking Bruno's arm. Throwing the machine off balance. Sending one bullet to the boss's head. Getting out.

The fire escape had been my first choice of exit, but because they'd been especially wary of me — I guessed they'd recognized me — the garbage chute had had to do. Boss killed, mess cleaned up, done deal. Still, I felt as if I was forgetting something …

"Roach? You want a hand?"

I lifted my eyes immediately at mention of the insect. The Blue-eye at the table brought me back to the present. I should take a sip from the glass that was soothing my wound.

"Deal me in."

———

Every Sunday poker night was the same: I lost most of the pot, then I got it all back, if only just enough to make a buck or two.

I sat with my glass of Scotch and a dart in my right hand, two cards in my left: King and Jack. To my left sat Paddy Sinclair, still antsy, tapping the tops of the two cards stacked together in his hand. Reynolds, a desk sergeant with too much time on his hands and not enough balls, sat across the table from me, trying to decide whether to fold or to stay in. And to my right sat our Automatic friend Tobias, Toby for short, the one Blue-eye I knew that could swear like a sailor. The metal man scanned the room and the cards with its blue bulbs, the lenses reflecting the light from the lamp hanging over us.

Sinclair always had this wild look about him, though it was only in his eyes. Clean-shaven with side-parted hair, at first glance he looked like a pretty boy from one of those military posters. He'd served for long enough to earn that look, too. He had broad shoulders and a bit more beef than the average guy on the street. With his classic New York accent, he was the golden boy of the 5th Precinct, and one of the few people I trusted there. I wished he'd stop wearing that damn polka-dot tie, though. He looked ridiculous.

"I ever tell ya guys what kinda case I handled on Friday night?"

Sinclair always started a story when he had a bad hand, trying to get us to fold by acting confident. He thought he was clever, but I'd caught on. I couldn't say the same of the other two at the table, though.

We all sighed and groaned. The Automatic's white pupils rolled in its blue eyes, and the buzzing electrodes of its voice box emitted a flanged, metallic voice: "Paddy, I couldn't care less about who you locked up. Play the goddamn game."

"Well, ya should care, because we got a Blue-eye who was runnin' some shipments across the border. It thought it could hollow out its carapace and slide in some bottles, sneak 'em over through the Lower City to Pennsylvania, and make a quick buck. That metal man is one of the reasons the politicians are getting wary of ya, Toby."

"Cute, asshole. You ain't looking so high and mighty with that in your hand." Toby pointed a metal finger to the snifter Sinclair held gingerly. He downed its contents and slid the glass under the table. "Don't you be ragging on us Blue-eyes," Toby continued. "There's not many of us left who haven't been turned off to be your little lapdogs."

"Easy, man, easy. Simple jab is all. Besides, ya can't catch me with this here alcohol."

"And why not?"

"No evidence, no crime." Sinclair laughed, and I couldn't help but chuckle a bit. "Exactly the logic the Blue-eye had when it got caught crossing from here to Penn. Except, unlike me, it didn't have to try too hard to hide what it was carrying, seeing as the goods were already out of sight. But, eh, stereotypes aside, no one trusts Blue-eyes these days."

"All right, get on with it." Toby looked at me with an expression I'd thought only humans could make in the face of something stupid.

I stifled another chuckle.

"Glassware, fine dinner plates — a lot of clutter, mostly covered in silver and gold. It was posing as a 'shipment official' for some tableware company near the docks. No idea where it got a story like that, since it was as far from a harbour as it's possible to be."

"Let me guess," Toby said. "They didn't catch on that it had booze, no matter how many times they roped it back into a cell?" Toby had fallen right into another of Sinclair's old tricks, getting caught up by the story.

"They hadn't a clue. It did this for months — until this Friday, that is, when it wasn't so lucky. It had passed through customs fine, but I got roped into Automatic screening on the Washington that day. This Automatic rolled in, and maybe it forgot to put extra padding in there to keep the bottles from knockin' around, because when it kept clinkin' after it set its luggage down, we knew somethin' was up."

"And what was the padding?" I had to ask. Lord knew if the Automatic was carrying something valuable, it would stuff as many illicit things alongside the booze as possible. I took a sip of Scotch and put the glass to my cheek again.

"Silica beads and oil. The metalhead was runnin' alcohol and cheap Automatic fluid over the border. Sounds like somethin' Toby might start doing soon, eh?"

"Too bad I couldn't have gotten some of that before you locked him up. That shit's expensive." Toby rotated its arms, and a faint creaking could be heard.

"Then ask for some, man. Y'know I'm a good cop. Good to the law and to my friends." Sinclair pulled a sealed plastic bag from the inside of his jacket and threw it into the pot. The tiny white beads and thick, viscous fluid inside the bag sloshed as it knocked over several piles of chips. "If you can win it, that is."

"Anytime, copper." Toby lifted its eyebrows in a sort of smirk, as its mouth wasn't capable of that expression — though it was quite adept at swallowing shot after shot.

Reynolds spoke up. "You up to anything, Roche?" He was a bigger guy — not unfit, but he definitely enjoyed his chair at work. No receding hairline, though — not yet, anyway. "Any crazy stories from your Night Calls? You look a smidge worse for wear tonight."

I did my best to keep the feeling of dizziness at bay as I tried to think of something. Night Calls had been sparse recently, but they were always interesting.

"Things are slow in my line of work … mostly. A couple weeks ago I was hunting down a guy who'd been running an Automatic prostitution ring for some hard cash. Hell, his excuse was 'It's the Depression; I'll get my money however I want.'"

"And how's that special in any way? Come on, when we were partners in '23, we busted at least a dozen a month," Sinclair piped up. He always loved hearing about the shit that the bigwigs from the 5th put me through. "The call girls were more human than Automatic, though, back in those days ..."

"While I was running this op, I realized I had to get close to this guy without him noticing me in any way. I spent weeks tailing all his escorts and call girls, mapping out their positions, until I found out which ones worked right out of his hideout. A few days later I went in, looking as legit as I could."

"What do you mean by *legit*?" Toby asked.

"Legit as in looking as inconspicuous as I can in a whorehouse."

"I don't get it."

I rolled my eyes. You had to spoon-feed information to these things. I wondered how they ever got work done without someone holding their hands.

Sinclair began to laugh. "You telling us you pitched a robot?"

I couldn't keep from grinning at that point. "Yeah, I pitched a robot. Then afterward, while the metal bird was counting the change I gave it, I busted the guy in his office, with my pants still around my ankles. You should've seen his face."

The table erupted in laughter. Sinclair put his face in his hands, trying to catch his breath. I had to laugh at that, too. My face hurt from smiling. We had to take whatever joy we could get these days. Even Toby laughed — after having the joke spoon-fed to it, that is.

After a while, we all died down, and the game was still standing motionless where we'd left it. Looking at the clock, I saw that it was tomorrow already; Sunday had turned to Monday, and my body was informing me that it was ready to go limp for a while after my little adventure.

"Shit, guys, I gotta roll. I got things to catch up on." I lifted myself from the chair as everyone shot out a sound of disappointment.

"C'mon, Roche, another hand?" Sinclair complained. "Or another smut story?"

"Can't. You know how it goes."

"If only I did. I'd rather be doin' what you do instead of pushin' paperwork for scraps." He chuckled glumly.

I nodded. He'd kill me if he knew how much I made these days, in this economy.

I bid them goodbye as I left the kitchen and passed through the front door, which led to a yard covered in dying grass. The blades crunched and crackled under my shoes as I strolled past the open gate and over to my car. I started the engine, listening to it hiccup and sputter for a few moments before quieting itself.

I stared out the window at the sleepless city as I began to drive. Jersey. Of all fucking places, Sinclair had to live in Jersey. Still, Union was a nice little town, and thankfully it was far enough away from the recent bloodbath.

I drove eastward, heading toward the Lower City and home. During the drive I had another distant glimpse of the Plate. I lost sight of the towering monstrosity for some time while passing through the Lincoln Tunnel, but it was much closer once I reached the other end.

I had to admit that the Plate was looking lovely this morning — a floating steel slab that held an entire city above our heads, mocking us silently, though the red and blue flickering lights along its support catwalks did look like stars twinkling in the darkness. Everything in the Lower City revolved around that damn piece of metal: billboards, skyscrapers, jobs, everything. But at least the Plate relied on us for support; the entire slab rested on several Control Points built out of taller buildings, including GE, the Empire, and even my own apartment building.

But the Plate wasn't enough to distract me from the filth of the Lower City. People there were robbed of hope, robbed of sunlight, living in eternal darkness. The prostitutes didn't work specific hours, and Mob killings weren't saved for the dead of night. Hell, even when the city lights went on at six in the morning, it still seemed damn dark. Nothing was as it should be down here. And because the sun was blocked from us twenty-two hours of the day — we got sunrise and sunset — we never really woke up from this enduring nightmare. We hadn't woken up since the Plate had been built.

The alcohol made me feel as if I were floating, and everything that had happened last night was coming through in flashes of lucidity. The only reason I didn't crash my car into a building was because my muscle memory helped me hit the brakes just in time.

My legs somehow pulled the rest of me out onto the sidewalk, and I stumbled past an empty street meat cart toward my building. I rode the elevator up to my floor and arrived in my apartment shortly afterward;

I didn't remember opening my door or locking it, for that matter.

Hot flashes — my mind was starting to go. I hadn't had that much to drink, had I? Last time I'd counted, I'd had a couple glasses of Scotch. Or were they bottles?

In my stupor and exhaustion, my body seemed to think the floor would be more comfortable than the couch, and I didn't have much power to protest as I collapsed. Not even the ringing phone stopped me.

———

The ringing in my head was overwhelmed by the ringing of my rotary phone. It shook with aggression on the glass and oak table in the centre of the room, claiming my attention before my own pain did. Had it been ringing all morning?

I felt drool running from my cheek and onto the floor. I dragged myself to my feet, stumbling slightly, and grabbed at the table to steady myself. I lifted the receiver off the base of the phone. There was some static as the switchboard operator plugged in a jack on the control board. A distorted voice finally came through.

"I'd like to make a Night Call."

CHAPTER 2

"I SAID I'D LIKE TO MAKE A NIGHT CALL."

The voice sounded professional and hard, even through the rusty technology. Familiar, too — probably Robins or Sinclair. And impatient. I must have blanked for a moment. My brain finally comprehended the words that had come through the speaker as I responded with a cough.

I looked at the calendar to see what day it was. I'd been losing sleep lately. Late nights pounding back bottles had distracted my eyes from the calendar long enough for confusion to set in. From the rough black streaks on the wall calendar, I gathered that it was Monday. The clock beside it said seven o'clock. Seven at night.

"Where?"

"Prince and Greene."

"Twenty minutes."

It was a short drive away, but I needed that time to sober up, or perhaps bleed the hangover out of my body.

I threw on my holster and straightened my outfit, trying to make myself somewhat professional. My holster was pretty light, and I realized I had left my weapon somewhere — again. Hopefully I hadn't put it in the pot last night. It was probably in my trunk. I'd get it later, when I needed it. *If* I needed it.

I stepped out into the hallway. Its condition seemed to grow worse by the day. My own apartment could use some cleaning, too, but it was nowhere near as bad as the neglected halls of this building.

As with all the other buildings that were Control Points for the Plate, everyone took great care to make the office space inside look respectable, as if it belonged in the Upper City. The residential area, however, was another story.

I walked down the hall and waited a few moments for an elevator. When the doors parted, the carriage was already occupied: a Green-eye was standing inside, eyeing me and speaking in its whirrs and buzzes. My hangover distorted every word. Hell, it barely had a brain. It was probably talking about the weather — not that the weather ever changed in the Lower City. A few minutes later, the rusted doors peeled back and we walked out.

The machine left through the revolving doors and joined the swarming sea of humans and Automatics running from or to their jobs.

The metalheads were everywhere; nearly half the foot traffic in this damn city was now machines. The metal men's rusted parts and peeling paint made for a terrible image. The Blue-eyes weren't bad — most of them, anyway — but the damn Green-eyes gave me the willies. Maybe the Blue-eyes were a bit more tolerable because they could think for themselves. But, like Toby had said, there weren't many left after Second Prohibition, when the law had required all Blue-eyes not employed by General Electrics to be made Green, for safety. It was more a sea of green than a sea of chrome.

I stepped out into Chinatown — at least, that was what they'd used to call the area. Nowadays it was called Manhattan's Anchor, because people didn't want to be referring to our main rival in the Automatics industry. Nor did the higher-ups want common folk complaining that the Chinese had once had a firm foothold on American soil.

I bought a newspaper and a hot dog just in front of the building. Yuri still made the best dogs in the city, and always gave me a discount on my nightly refuels at his stand. He was a shortish man, a bit chubby in the cheeks, his weight having suffered from eating his own merchandise. No doubt it was all he could afford. A *privyet* and a *paka* later, I was walking along the crowded street once more.

The newspaper was far less comforting than the street meat and full of the same shit: politics, Plate expansion, threats from China, robotic advancements, crashing stocks. Today there was also a short piece about a Mafia gunfight in the Heights the previous night, with five dead gunmen and no suspects. Nothing unusual in the news — and hopefully there wouldn't be for some time.

I finished the dog and gave the newspaper to the old man who lived on the sixtieth floor as we passed each other. Couldn't remember his name, but he always took a stroll at that hour. Said it cleared his head. Was it Charles? Probably.

The one thing that had improved after they'd forced out the old residents of this neighbourhood was the parking situation. I would be able to move my car to the front of the building, or at least damn close. It beat parking in some skyscraper-like garage.

I reached my Talbot 140 and slipped inside. The leather felt a bit less comfortable than it had the previous night. My car was unique for this side of the city — for this side of the world, for that matter — as most people scraped by with Packards and Fords. I made enough to pay this one off, though it had cost me a small fortune to get it shipped in from France, since it was a concept car.

I'd just had to have it.

I still had sixteen minutes. Sixteen minutes to sober up in the seat's leather embrace. I closed my eyes for a moment, and it was the most heavenly feeling I had experienced in months. I would have nodded off if not for the Green-eye with the buzzer who saw me sleeping in my car.

"Identification, sir?"

It was too formal. It creeped me out. The precincts employed Green-eyes for labour they couldn't be bothered to do themselves, like writing parking and jaywalking tickets — or to be bullet fodder. This one kept staring into me with its green bulbs until I flipped open my coat and reached for my own badge. Not the most convincing fake, but I wasn't trying to convince a human.

After one look, it stiffened up and retracted. "Thank you, sir."

"Any time." My throat was parched. I needed a drink — non-alcoholic. Looking at my watch, I saw I was late. Time flies when you're nursing a hangover.

I started the car. The modified straight-10 engine croaked as exhaust funnelled out. The force of gravity hit me as I pressed my foot on the gas pedal, swerving into traffic to merge with the innumerable black boxes populating the American automobile market.

I knew the Prince well — far too well. After all, I'd often come here back in my heyday. It was half speakeasy, half red-light stop and drop, well known to criminals and cops alike. No one wanted to ruin it, since it was the best place to get liquored up or get laid in Lower Manhattan — the district, not the city. There were far better places in the East Village.

The building itself was taped off by yellow and black. Most of the people on site were either paramedics or recovering victims. The presence of body bags wasn't comforting.

The Night Call had come from the senior officer on scene, Sinclair. He looked a lot more professional in his uniform than he had last night. Or was it this morning? I moved to approach him when one of the lesser cops from the 5th decided to get in my way. I couldn't get mad at the greenhorn, though. Proper procedure, was all. He didn't shove me, didn't yell, but definitely put himself directly in my path. "Sorry, sir, we have a situation. Afraid you won't be able to come near for some time, as —"

"Hoyte! Civilians over there. Keep 'em busy until the ambulances show up," Sinclair snapped at the officer.

The young constable flushed red before running off toward the crowd of people who had previously been enjoying their night, and I resumed my path.

Sinclair pulled a long drag off his cigarette. "You look like hell, Roche. You sure you're good to go?"

"Just fashionably late," I said, stumbling a bit as I tried to jump over the yellow tape. A headache pierced my skull like a buzz saw, making everything more intense: the lights, the smells, the sounds. "Not all of us can fly Rotorbirds, you know. It takes time to travel places." I looked around. "Goddamn, though ... we used to love this place, didn't we? It was only a matter of time, I suppose."

"Yeah. Good girls, they had here. Guess they'll be scroungin' up residence someplace else."

"I just came for the drinks, Paddy. I didn't know what you got into behind closed doors."

Sinclair turned to me, a bit less jovial. "Don't call me that. Not on the job."

"What? I've been calling you that since '16: Ol' Paddy Sinclair." I winked, showing him a grin as he turned away and led me toward ground zero. Was he trying to look good for the new kids out front wrangling the passersby and patrons? Well, if he really wanted to impress them, he shouldn't have called me in. "So, what's the lowdown?" I asked.

"Worse than I can put it." Sinclair led me into the cordoned-off speakeasy — or what was left of it — through the open double doors. It took some time for my vision to adjust to the low light, but soon enough I could make out nooks and tables covered in an assortment of glasses. The smell of alcohol was revolting to me at the moment. But the stench of blood was worse.

I've got to keep it down. Can't throw up on the job.

The second-floor balcony that overlooked the main area looked more torn up than the ground floor; the safety bar at the edge of the landing had been torn from its sockets, twisted and bent like plastic. It was obvious that a Red-eye had done that damage, because no human could. Well, no regular human, and I hadn't seen any Augers outside getting medical treatment.

My eyes were fixed upward on the second floor as I kept walking, until Sinclair's hand on my chest stopped me in my tracks. I looked down and saw the reason for the Night Call. I nearly stepped in it, too.

There were at least half a dozen bodies, all of them dressed well and none of them moving. Blood caked the ground, along with spilled food and drink. Pale skin was visible between folds of black, burgundy, and blue fabric that was stained dark. This wasn't just some hit — it was a massacre, and a particularly ugly one at that. The perp seemed to have taken their time to wreak enough havoc that stomachs would turn at the mere thought of the scene. Some had been shot in the chest, some in the head; others had had limbs blown off and then probably had bled out.

Four men, two women. Two of the men in the centre of the room were well-dressed, with burgundy corduroy jackets, grey slacks, and just enough class to pass for the sort of gangsters the dames swooned over. Then again, maybe it was the holes in them that made them look like pretty authentic mobsters.

"Hit and run?"

"Ain't never that simple," Sinclair said, nudging open one of their jackets with his foot. A buzzer threw its golden gleam at my face. Dead cops. Long case, then. "The patrons started to run outside after the first few shots, and after the gun went automatic, the place was crazy. Supposedly two Red-eyes tore this place a new asshole. One lunatic pulled apart half the joint before it took off. The other stuck around and got canned by the cops that showed up."

"Fifth boys, right?"

He nodded. "No other precinct has the stomach for this sort of crime."

"Where'd the carnage start?"

"Few testimonials said the first Red-eye was up there, shot some poor bastard before throwing him off the landing, fuckin' up the railing." Sinclair pointed upward before kneeling on the floor to look the dead cops in their lifeless eyes. "Second one came in through the doors, started spraying Typewriter bullets, and the rest went down. First cops on the scene were Ozzy and Marv. They put down the second Red-eye by the door. The first one was able to push past, get out onto the street."

"Fuck, that's just bad shit. These the only notable corpses?" I rummaged through the cops' jackets while Sinclair stood and walked over to another male corpse.

The stiff looked like it had been through a blender, and I guessed that he'd had the fortune of being thrown from the rafters.

"Another dead cop here, separate from those ones. Three dead badges is one hell of a haul for the Mob if they were the ones gunning us down. You think they'd use their fuckin' brains pullin' something like this. Killing cops will get you a target on your back in this city."

"Didn't stop Murder, Inc., and it won't stop whoever did this. If the 5th can contain this, they better be quick." I turned over one of the bodies. Thick face, long moustache, clean-shaven everywhere else. The hair on his head was matted down with blood. Even grey and dead, I recognized the stiff. "Shit, I know this fella."

"Yup, 5th Precinct, worked here since the early days. Name on the badge is Travis Barton. The other one is Bill Ewing. Ya probably ran some raids with him over the years."

"Never did, but I saw him in the station a while back. What about the third fella?"

"ID says Marco Coons, undercover for the 11th. I gave them a ring. Waitin' for them now."

I let the grey head roll back to its relaxed position. It felt weird touching a corpse again. Like touching a robot, but squishier, stranger. Like stepping into a house that had recently been occupied and bustling each day. A husk that shouldn't be a husk.

The guy from the 11th's wounds weren't that bad, all things considered. One shot to the gut, another to the shoulder, and several broken ribs and ruptured organs from the throw. So the first machine hadn't been as trigger-happy as the second one — interesting.

"There's hell to pay for a cop killing in the 5th. Everyone in the Lower City knows that, I'm sure. You've dealt with cop killers before. Why did you need to call *me* in?"

Sinclair beckoned me over. In a small corner half-way between the stiffs and the door was a riddled husk of an Automatic, its limbs twisted and mangled, its boxy head dented in all the wrong places, wires poking out, the Tesla Battery inside trying to power the broken machine. He grabbed the lifeless head — lifeless wasn't the most accurate word to use — and forced it open, revealing the Automatic's brain. And therein lay the problem: there wasn't one. The Neural-Interface was missing, which meant that this machine shouldn't have been walking, let alone shooting up a speakeasy.

"Fuck," I managed to croak out.

Sinclair pulled out a second dart and lit it, replacing the old stub in his lips, and refilling his lungs with fresh tobacco. And him always saying he'd quit smoking. "Fuck is right. Put it together: dead cops, slaughtered patrons, two Red-eyes, and a dead perp with no head? I've heard of cops chasing ghosts, but this is pushin' it."

I rubbed the back of my head. I wished I'd stayed in school before the War. Might have learned a thing or two to help me. "That's one way of putting it. Fuck if I know anything about Automatics. Shouldn't you defer to Red-eye Law?"

"Red-eye Law still requires a human to be present to take the blame, and a Neural-Interface present to tell us who did it. We have nothin' other than the shell, which is less than useful. Fuckin' Grifter capek." He kicked the empty-headed Automatic, causing it to lurch a bit, then walked around to try to ease the pain in his toe. I was surprised. Sinclair wasn't usually one for vulgarity.

"What'd the other Automatic look like? Anyone get a description?"

"A few of the patrons got a look, but nothin' concrete." He pulled out a small notepad from his pocket. Probably not his, though; he wasn't the type for writing things down. "Uh … six feet, rusted, red eyes obviously, older model. Some said a Swinger model, but those are pretty rare these days."

"Anything else?"

"Nothing else. We're runnin' on nothin' but gut feelings." Sinclair wiped his brow. Sweat was beading on his forehead, even though the place was freezing now that the doors were open to the November air. "Keep this on the DL, 'specially now. When it comes to the Automatic trade, things pick up in December. People try to smuggle shit in from China during the Christmas confusion. Talk to Robins. This is fresh news, and I need to hide their buzzers before the other boys outside start spreadin' shit …"

Sinclair didn't get the chance to finish his thought. Tires screeched, doors slammed, and Constable Hoyte was heard trying to assert his authority. Whoever had arrived must have superseded him, however, and their approaching footsteps told me that they meant business. I bent down over the dead Automatic and reached behind its head as I searched for its serial number, something Sinclair wouldn't have thought to look for. Whoever had programmed the Red-eye had stupidly left it on. A quick pull ripped it from the metal, and I stuffed it into my pocket.

Through the open doors of the speakeasy came a small collective of men and women in black suits. They spread out through the area, covering every possible angle and corner. A man who looked more important than the rest approached me and Sinclair. He was tall and quite lanky, with a receding hairline and stubble on his chin. Dark glasses were a nice touch — an attempt to look imposing, I guessed.

"Officers, please remove yourselves from the area. This crime scene is now under the jurisdiction of the Automatic Crimes Unit of the FBI, as denoted in section six, subsection four of the Automatic Rights Charter."

Sinclair and I weren't convinced. My friend was still puffing on his dart, and I readied my stance a bit. The G-man's blank face made him seem almost as dead as the stiffs on the floor.

Sinclair spoke first, dropping his dart and crushing it with the toe of his shoe. "You got a name, boy?"

"Agent Masters." I snickered, and he snapped his head around to look at me. "Need I repeat myself, officers?"

"No, sir," I snarled, putting my hand on Sinclair's shoulder to urge him forward. I could have stayed and flexed some muscle, but Robins would have had my head if I pissed off any Black Hats. I followed Sinclair out, with Agent Masters's glasses still tracking me as I exited the speakeasy onto the cold street.

"If it weren't a Night Call before, it would be now," I said.

Sinclair rounded up his officers, yelling to them to pack up and get out of the Black Hats' way. "Hope you got some ideas, Roche. We're runnin' on borrowed time now," he said.

"I got a plan," I said. "It's stupid, but it might pay off." He didn't need to know any more than that lest the G-men "question" him and try to pull information he wouldn't give willingly. This way, both our asses were covered. "I've got to see Robins first."

"Get this news to him quick, before he gets blind-sided by it. Be safe out there, Roche." Sinclair started toward his unit, grinding his teeth.

"Paddy, one last thing." He turned back to me with a look of impatience. "The Swinger model Red-eye had enough trigger discipline to shoot only one target, then let another machine cover its escape with .45-calibre bullets. Regular Red-eyes ain't this precise. They'd have filled Coons through with holes. This was some top-notch police programming it had to put holes that clean into two targets."

"Police programming is pretty good these days, El. What else do you want me to say?"

"No, it isn't this good. This is custom … I know this programming."

Sinclair looked up at me, his gaze lingering, trying to draw my eyes to meet his own. "El … he's dead."

"I'm not so sure, given the evidence."

I decided to make myself scarce after that.

Dodging the gaze of the other officers on scene, I slid into my car. I stabbed the key in and turned it, and the engine roared to life, crying in anguish. I felt eyes on my back, but not Sinclair's. No, I felt watched. I hadn't had dead cops on my plate for years — two years, to be exact — and I'd rather it had stayed that way. Something about this gave me the chills. Maybe it was the pressure, or maybe the hangover. That evidence didn't calm my mind, either.

I couldn't get it out of my head: a gut shot and a secondary one up higher. Perfect double tap, something only implemented by old police programming. Swinger model, too. The Automatic I was thinking about had died a while ago — I knew that for a fact — but tech was improving every day. Its body was probably long gone, but the Neural-Interface could have been saved, along with the programming that I myself had made sure was in there. But, hell, if that dead machine at the scene was any indication, Automatics didn't need Neural-Interfaces to kill anymore. That wasn't a pretty thought.

Could it be him?

It, I mean. Not him.

Sinclair gave me a wave as I punched the car into gear and ran it down the street. The Talbot was purring, but creaking as well. It sounded like it was struggling to survive, just like me, or my career. I'd have to check the car, maybe do some repairs.

Eventually.

CHAPTER 3

WHOEVER HAD SENT THOSE RED-EYES to tear up that speakeasy was either brave and stupid, or smart enough to know that they could get away with it if they played it close to the precinct. After all, the 5th was only a stone's throw from ground zero. The precinct had gotten under the skin of quite a few organizations — especially the Mob — which made nearly anyone in southern Manhattan a suspect. Still, while too many people had it out for us, far fewer had the means to pull off something of this calibre.

I coasted up to the front of the 5th Precinct and cut the engine. I always forgot how tall the actual building was. I still expected to see the tiny, three-floor office it had been in my childhood. The 5th was one of the few buildings in the area whose top hadn't been cleared for wireless power services. Instead, it boasted a helipad to accommodate a Rotorbird. The air was still and silent at the moment, meaning the vehicle was absent. It was a useful contraption for cops to zip across town from SoHo to Greenwich faster than a bullet.

Traffic was thinner in this area, maybe because people didn't want to get in the 5th's way, or maybe because this was one of the many backwater streets forgotten by the ever-shifting populace. It was dark down here, so deep in the Lower City that a lot of lights were needed. One of the lights outside the station was burnt out again. Or was it the same one I'd noticed months back? I walked up with some difficulty, tripping a few times on the cracked sidewalk.

The station was bustling with activity. The interior was the same as it had been back in the '20s, with wooden door frames and asbestos ceilings. It had a charm that had always made me happy when I'd worked here. Stepping through the glass doors into the central area, I nearly toppled over a small trash bin. Thankfully, my blunder went unnoticed by the apathetic cops nearby.

The corridor to the right of the central area led to Commissioner Robins's office. The wooden door at the far end of the hall looked darker than it had before, possibly because it had been painted over, or maybe due to rot. Light poured through the crack under the door, and I could hear people talking. Robins would kill me if I interrupted something important, so I took the opportunity to head to the bathroom and make myself somewhat presentable.

Inside the tiny washroom was a porcelain sink, a toilet, filthy tiles, and a blinking light that begged to be replaced. It was bright enough for me to make out my reflection, at least. I placed my hands on the edge of the sink and let my head hang for a few minutes, trying to collect myself.

I turned the taps on and splashed water into my face, watching the dried blood and soot of last night run down the drain, before looking up into the mirror.

I almost didn't want to.

My jaw was a bit worse for wear, but it was still square and sharp. A thick mat of hair covered much of my face, going down to my neck, though some sloppy shaving had cleaned up the area under my chin somewhat. I should shave again soon. My cheeks were sunken and gaunt, reminding me that I needed to start eating properly again. My hair was a little long, but it had some style to it. The cut on my cheek was scabbing over and looked far better after the wash.

The cuffs of my polo shirt were a smidge looser now. Losing muscle mass was the one sign I'd told myself I wouldn't ignore. Just looking at myself made my stomach grumble in dissatisfaction. I'd grab something to eat after meeting with Robins.

The slam of a door told me that Robins's visitor had left. As I headed out, I caught sight of the long greying hair of the woman storming from Robins's office. I retreated back into the bathroom and held my breath as her heavy footsteps approached, then turned to leave. Who knew the director of the FBI would take such an interest in the 5th?

I had a feeling I wouldn't have to tell Robins what had happened at Prince and Greene.

I emerged once more and made for Robins's office. The slammed door had blown open again. Robins sat down in his chair with a thud, his overweight body making the chair creak and groan as he settled in. He was a man who loved his job, though you wouldn't have suspected it, looking at him now. He froze when he saw me and licked his lips in preparation to speak.

"I tried to get here quickly," I interjected, and was met with a groan.

"Yeah. Not fast enough. You would have been a good chew toy for Greaves instead of me."

I closed the door behind me and fell into one of the chairs in front of his desk, which was as dishevelled as I was: papers here and there, open folders, and his M1911 resting on top of several files, one of which was mine, I saw from a quick glance. He definitely needed some time off, and I was about to tell him so when his low voice shut me down.

"What the hell are you doing here, Elias? You only come to the station when I call you or when you need something. And seeing as I haven't called you, I'm really not in the mood for the second option."

"Paddy gave me the ring about the shooting."

"Shooting?" *Shit.* Maybe the FBI director hadn't been here about that. "What shooting?"

"Speakeasy at Prince and Greene. Two Red-eyes tore up the place. Three dead patrons and three dead cops, two of them from the 5th."

"In the shop or on the street?" The way he said this gave me the impression he was more accustomed to the latter.

"The shop. A few hours ago, maybe earlier. I'm surprised you haven't heard anything."

"There's too much to hear in this city, especially these days. I can barely focus on one thing before getting jostled into another fiasco. I thought people would be smart enough not to kill cops *near* the 5th, let alone cops *from* the 5th."

"You give people in this city too much credit."

"I suppose you're right. For once."

Robins stood and walked over to the window. I knew what he was looking at: that damn fountain. Everyone knew that whenever he felt stressed, he'd eye that stone relic, never mind the fact it hadn't run for years. "We've been setting up a raid on Prince and Greene for a couple months. The cops were probably scouting it out. Of all the times this could happen, did it have to be when fucking federal agents decided to come down to the Lower City for a spell?"

"Ballsy doing it near the 5th. Dead cops are enough to get you a bull's eye painted on you — on the street and in the big house. They might as well have walked right up to the precinct and tried to gun it down."

Robins paced for a while before sitting down at the desk again and putting his head in his hands. He wasn't usually this calm; some days he was like a tsunami. It all came back eventually. "You have any leads?"

"A serial number I haven't yet run. I could use someone to make head or tail of it in the Automatic Division. And —"

"No time," Robins interrupted before I could finish. "I can't have the FBI coming down from their perch to see a former cop running side ops for us. One of the main reasons they're coming is all the recent Automatic crime.

Shootings, stabbings, Mob fights, bootlegging. Red-eyes mostly, though no machine will be off the table when they start their inspections. How do you think they'll react if they spot a serial code search with no records of who looked it up? If they find any connection between us, they'll toss you in prison and cart me off the island."

"That hasn't been an issue before. Either you're getting paranoid, or there's some shit-stirring going on here."

"These FBI agents are everywhere, from the 5th up to the 9th on the Upper West Side. Something poked the nest, and the bees are swarming now. Whatever that something was, they think we caused it — we being the Lower City, of course."

"Of course."

"And the problem is, we don't know what they want. They've pulled a ton of big names from the other precincts up to the Plate for questioning, and I might be next. Were there any agents on the scene?"

"One guy from the Automatic Crimes Unit. Agent Masters."

"What a stupid name," Robins chuckled, leaning back in his chair. "Fuck, it'll get back to her eventually. Then the shit will really start flying."

"We talking about Greaves? Annual inspections, I presume."

"Same time of year — it never changes. Greaves is punctual, I'll give her that. You've got to tread carefully while they're here, especially if they already have agents on the case. One whiff of you near a crime scene they're investigating, and it'll be both our asses. And I'm far too young to retire."

I snickered. In response, his face twisted into a scowl.

"Sorry. Well, in that case, I'll be off to solve this case properly."

"Not so fast. I need a favour."

I groaned. *Fuck.* "I'm already solving a crime for you. Can't you put a hold on it?"

"I really can't. This news has forced my hand. Given the context of your investigation, as well as your reputation for dealing with Black Hats ... well ..." Robins stared at me for some time. Not like he was disappointed with me — I knew that expression quite well. He looked almost concerned. "You won't like me."

"I don't need a reason, but I'll take one regardless."

"If the FBI decide to question you, we need you to look completely legit."

"I agree."

"In every aspect, right down to the badge, which I'll have for you in the next few days."

"Excellent, new badge, whatever. You're stalling. What's your big idea for making me look on the level?"

Robins tapped a device on his desk. A buzz emanated for several seconds, then stopped. After a moment, there was a knock on the door. He got up, walked around the desk, and grasped the door handle before continuing. "You're going to have a partner for the time being."

"What the fuck!" I jumped up so quickly that it knocked my chair back. Robins looked surprised by my reaction, but his expression was resigned.

"Elias, relax."

"Where the hell do you get off slotting me with some pill?"

"If it weren't for that last 'pill,' you'd be dead. You're welcome."

"Are you talking about Joan or Desmond? Because I don't think ride-alongs count as partners. In any case, distracting a guy aiming a Foldgun at me hardly counts as saving my life."

"They took the heat for you, and both of them were found by our patrols wandering around 90th Street, where you always leave them. You can't keep blowing this off. You'll need someone watching your back, so this time, you'll have an *official* partner, like it or not. And if any agents corner you, you can shove the new guy at them, and he'll answer all the questions they shoot your way. Besides, I need him out of here while this investigation into Red-eyes is going on. They won't spare any Automatic — Red, Blue, or Green."

I sat back down. "Speaking of partners ... you interrupted me earlier. There's something else about the killer."

"Other than the serial number?" Robins asked, his hand still resting on the doorknob.

"Yeah. The Red-eye that helped shoot up the place was a Swinger model, quite a strong one to be able to throw an undercover cop across the room, and with pretty precise firearm handiwork, if I do say so myself."

"What are you implying?"

"I mean ... of all the Green-eyes working for the cops and all the Blue-eyes that've been laid off, how many are Swinger models? And how many have custom police programming good enough to pull double taps?"

Robins looked down for a moment, sighing. "Elias, there's no use chasing ghosts ..."

"We never recovered its body, remember? Someone could have repaired it or ripped its NI. It could be James."

"I sincerely doubt that … and you should have led with that information. You are really going to hate me."

He opened the door a crack to regard the person waiting outside, then swung it wide open.

An Automatic walked in and sat beside me, its unblinking blue lights staring straight ahead at the desk. The tension in the air was palpable. This had to be a fucking joke.

"Roche, I'm assigning him" ("It," I interrupted, but he just shook his head and continued) "to be your partner, at least until this case gets resolved and the FBI crawl back up to the Plate. More inspectors from the Upper City are arriving soon, and we really don't need information about this incident being spread around."

"Incident?" The Automatic's head jerked to lock on to Robins.

"A massacre at a speakeasy perpetrated by a couple of Automatics, which makes the precinct a dangerous place for you to be in. Detective Roche here will explain further … away from here." I'd felt him strain to say those words again: *Detective* Roche. I hadn't heard that title for nearly three years.

The Automatic had a strange face. Not the usual egg- or box-shaped head, but one that looked much more human — though the top of its head was flatter and its cheeks were more sunken in than a human's. Rather than the shitty latches and voice boxes the rest of them had, this Automatic had hundreds of joints and servos on its face, making its mouth move

convincingly, even with small twitches. It had gleaming metal skin and steel eyebrows over its blue bulbs.
The unblinking lamps still gave me chills. It was wearing a black suit, a white shirt, and a black tie, dressed
all fine and proper and convincing enough for most
people. It extended a hand to me and waited for me to
reciprocate. I did so reluctantly.

"Elias Roche," I said with as much spite as I could
muster.

"My designation is Forty-One-Echo-November,
Detective Roche." Damn thing had a shrill voice. Not
as monotonous as the other tin men, but with the
same flanging and metallic tone they all had. I hoped it
wouldn't make a habit of calling me "Detective." I kept
an eye on the Automatic as I turned to Robins.

"You're hiring Blue-eyes again? That's going to cause
even more issues with the Black Hats. You forget what
year it is?"

Robins chewed on his bottom lip. "It's a complicated issue, Roche. Let it slide for now. Now, with shit
as tight as it currently is, I'll need both of you off the
grid for a while, which means no arrests, no deaths, no
explosions. Forty-One, Detective Roche over here has
already begun …"

As Robins filled the robot in on the state of things, I
peered at it beside me. I hadn't had an Automatic partner since '28, and I would have liked to have kept it that
way. This thing was just as complacent as the Green-
eyes in the station, hanging on every one of Robins's
words. I couldn't help glaring at it. I wasn't sure whether
it knew I was doing so. These days, the only Automatic

I ever exchanged more than a few syllables with was Toby. I doubted that I could get used to another one. At least Toby and I had a history. This bastard looked fresh off the production line. It looked like the same model as my old partner, which didn't exactly help. It was as if Robins was trying to replace my old partner with this new machine. I shook my head. *I'm getting to the bottom of this, and I won't let this pill chain me down and keep me from doing my job.*

"Elias, are you listening?"

Robins must have known that I wasn't, not with my mind rattling around like this. I responded by standing up, and opening the door to the office. He barked at me to sit down. I looked back for several seconds before walking out.

My body had taken matters into its own hands, removing me from the situation without my brain's consent. Everything was a blur as I entered the main area of the precinct. I couldn't handle this. Maybe it was the hooch or the lack thereof, maybe the metal man, maybe the dead cops. Something was fucking me up.

The yelling from Robins's office continued, and the station's buzz ceased momentarily as everyone within earshot stared at me. Most of the officers were regarding me in shock and awe, astonished that I had the balls to walk away from Robins. I pushed open the front door of the station and walked to my car. Inside, I rolled up the windows all the way, isolating myself from the world.

The relative quiet inside my Talbot was comforting; I heard nothing but the hum of electricity around me.

I preferred sirens and the noise of the city to Robins's office and its occupants right now. Would Robins chase after me? He knew why I'd left. He might try again later, but not now.

Feeling calmer, I lit a dart and rolled the window down to let the smoke escape. There was far too much to think about now, especially with this *partner* bullshit. I hadn't thought Blue-eyes were allowed to work on the Force anymore, which meant that either something weird was going on in the Lower City, or Robins had pulled strings to make this happen. *Welcome to the brave new world of 1933*, I thought.

I had only a minute to myself before the Black Hat walked up to my open window. It was Agent Masters, the lanky asshole who acted as if he had muscles bigger than my head. He bent down to look inside the cabin, stone-faced.

"Disagreement with your boss?" Masters sounded too posh, too pristine, too entitled. Sometimes it was hard to identify FBI agents just by looking at them, but it got easier after they opened their mouths.

"Go foreclose on someone's home, shithead."

"Edgy, are we?" He moved to kneel more comfortably, like he owned me. God, he was irritating. "I could hear him yelling from out here. Anything the matter?"

"Fuck off, G-man."

Masters was actually taken aback by that. But, of course, he had to get in the last word. "It's an odd world we live in, son. You and the rest of the Humanists need to get with the program and realize there are worse things to fear than a soulless machine."

"Such as?"

"A machine with a soul, perhaps. I haven't seen many Blue-eyes working in the Force these days." He placed a hand on the roof of the car and hoisted himself up. He might have a point, but I wouldn't give him the satisfaction of hearing me say so. "Be seeing you, Constable."

I could have retorted, but then he'd have kept talking. I watched him enter the station, probably to tell Robins all about the massacre and how it was "being handled" by the FBI. As laughable as the statement was, Robins would have to keep a straight face so that the real investigation could continue away from the Black Hats' prying eyes. After Masters had disappeared into the precinct, I kicked the Talbot to life and rolled into the street.

FBI, Automatics, cop killings. They were usually few and far between, but when odd things did start to happen, they always piled on top of one another. The first thing I had to do was run that serial number I'd gotten, but I couldn't do it at a police station. I'd have cuffs on me the second I walked into any other precinct besides the 5th. There was only one other place where I could run this number.

Maybe they'd be more helpful. Or at least complacent.

CHAPTER 4

MY DESTINATION WASN'T TOO FAR AWAY, though it took longer than it should have to drive there, what with the traffic that congested the streets day in and day out. You could see it from anywhere in the Lower City. Hell, you could see it from the mainland on some days.

To call the monstrosity that was the GE a "building" almost seemed disrespectful of the engineering that had been required to build it. The square footage of the building encompassed more city blocks than many believed necessary. But it had to be big, since it was the central Control Point for the entire Plate and, therefore, for the Upper City. Looking upward, I could see the massive slab of metal moving downward several dozen meters. Small mechanical spokes acted like fingers as the Plate crawled down the building. The snowfall was late this season, and so the Plate had only now started moving to prepare for the onslaught of snow. If the Plate stayed up as high as it was usually, the sheer weight of the snow would cause mechanical issues. Some regarded this building as a lighthouse for those of less desirable status, bringing money back down to the workers and taxpayers who dwelt alongside me. However, others said it was a wall that blocked them from the sun and from the rich spaces and luscious opportunities of the Upper City, and that corroded the thin line of tolerance drawn between man and machine. After all, GE was the heart of the Automatic market, eclipsing even Detroit.

Beside the main building was a tall structure about half its height: a parkade, one of the largest ever built, for all the people who came to work for GE each day. Parking in there would be inconvenient, though, so I decided to use the executive parking lot, a small gated lot at street level. Both the size and security of the lot could be explained by the fact that not many executives wanted to be caught dead in the Lower City — and I had to agree. This wasn't a place for bigwigs. I opened my glovebox and removed a large aluminum plate that gave me the right to commandeer a spot, placed it on the dash, and exited my car to approach the building on foot. Hopefully if any guards came by to check up on the cars in the lot, they wouldn't look too closely at the numbers on the aluminum plate. One of the security guards patrolling the area spotted me. I flashed my badge, and he gave a nod and let me be. The guard's head was encased in a thick helmet designed to deflect rifle rounds and a similarly thick coating of Kevlar and body armour. I just hoped that the guard was human. GE was the last company in the Lower City that still employed Blue-eyes, so it was possible it could be a bulletproof machine under all that armour.

The lawn in front of the main door of the factory was a dozen meters from the street, with grass that was green and luscious despite the lack of direct sunlight. With the money the company made, it seemed they could afford honest-to-God UV. Night-shift workers were exiting through the main door in the opposite direction to me, going off to scrounge up some street meat during their ten-minute break before returning to their twelve-hour day. GE always touted their dedication to the working class, even going so far as to allow the assembly-line workers to use the building's main entrance, which made them feel more human. And those underpaid slaves needed all the respect they could get.

I crossed under the massive arch of the doorway, whose rustic stonework was peeling away, and a silver and white gleam from the interior shone onto my face. In this area, the old-fashioned and modern architecture of wood and stone had been pushed aside to make way for the steel and white of the Upper City. The foyer of GE felt like the interior of a spaceship from one of those outrageous movies and was a marvel to look at, let alone stand in.

The reception centre sat under a triplet of magnificent statues each more than thirty feet high. The first figure was the CEO of GE, great leader of the Automatic industry and owner of the Upper City J.D. Rockefeller. To the right of his statue was one of a Grifter model Automatic. It looked finer than most Grifters on the street did, with square shoulders, thick limbs, and a Great War rifle in hand. To Rockefeller's left was a figure representing the company's past: the Manual, a war on two legs, father of the Automatic, and now obsolete. It was significantly scaled down; most Manuals had been far larger than the statue and bristling with enough firepower to take down a trench single-handed. The Manual had been the saviour of Europe back in the War, with Henry Ford taking the reins mass producing the war machine for the Allies. Of course, when the money-hungry bastard had wanted to keep the War going for his own benefit, Rockefeller stepped in, and so one era was pushed aside for another — Manual for Automatic.

Underneath the statues was a monstrous plaque that read, *From past to future, blood and metal, science and spirit.*

I wasn't too fond of coming here. As I approached the desk, the receptionist peered up at me, irritated at being made to look up from her paperwork.

"Yes?" She had a thick Brooklyn accent, sounded like a showgirl from one of the theatres around town. Maybe this was a part-time job to help her pay rent or for other amenities. There was no uniform required at GE, and I knew the suit she was wearing was far too expensive for her to have purchased on her own dime.

"Detective Roche." I flashed her the badge. She had no way of knowing it wasn't my number on the front. "I need access to your Automatic database. Official police business."

"Sorry, no can do." She turned to the terminal next to her and started clicking on the metal keyboard until I cleared my throat to get her attention again. She looked back to me with annoyance — a look I knew well.

"This is official police business, and I'm demanding access."

"You can have all the access you want ... down here. But unless you know how to go through that database — which you don't — or unless there's someone on duty who can — which there isn't — you ain't getting in and you ain't doin' your job until tomorrow."

She turned away before I could respond, so I placed the badge back in my pocket and retreated from the desk. Away from her gaze, I circled the desk and found a small directory on the wall, which I scanned until I found what I needed: Depository and Database Access, floor fifty-three. The only way to get up there was for me to be an assembly-line worker or a Tinkerman. Thankfully, both types of employees used the same elevators. I definitely couldn't pass for a Tinkerman, but I sure fit the bill as a worker. Thank Rockefeller for saving costs by not allotting separate elevators.

I leaned against one of the walls in the main foyer, taking my time scanning for workers. While I waited, I examined the strip of metal bearing a serial number that I'd removed from the dead Automatic. It was remarkably intact, as though it had already begun to peel away before I'd torn it off. What sort of idiot Mob Tinkerman would have left it on? Maybe they'd just forgotten. But something about that idea didn't sit right with me.

I planned my route carefully. I had to slip into the stream of returning workers nonchalantly, lest the receptionist catch a glimpse of me gaining "access." As the train of dirty men approached, I began walking forward and grabbed one aside as we slowed down, making sure he saw the glimmer of my badge before he called for assistance. The man had a gaunt face, thin arms, and dirty overalls. Poor bastard could have been in his thirties or his fifties — I wasn't sure.

The only way into the elevator was with a temporary access card workers received every morning at roll call. I slipped a twenty into his hand and he passed me his card, as I'd known he would. I joined the line of workers funnelling into the main elevator, flashing my card in front of the blue light just outside the doors. A high-pitched chime confirmed that it had been successfully scanned. I entered and asked the elevator operator — he looked slightly less dishevelled than everyone else — to press the button for level fifty-three as the elevator shot upward with intense speed.

GE had tech the world wouldn't see for years. Though their cameras were rudimentary, anyone running security would know something was up if they saw someone looking like me on a technician-only floor. Once I got up there, I'd have little time to try getting in and out unscathed.

I felt like a bullet shaken in a barrel as the elevator stopped intermittently to let workers exit at various floors to get to their stations. Whenever the silver door slid open, I could see presses, assembly lines, power tools, Tesla Batteries — the works. The air that seeped inside the elevator as it stopped at each floor was rank and smelled of oil, making me choke. I got a suspicious look from the elevator operator. Probably most everyone who worked here was accustomed to the air by now. But before long, the doors slid apart at my destination. I exited as though I knew where I was going, trying to look confident for the benefit of anyone who might be spying on me. In truth, I had no clue where I was going.

The sound of typing emanated from most of the small offices that lined the many corridors sprouting away from the elevator doors. Most of the people there looked to be catalogue workers, who made sure that every metal man pushed out or brought in was accounted for. Directly across from the elevator was a solid glass wall and a set of double doors leading to a mainframe. I could have walked right in and used that main terminal, but someone accessing it at this time of night might arouse suspicion. Instead, I found my way into an empty office. Tinkerman offices were often the largest on a floor, so didn't take much effort to find one.

The office I'd chosen was close to the elevator and about twelve feet square, with a large, boxy terminal and a lamp sitting on an L-shaped desk. The rest of the desk's real estate was covered in loose papers, which made the room feel smaller than it really was. I sat at the chair and booted up the green-screened terminal. A blinking white box appeared, prompting me for my identification. While the guy's identification was easy to find on some of the forms on his desk, the password was trickier. Typing *PASSWORD* elicited exactly the response I'd expected: *Access Denied*. Looking for some clue, I glanced again at the letters from his wife and reminder notes strewn about the desk. Tinkermen were notorious for wasting their lives at their jobs, and yet this one was away from his office at the moment. I found out why when I discovered the lawyer's bills; the amount due made my paycheck look like small potatoes.

I spied a small button labelled *ASSISTANCE* on the side of the terminal's keyboard. I jammed my thumb into it and waited a minute or two until a Green-eye let itself into the office. Most of its body was stripped down to basics, with a very simple base and limbs. The friendly, simple design made people feel safe. Quite the opposite of the Grifter statue downstairs.

"May I be of assistance, Mr. McEwen?"

"I need access to the — I mean, to *my* terminal, but I've forgotten my password."

I should have thanked my lucky stars that these assistance models were dumber than most. They were built without visual recognition to reduce costs. The Automatic plugged a small cord from its palm into the terminal and turned to me.

"I need confirmation of your identity, sir. Access code?"

"Password?"

"Incorrect."

Why had I thought a second time that that would work? My eyes fell on the lawyer's bill, which included the name of the guy's wife. "Beatrice?"

"Correct, sir. Thank you." He retracted from the terminal and slid out the door to parts unknown. I guessed the fellow in this office wouldn't have the same access code for much longer.

I made sure the machine was gone before I started searching the directory for the serial number. Hundreds of lines of code ran in front of my eyes, and my body tensed up from the onslaught of information. I had far more respect for those Tinkermen now. I'd never done this alone. They performed such searches in mere seconds, which now seemed like a miracle. A few lucky clicks of the keys to select anything saying *serial* or *number*, and the white rectangle finally lit up, blinking to signal me to input orders. I pulled out the small strip and entered the Automatic's serial number into the terminal. After several moments, the computer spit out a list of information: the Automatic was listed with the model code RU-D1, and had been bought two years ago by Johann Jaeger of Jaeger's Electrics in SoHo.

Jaeger. That was a name I hadn't heard in a while. I wondered if it was the same man I'd used to know.

No matter. I had what I came for. I shut down the terminal and left the office. Just as I was about to press my thumb on the down button, the elevator car arrived with a chime, and the silver doors parted to reveal two men in uniform. Not cops — GE hated having police on their premises — but security guards.

All three of us froze — the guards were surprised that I had gone for the elevator, like an idiot, and I was surprised at how much faster their response time was. I looked behind me for a way out, but heard them draw their weapons from their holsters. The guns were only for show, though. I knew they wouldn't fire while civilians were on the floor. I was another story altogether.

It was too bad my own revolver wasn't in my holster. Then again, I wouldn't have made it past the front door if I'd been carrying heat. Right now, my only options were to put up my hands or to run. I settled on the latter, turning and booking it down the hallway.

As I ran, the pattering of feet behind me was getting louder. These guards were in better shape than I was. Several pencil-pushers working at their terminals turned in surprise as the guards chased after me. I noticed that there weren't any security cameras in the area and surmised that security had been tipped off by the Green-eye's coming to the office I was in — they must have known that no one was supposed to be in there. I'd had no idea that GE was able to keep such close tabs on their Green-eyes, but I should have expected it. I kept forgetting that the old rules didn't apply, here in GE. They probably knew everyone who even breathed on their building below the Plate.

The offices to the left and right ended just before I reached the doors to the mainframe. Now the corridor diverged in two directions. The hallway running perpendicular to me terminated on either side in windows. Hopefully this meant that the floor was set up in the shape of a figure eight, and the hallways looped back to the elevators on the other side of the offices. I took a chance and went left. Maybe I could swing around these guards and catch the elevator, or perhaps there was another set of elevators. There had to be.

I took a left. When I reached the windows, I nearly tumbled over a table and some chairs. I turned left again, hoping I could make it back to the elevators before the guards caught up to me. But I was unlucky. These guards had brains; while one had chased me, the other had gone around the other way to cut me off.

"Shit," I muttered just as the guard chasing me grabbed my arm and twisted it behind me. He stuck the barrel of his weapon into the small of my back as the other guard approached.

"What the hell are you doing? No fuckin' cops are allowed here, especially not without an escort."

"Well, this was important, and I didn't have time to wait."

"And look where that got you." They searched me, finding my car keys, my deteriorating wallet, and the temp card that definitely wasn't mine. They held on to me, taking the card and tearing it up before leading me to the elevator. One of them put a hand on the radio attached to his shoulder and spoke into it as the other made sure I couldn't pull another fast one on them. They both wore polymer protection vests, two-way cordless radios, and what looked like crowd-control batons with electric pads for frying Automatics. Most precincts likely wouldn't see that kind of tech for another decade. These security guards were carrying more advanced stuff than me or anyone on the Force.

The guard on his radio turned back to me. "No warrant?"

"No, of course not. Why the fuck would a cop need a warrant to get into GE?"

"Because unlike you cops, we're doing actual work here. What were you looking for in that office?"

"None of your goddamn business."

A firm punch to my jaw knocked my orientation out of whack. When my eyes refocused a few moments later, I realized that I was on the floor. I felt blood start running down my face after the guard yanked me back up.

"Try again, copper."

"Fine, I needed an Automatic's information. I didn't get into the damn computer, though. Happy?"

He turned away from me and began to speak on his radio again.

The one who was holding me seemed far quieter, and I decided to press my luck.

"You reach in my back pocket and we can forget this ever happened. Just look behind you for a few minutes when we get to the ground floor." I moved my fingers enough to pull the tip of a twenty out of my pants pocket, but the guard looked away. They must have loved their jobs if they weren't willing to take a bribe.

"Got a name, copper?"

"Nope. I didn't get one from my parents. Still trying to decide what to call myself."

The second punch hurt much more, but I had to smile. The fact that they were using violence meant either that I was getting under their skin, or that this kind of thing had happened recently. And I knew for a fact that no contract cop was brave enough to even step on GE's lawn.

The security boy took my badge and looked it over, turned his back to me, and radioed in the information. The radio handler on the other side soon responded, stating that the number on my badge wasn't in circulation. I should have waited to get that fresh badge from Robins.

We finally reached the main foyer, where the receptionist refrained from looking at us as the guards dragged me toward the front door roughly enough to make me an example to any ne'er-do-wells in the foyer. I looked down to see spots of blood falling from my mouth and dotting the floor behind me — that would piss off some bigwigs. The situation sucked, but even little silver linings made things more bearable.

Outside, the sidewalk and lawn were devoid of human life. They threw me onto the grass — which was colder than I was expecting. I opened my eyes and saw that snow was beginning to fall. That was why the Plate was moving tonight. Most of the snow would be converted to water for the Upper City, but some would be filtered through the Plate with fans to alleviate pressure. The falling snowflakes and chill helped comfort my wounds.

I looked over to see a tow truck hooking up my car. Before I could get up to make my way over, the truck had driven off with it. Security must have found out it was mine and called for it to be impounded. Just my luck. And fuck me if that tow truck wasn't the fastest one in the city.

I flopped back on the grass, looking up at the Plate and the tiny snowflakes falling onto my face. I wanted to scream in frustration. The cold made my jaw feel somewhat better, though the humiliation had done little for my self-esteem. I was surprised that I had even gotten so far as to pull the Red-eye's numbers. This would be a story to share with the boys next poker night, right after I got my car back.

I was pulled out of my self-loathing by a shadow appearing over me, its blue eyes staring down at me. "Hello, Detective Roche."

I pushed myself up from the thick grass to see the Blue-eye from Robins's office standing there. It gestured to the police cruiser that was parked at the side of the street. Well, damn, it could drive. More than I could say for Toby.

"I am here to take you home."

CHAPTER 5

CEILING FANS HAD A WAY OF CALMING ME. The swift, fluid movement was like a ticking clock, mesmerizing. I realized I'd been staring at this one for quite some time since waking up. I felt around with my hands for a few seconds and came to the conclusion that I was on a couch. My couch. I looked down to see the same button-down shirt and wrinkled, stained black slacks I'd been wearing during my meeting with the grass. I couldn't remember how I'd gotten home. The bleeding in my mouth had subsided, and dried blood clogged my nose and covered my face. My shoes were still on my feet, and I'd tracked dirt along the carpet and onto the couch. "Shit!"

Something stirred to my left. I looked over to see the suited figure of the Blue-eye peering through my window at the city below.

I grasped the sides of my leather couch and pulled myself upright. My face was on fire. I knew, though, that I could do little for the pain besides put some ice on it. I looked at my watch. It was four in the morning. All I could remember was getting in a police cruiser and closing my eyes for a moment.

"How did you find me?" I asked.

At this question the robot turned, its blue eyes gleaming brightly.

"It was not hard to find you, Detective Roche. The commissioner told me that you had a serial number in your possession, and I deduced that you would want to get some information on it promptly. Therefore, going to the General Electrics building was my best option — though in the end, it proved easier to find you than I'd initially expected."

"Why'd you guess GE? I might have gone to another precinct."

"Commissioner Robins informed me that you are … less co-operative, let's say, with other commissioners than you are with him."

"Also, why couldn't you stop my car from being impounded?"

"On the contrary — I've arranged for one of our associates — or, constables, rather — to bring it here."

I felt a chill when it said *associates*. Too formal, too inorganic. "Why did you help me? You feel some kind of responsibility to keep me from risking my ass too much?"

"I believe that if we are to work together as partners, I should —"

"No." I stopped it from speaking and found myself walking away into the kitchen. The small cooking area was separated from the living room by a small waist-high countertop. I rested my weight on it. "We're not partners, we're not working together. I work better alone, and the *only* reason you are here is because Robins needs a babysitter for you. Or maybe me; I don't know. You can tag along, but you are not my partner in any sense of the word."

"I would refer to your file regarding this behaviour. However, it seems this information has been expunged."

"You've been going through my file?" That explained why it had been on Robins's desk.

"Of course. I wanted insight as to your history, methods, and general personality."

"Well, shit." This was too much for me. Fucking Blue-eyes.

I slotted a cup into my coffee machine, spooling up the wall-mounted Tesla Battery as black liquid spewed into the cup. I turned to see where the Automatic had gone and found it standing mere inches from me. *Goddamn!* I nearly threw my cup up into the ceiling in surprise.

"You need something, metal man?"

"I'd like to inquire as whether you have any leads in … your investigation."

It had avoided saying "*our* investigation." Good, it was a quick learner. I supposed that I'd better say something constructive, make sure it didn't think it was chasing a lost cause. "I made some headway and got the serial number registration. The Auto belongs to some guy at Jaeger Electrics in SoHo."

"I am familiar with the establishment. I could direct us there, if you would have me join you in the investigation."

I looked at it, still astonished and unable to think of a retort just now. I thought for a few seconds before responding. "You ain't a regular Automatic."

"I believe you're correct."

"New model?"

It stuttered as it tried to think of a response. "In a sense, yes."

I pulled the cup from the coffee machine and drank, letting the scalding liquid hit my tongue and slither down my throat. It hurt, but I needed a wake-up call; I couldn't be investigating only half-awake. I waited a few more seconds before walking around the Automatic and grabbing my car keys from my jacket pocket and my vest from the coat hanger. "One chance, coppertop. You make yourself useful, we'll work together after this. You're already more useful than any regular Blue-eye."

"Thank you, Detective Roche." It followed me into the hallway and matched my stride. "While at the 5th Precinct, I put together a small file of information on our case, so as to organize our thoughts better. It might prove useful."

"We shall see, tin head."

"Will you be finishing your coffee?"

"Nah ... only needed a sip."

It hesitated, trying to process what I meant, then forgot about it a moment later. "Shall I drive to this location?"

"No. My car — let's roll. Hopefully it's here already." We entered the elevator and shot downward to our objective. A temporary partner wouldn't be too bad. Maybe.

They'd better not have scratched up my car, though.

The shop was in the lower quarter of SoHo, a stone's throw from my place. Getting there, however, was a slog, as we had to pass through the west side of the Anchor, which was rife with traffic even at this time of morning. Once we reached SoHo, the congestion dropped off considerably. We parked outside the shop at half past four. It was dark under the Plate at this time; the sun hadn't even reached the horizon yet. My car was one of the few on the street. For the most part, the area was clear of man or machine, as everyone was either sleeping or working the graveyard shift. The subway tracks above me were rusted and long since abandoned. Most avoided the subway, whether above ground or underground. Stepping out, I smelled the unforgettable stench — rotting wood and rusted metal with a hint of cannabis — of one of the largest decrepit neighbourhoods in the city. Or in the country, for that matter — this was as bad as it got anywhere outside the Grotto.

With its glowing neon sign and faint bulbs over the door, Jaeger Electrics looked far more respectable than the rest of the neighbourhood it resided in. The only other manned establishment was the Brass and Pass, a local speakeasy for any wandering Blue-eyes. I opened the trunk of my Talbot and rummaged through the junk I tossed in here time and time again. The metal man opened its door and came to my side to see what I was doing.

"Now listen, this'll be a delicate situation. I need you to do exactly what I do, and don't make any moves without my say. I don't need the guy freaking out when we tell him his Automatic may have killed two cops. Regardless, there's a body going in this trunk tonight."

"Understood … except for that last part."

"And if I get shit on, your job is to back my ass up. Especially if he is who I think he is." There was a damn good chance that there was a cop killer in there. All I needed was confirmation of that and my handgun would do the rest.

"Of course, Detective, but … who exactly would he be?" it asked.

I ignored the Automatic, feeling something cold and rough grace my palm. I wrapped my fingers around it to feel the soft leather of my revolver's grip. Of course it was in here — the trunk was my go-to place for hiding things. I pulled out the large revolver, cracking open the breech as I spun the cylinder. Seven bullets, perfect. I must have remembered to load it after last time. The robot took one look at the weapon and piped up again. "That is a .46-calibre Diamondback revolver, banned in New York and several other states on the grounds of —"

"That doesn't matter, tin top. This thing has saved my ass more times than any partner has. And it's a .38 calibre, same as standard-issue police pistols."

"Sir, I will have to confiscate the weapon if you plan on carrying it."

I closed the breech with a loud *click*, fitting it into the holster under my left arm as I turned. "Take it from me, then."

The machine was smarter than most. It dropped the subject. We stepped up to look through the murky window of the store. Most of it was falling apart, but the shelving units were new and lined with shiny chrome parts and electronics. From the looks of things, whoever ran this joint was used to staying open through the night. I turned to the tin man again.

"Just follow suit, and don't mention any of this being off the record. And for Christ's sake, try to look convincing."

I wondered if it had picked up on the irony of my last statement. I turned the handle and entered the small shop. The machine followed me in, approached the counter, and waited. I scanned the room and found one security camera in the upper corner, some locks and bars on the windows, and a few folding chairs under the shelves. Judging by the size of the place, the owner might live above or behind the shop. The countertop was vinyl, a rare sight in the older part of town. It smelled like mint in here.

The door behind the counter creaked open, and a casually dressed man walked through, surprised to see people in his shop at this hour. He must have seen us on the camera. His beard was thick, with grey streaks. Most of the hair on his head was grey and thin enough to see his scalp. His face, though, looked no older than forty.

"Gentlemen, how may I be of service at this hour?" Weird German accent. His voice sounded posh, yet unrefined, a bit gravelly.

"Detective Roche of the NYPD, 5th Precinct. This is my partner …" Shit, I hadn't given the damn thing a name. Luckily, it heard me trailing off and spoke up.

"Designation Forty-One-Echo-November."

Thanks, tin man.

"Would I be right in assuming you are the Jaeger of Jaeger Electrics?"

"*Ja*, Johann Jaeger." Funny name, funny man. He forced an uncomfortable smile, probably nervous about having coppers in his establishment. The last Jaeger to be thrown in the slammer had been taken down by the 5th.

"Last night at around twenty-three hundred hours, two Red-eyes tore up the speakeasy at Prince and Greene. One of them was destroyed by the police. We looked up its serial number and found it to be registered to here. Do you have any idea why that would be?"

I passed Jaeger the strip with the serial number. He paused before what I was saying seemed to click in his head.

"My Automatic was destroyed? No, not Rudi." He sat down in a chair behind the counter, stunned. "He went to see a supplier, to pick up a shipment for the shop. I thought he was just running late ... *Gott im Himmel*."

"Do you have any idea why your Automatic would have been Red-eyed? "

"I have no idea. I don't know what makes the machines run, and I don't understand why they might have taken my Automatic."

"You have any experience programming Automatics? Police Green-eyes, even any who come in for maintenance?"

"No, no, I'm just the proprietor. I've never programmed in my life."

"No ties to the police?"

"No. Would you please excuse me? I must go to the back."

"I'm not done asking questions, sir."

"I'm an old man, and my only companion has been destroyed. I need a moment alone."

He wasn't *that* old. I guessed there was something other than sadness and shock motivating him right now. He tried to get up, but I approached and forced him back in his seat. "Let's start over, and this time —"

"Excuse me, sir, may I ask you something?" the tin man piped up. Jaeger turned his head to meet the robot's gaze. "What kind of electronics do you sell?"

"This ain't the time for that, robot, we need —"

"I know what I'm doing, Detective Roche. Please allow me to do my job," the Automatic said. It had interrupted me. This was new. This I had to see play out. I stood back and let it continue, but I put my hand on the handle of my Diamondback in its holster.

"I do not understand what you're asking," Jaeger said, looking confused. No, concerned.

No, terrified.

"I'm inquiring what electronics you sell in this shop. The prices of various items, such as this feedback terminator and even this cord splitter, are substantially lower than identical items in other shops in the city."

"Well, I'm a purveyor of cheap wares —"

"Any wares which have oil in them?"

"Excuse me?" Jaeger's face broke. I tightened my grip on the revolver, but kept it in its leather cradle.

"There's oil underneath your fingernails. You've wiped them carefully, but not thoroughly enough. Your jeans are torn at the knees and ankles, and your wrists and temples bear the marks of worn leather goods. Your demeanor and dress suggest a modest lifestyle. As well, from outside, the upstairs window reveals a lamp, a bedpost, and the edge of a small kitchen. I have also noticed several Automatic-specific items hidden behind some of the larger objects in this store. I do not, therefore, believe that there is more living space behind that door. In fact, based on the red chain mark on your left wrist, the burn marks on your shirt, the spark burns on your jeans, and the oil on your hands — the mint air freshener masked the smell of it well, but not entirely — it is my belief that the space in the back holds hoisting chains, welders, rewiring kits, and pneumatic pumps."

Jaeger froze, wide-eyed, as did I. An Automatic that could think — that was not something I'd been prepared for. The old man hesitated for a few seconds before slamming his hands into the rear door, jumping out of his chair, kicking it toward me, barrelling through the rear door, and breaking into a sprint. I broke from my own stupor, pulled out my revolver, and hopped over the thrown chair after him.

"We don't have a warrant, Detective!" the metal man yelled after me.

Most of the room was in darkness, but faint light revealed the back door standing ajar — obviously Jaeger's objective. Next to said door was a small red cylinder: a fire extinguisher. As I ran, I levelled my gun, aimed at the extinguisher, and popped off a shot. The heated round instead slammed into the concrete wall, boring a hole the size of a dinner plate. The gunshot caused

Jaeger to freeze, giving me plenty of time to catch up to him. The metal man sprinted past me to bind Jaeger's hands in a pair of cuffs. I grabbed Jaeger by the neck and pointed the barrel of my revolver at his stomach, then nodded to the machine. It released our captive and went off to switch on the lights.

Needless to say, the machine's hunch was right. The space looked like an old car garage. The car jacks in the floor had been mangled and converted into work-benches for Automatics. Several dozen scrap parts lay on the floor and on shelves, with even more loose bits and bolts dotting the floor around the workspaces. In the corner next to the door was a terminal with a re-wiring kit next to it, and near the back door there was a chain and sling for Automatic torso removal, as well as various other machines I'd only ever seen in the bowels of the GE building.

"What made you start to suspect?" I asked the tin man as it returned to where I was standing with my new prisoner.

"The retail prices in the store were half of the mar-ket price for those items. His business would have been unsustainable ... unless he had a more profitable opera-tion as well. My other observations filled in the blanks."

I was impressed, to say the least. Most Automatics just looked at things and said what they saw. Blue-eyes didn't think too hard. And Green-eyes thought even less.

"Check if there are any Neural-Interfaces here. Be thorough," I added. The machine nodded and walked away, and I turned to the German. "Now, Jaeger, would you like to explain yourself?"

"Please, you must understand, I have nothing else but this."

"You won't even have this pretty soon, *Karl*." Both he and my temporary partner — God, was I actually going along with this? — shot a glance at me. "Robot, this is Karl Jaeger. He worked for the Mafia for years, bootlegging parts for the Red-eyes that they used for contract killings, smuggling, and everything in between."

"That was over a decade ago!" Jaeger protested. "I did my time, Detective. I'm trying to run an honest business."

"Honest? Only half of it is legit, and it's not even the half I'm standing in. So, let's cut to the chase: Why was your robot at the site of a murder?"

"I don't know! I sent him to get supplies for us but he never returned. I've done work on hundreds of Automatics, but I never tampered with Rudi. I never could, for this exact reason. If he was ever found, they'd track it back to me, and I'd be locked away again."

The metal man started turning its head to sweep the place for any sign of a Neural-Interface. I had a gut feeling it wouldn't find anything.

"What time was Rudi taken?" I asked Jaeger.

"Rudi left for the pickup at ten forty-five. One half hour to requisition, pay, and return. He should have been back by quarter past eleven at the latest. When did the shooting happen?"

"Around eleven. So it had fifteen minutes to turn Red-eye … doesn't sound unreasonable to me."

"It takes an average of one hour and twenty minutes to assess an Automatic and rewire it to take hostile action," the robot butted in, silencing me and Jaeger. In truth, this was a subject I knew very little about. "The crime was committed at approximately seven minutes after eleven. There wasn't enough time for a rewire to have been performed. I believe the precincts would allow this substantial evidence to be used in Jaeger's defence."

"That remains to be seen, metal man. Jaeger here was the most talented bootlegger and Tinkerman in New York back in the early '20s. He was put away eleven years ago, and yet here he is, out and about with a new shop to tinker in. I'd put money on him being a whiz at rewiring an Auto."

"His skill has no bearing on what is mechanically and physically possible, Detective. The time frame does not support his machine being one of the Red-eye perpetrators."

I had to let on what I knew, or we'd just keep spinning our wheels. "Capek, listen to me! There was no Neural-Interface! It didn't *get* Red-eyed — it simply was!"

Both the German and the machine were silent for a moment. Jaeger spoke first. "You must be mistaken, Detective. No Neural-Interface? A machine cannot operate without one. Perhaps someone allocated it to somewhere else in the machine."

"I ain't stupid, Karl. Automatics are too crammed full of wiring to fit a Neural-Interface anywhere but inside their noggin. There's barely enough room in the new models for the Tesla Battery. I assure you, this thing was as empty as a poor man's pocket."

"No, I do not believe it. Impossible …" Jaeger seemed shaken. I gestured for the machine to bring him a chair.

"Let's move on to an easier question: Any reason you know of that your Automatic was used in a shooting?"

"I am lost on all fronts, Detective. I work for myself repairing Automatics for people who cannot afford the legitimate mechanics. I will never work for the Mob again. Back when I was captured, Murder, Inc. found out, but because the police couldn't track them through me, I was left alone. No one came after me in prison or after I got out. I was a tied-up end, an issue fixed before it even began. Even if I had told anyone that I'd worked for the Mafia, they never would have believed me. My identity was erased, most of my money liquidated — I had nothing left. Why would I risk a cop killing when I could get thrown back inside for jaywalking?"

Jaeger had a decent alibi and enough fear for me to believe him. The Automatic had brought over a small chair and placed it behind him, so I forced the old German to take a seat.

"Metal man, you bring anything from the office?"

"I have the relevant information and pictures of the victims."

I snapped my fingers, and it pulled out the light-brown folder from the confines of its suit and handed it to me. Inside were the crude photographs Sinclair had taken at the scene. I tore them from the folder, crouched down in front of Jaeger, and showed him the faces of the dead cops. "Do you at least recognize any of them? Maybe you know why someone would gun them down and supposedly frame you?"

"*Mein Gott* … I know them." He grabbed the pictures from me and stared at them. "These two put me away eleven years ago, in '22," he said, indicating the cops from the 5th. "And three others, they were at my hearing. They arrested me and seized my assets. When I got out in '26, it took forever to get this shop up and running."

I ran my hands through my hair. *Fuck, too perfect a crime to be a revenge killing. There ain't no freebies in this business.* The situation lined up so perfectly that it was right out of a movie plot. I'd dealt with enough crimes to know that if the facts fit too well, you were missing something. Jaeger's Automatic being on the scene would be enough to make him a prime suspect, and I knew for a fact that the FBI agents wouldn't give two shits about what was or was not inside the Automatic's head.

I stood up and backed away, looking at the robot and jerking my head toward Jaeger. Seconds later, the old man was standing next to me, uncuffed and far less likely to run. I slid my gun back into its holster to make him more comfortable.

"So, if you didn't cook your Auto's NI and send it out to shoot up a speakeasy, who did?"

He shook his head. "Rudi went to meet one of my suppliers to retrieve cheap parts. Perhaps it was them. He was an easy target to kidnap and plant as evidence. *Arschgeige.*"

"What they did to your machine was more than just plant evidence. Who is this supplier?"

"I have never dealt with them directly. I would send Rudi to a specific address in the city for the pickups and exchanges."

"Poor business practice on your part, huh, Karl?"

"When you're avoiding the Iron Hands, you'll do anything to get cheap parts," he said, looking at me like I knew what he meant. I did, of course, but wouldn't admit it in front of the robot. "Rudi learned of them through some other Automatics he was close with. He only ever went to one meeting place, but there was a list of several backup locations, in case they were compromised. I'll show it to you."

Most of the places on the list were high-traffic parts of the Lower City. Perfect for an exchange. It would be impossible to identify any specific suspicious person, seeing as everyone in the Lower City was suspicious. One noteworthy fact was that three of the locations were a stone's throw from one another in Times Square. Those involved in smuggling and Mob activity loved Times Square — human cover was the best cover — so this wasn't a substantial lead. Still, it wouldn't hurt to check the area out.

I put the list in my pocket. "Can you give me the names of the other three cops who put you away? We need to start somewhere."

"Cory Belik, Davin Morris, and Andrew Stern." He recited the names as if he had been waiting all these years to tell someone. "I wish for this to be cleared up as fast as possible, Detective. And so, I offer you whatever services I can provide, on the condition I remain anonymous to anyone else you may encounter."

"Can do. Robot, go spin up the car. I'll be there in a minute." I threw the machine my keys and watched it walk out of the room before turning to Jaeger. "Got some questions I can't have the new partner hearing. In the past few months, have you done any work on Swinger models?"

"Swingers?" Jaeger rubbed the back of his head, thinking. "That's an old model. There aren't many left in the city … But I have done work on a few."

"Any with the designation J4-35?"

"I'll have to consult my logs. I'll let you know."

"Excellent. One last question: I know this is new for you, but *can* an Automatic run without an NI installed? Like how a chicken with its head cut off can run around for quite some time before it dies?"

"Machines are not comparable to chickens, Detective. By all accounts, it is quite impossible. But I'll try to formulate some idea as to how it might happen. Removing a Neural-Interface is a challenging task. It can be done in about a week with finesse and patience, but it's traumatic."

I popped an eyebrow up. "For you?"

"For the machine. Imagine having your brain ripped out while you're awake for the entire procedure. They might be metal, but they have personalities, too. I hope, wherever Rudi is — if his Neural-Interface was indeed removed — that he is all right."

"I'll be seeing you. Have a good night, Karl."

With that, I left the establishment and returned to the car. The machine was sitting in the passenger seat. Any other cop who'd come to investigate would've booked Jaeger, case closed. If I'd come alone, there would've been a corpse.

But the robot had been able to look past the facade. It seemed that Jaeger was being set up as the perfect patsy to mislead us from the truth. That made things easy and hard at the same time: longer case, but one less major suspect on the watch list. The tin man seemed as exasperated as I was, which was off-putting. Was it seriously feeling drained, or was it mocking me?

"You did good there. You have one hell of an eye," I said, breaking the tension and grinning.

"I go out of my way to notice things others would miss. The smallest things are often the most telling in an investigation."

I smiled again, amused. "Before we go anywhere, we've got to settle something. I'm not calling you Forty-One-Echo-bullshit. You need a name."

"Will that make our investigation easier?"

"Yes. A lot of Automatics have human names. It helps in the public eye."

"Well, what should it be? I'm not sure what kind of name would fit me."

I mulled over it for a while. Hmm ... Forty-One-Echo-November, or 41-EN. The numeral 4 looked like an *A*, and 1 looked like an *L*.

"How about Allen?"

The tin man thought about it. "Allen Erzly."

"Erzly?"

"I'm based off of the Erzly model, which was a restoration of the old Swinger model from the Great War. Allen Erzly would be my full name, as humans put it."

"All right. I can roll with that."

The old Swinger model ... could my old partner, James, have been slotted into a new model? I'd come back later, once Jaeger had something substantial, but right now, we had three cops to question.

Allen reclined in its seat, and I brought the engine to life and headed out to continue our investigation. Yeah, *Allen* was a much better name than some string of numbers and letters. Still, you get attached to things when you name them.

I shouldn't make that mistake again.

CHAPTER 6

"I'D CALL THE BOTH OF YOU blundering fucking idiots, but that'd be too generous."

Robins had a way with words, and since our arrival at his office, he had shown us how creative he could be. I remained quiet and allowed him to continue. "You're goddamn lucky that GE's security called me and not someone like Viessman at the 7th. We are trying to keep this case from the public, not throw it in their goddamn faces!"

The metal man and I had already worked out how we'd discuss our discoveries with Robins. Now Allen took the stage. "Sir, we have uncovered new developments in the case. We tracked the serial number of the Automatic ..."

"I can't be bothered with what you did or how you did it." Robins turned away from us and stared out the window — at that damn fountain, again. "Just tell me you know who killed those cops."

"We have a lead, but I'm afraid the circumstances won't give us much legroom, as the evidence was meant to mislead us," Allen explained. "Two of the deceased officers were connected to a case which led to the conviction of our previous prime suspect. Therefore, we must assume that the three other members involved in that case must have some connection to these events."

Robins's hands twitched. I could tell his worst fears were realized. I'd have hated to be the one to tell him. He turned and, with eyes downcast, slumped into his chair. "Goddamn it. So if someone else catches wind of this and digs deeper, we're shafted. Is working here that terrible that my own boys need to turn their guns against one another?"

"Terrible pay, horrible hours, and constant threat of getting a bullet in the head aside, this precinct is one of the best work environments I've ever been in."

Robins snickered. Even a little humour helped.

"Well, it's only a lead so far. There's a chance that this can be a misunderstanding, or a scheme to frame cops. It's a slim chance, and I know that maybe not all my men are clean ... but they should know better than to shoot down people they trained and worked beside for years."

"You'd hope so. But everything is up in the air until we find out what the truth is. So ... regular pay times two. Call it cop-killer pay."

"Times two? What do you need with five thousand bucks? The precinct isn't made of money, Roche. I barely have enough to buy a new piece for anyone who asks for a position here."

"Pay?" Allen piped up. But I kept the negotiation rolling.

"Welcome to my business, Robins. Would you really risk leaving this case to someone who wasn't devoted to the 5th? Do you think that thing could solve this alone, without someone like me doing the dirty work?" I said, pointing to Allen, who, though silent, remained ever vigilant.

"Commissioner, are you saying Detective Roche is an outside contractor for the police force?"

"You could say that. He's still part of it ... just not entirely," Robins said.

"Any thoughts, Allen? Even a quip or two about the massacre?"

"I ... suppose that the evidence could be miscon-strued, though the likelihood of that has diminished significantly. Our best bet as of this moment is to inter-view the other three police members who initially arrested Jaeger eleven years ago in the hopes that one of them has information leading us to the killer, or to other outcomes and possibilities. There is still a small chance that this has nothing to do with members of this precinct assassinating one another," Allen stuttered.

"I like the metal man's thinking," Robins said. "There's still a chance. Run that plan, and I'll do my best from here. I have the home addresses of those boys from several months ago, but who knows if they've moved. You're pretty good at getting recent information, right, Roche?" He winked, causing me to jerk my head over to see if Allen had noticed. No idea if it had or hadn't, though I doubt it'd think much of the wink either way.

"Will do," I said. "How often you want updates?"

"That's the issue. The FBI agents from the Plate will be arriving soon — as in minutes from now — and if they run your numbers and see a dead man's name attached to them, we're all in deep shit. So, for now, you're fully off the books, and so is your partner." Robins looked at me matter-of-factly. "We're in a tough bind, so report to me only when you feel it's absolutely necessary, and try not to cause too much of a ruckus. Everything about this is off the books so long as the Black Hats are here, including arrests, evidence — the works. Forty-One, keep a close eye on him. He's a snake some days."

"Yes, sir."

We turned to leave, only to hear a knock on the door. Robins snapped his fingers, commanding Allen to open the door. Four black-clad figures entered the small room and immediately surrounded us and the desk. They were led by our favourite Black Hat, Agent Masters.

"Robins." To my ears, his voice was like nails on a chalkboard.

"Agent Masters."

"Commissioner, if you please, we'll be getting on with the inspections that Director Greaves insists we take part in."

"By all means." Robins leaned back on his chair, lighting a dart as the men and women in black all turned to me and Allen.

"Constables," Masters said, as if informing us our presence was no longer welcome.

"How'd that shooting investigation go? Any leads?" I asked him. He didn't return my grin.

"What shooting, Constable? Perhaps you're mistaken."

I saw Robins looking shifty. Thank God all the G-men were looking at me. I dropped the smile and nodded. "You're right, my mistake."

"I thought as much."

Without another word, we exited the office and strolled through the precinct. The place was empty. No constables at their desks doing busywork, no one running out to their cars — nothing. I had never seen the place like this. Thank God I was heading out. It gave me the creeps.

Out front, I slid into the Talbot and put my hands on the wheel, frozen in thought. Allen soon brought me back to reality.

"Was that agent unaware of the crime that occurred at Prince and Greene? It would make sense for you to hide it from him."

"No, Allen, he was right there when Sinclair and I left the scene. He took over the investigation minutes after I saw it." Allen looked as perplexed as I was suspicious. "You any good at investigating crime scenes?"

"I believe I am."

"We're going back there. With any luck, they haven't moved the Automatic bodies yet. Cops have a nasty habit of letting shells rot wherever they fall."

But of course, we weren't anything close to lucky. This was a worst-case scenario, in every way possible.

The exterior of the speakeasy had been mopped and fixed up to a presentable level, though it still felt like I was walking into a corpse. The yellow tape was gone, but the signs plastered across the shop were now red, meaning it was only a matter of time before a construction crew broke it all down and refurbished it. The owner would hardly want to keep running the place known for being the site of a massacre. The door was unlocked. The floor was still slick with blood and alcohol, and the stench made me gag. I supposed the owner hadn't bothered to have the place cleaned since it was already slated to be renovated.

The fact that there weren't any agents outside to keep out curious members of the public and investigators was a worrying sign. I was glad that I had my Diamondback with me.

I noticed some things that I hadn't before, when I'd been hungover. On the upper level, beyond that broken railing, there was nothing but seating space. No exit door or hatch leading outside. That meant that the upstairs assailant would have been waiting for quite some time before Rudi showed up to blow everyone away with the Thompson. It wouldn't have taken much effort for an Automatic to get past a few screaming, inebriated patrons, but getting past those cops would have been difficult, especially if they'd been armed with shock batons. It would have needed advanced close-quarters-combat programming — more credence to my private theory.

The bodies were still there … interesting. The blood had been mopped up, and body bags lay next to the corpses, ready to carry them out. The dead Automatic, however, was gone, not a single part of its hull left on the floor.

I could see where the G-men's priorities lay.

"Huh. First time I've ever seen them do the ol' switcheroo."

"Excuse me, Detective?" Allen asked.

"Oh, just … you know, bodies shouldn't just be sitting there, you know?"

"Quite odd, yes."

The metal man leaned down over the bodies, inspecting them without touching. I stood there and watched Allen run from one area to the next, scanning the walls, the grime on the stairs, even the stain left by pooling blood. It looked around with such intense concentration that the place could have caught fire. I'd never seen an Automatic focus or think this hard. It was unnerving, but impressive. Damn impressive.

"Where did the first shots come from?" Allen's ringing metallic voice ripped through the silence, startling me. It got up from its low crouch, the plates on its legs moving under its pants in odd shapes.

"First shots came from there, I believe." I pointed up at the twisted, broken railing of the balcony. "The rounds double-tapped through an undercover officer — one in the gut and one in the shoulder. He was thrown from the balcony, and then the second Red-eye came in and sprayed the place with .45s."

"How many rounds were fired?"

"Fuck, you want to count the holes? Be my guest."

Allen took its time circling each of the bloodstains on the floor, eyes blinking and whirring as — I believe — it tried to rip whatever evidence it could from just gleaming at the bodies. It waved me over to the two cops in the centre of the floor, the ones who had put Jaeger away.

"Notice anything interesting about these men, Detective?"

"Other than the fact that they're dead?"

"Sarcasm aside … look at their wounds. They did not sustain fire from an automatic weapon. While the patrons around them have been hit by submachine gun fire, these cops are spotless, save for two shots each. The only way they could have avoided being sprayed by the automatic weapon is if —"

"If they were already on the ground." I knelt down, inspecting the bullet wounds. On both corpses, there was one in the head and another in the chest. The officer on the landing had taken a bad hit, but that was a reactionary double tap. These shots had been very precisely taken. The Automatic up above hadn't been fucking around; it had targeted these boys. "I think the G-men hid the wrong bodies."

"I agree. The Automatic's body might be useful evidence, but these wounds are equally so."

"The massacre — or attempted massacre — was a cover for the two real targets. Something tells me we should get started on that lead Jaeger gave us."

"Agreed. I shall be ready to depart in a few moments. I have one last thing to investigate."

I turned from Allen and put my hand over my revolver in its holster, spinning the cylinder with one finger to keep my hands busy. Something felt odd about this place, like I should get out of here. I still felt watched. Was I getting paranoid, or was someone actually watching us? We had to get out of here soon and get on with the investigation, or at least discuss things in a more secure location.

I didn't want to tell Allen that I thought there was a chance it was my old partner who'd put holes in those cops. Best to explore that theory without Allen looking over my shoulder. However, Allen seemed to have a good instinct for these things, and I needed its opinion.

"What are you looking for, Allen?"

"Footprints ... the assassin approached and, before departing, took something from these corpses — something easy to hide, given the chaos they were surrounded by. Once we find the machine, we can discover what that object was."

"Unless the Automatic is just a shell, like the last one." Allen didn't seem to believe me that the now-missing Automatic had been lacking a Neural-Interface. But I knew what I had seen, and I needed more information as to how it was possible. "If that machine did take something from the bodies before running out of the speakeasy, it would have blood on its feet ..."

"And in that case, it would be quite easy to track it."

"Exactly what I was thinking, metal man. Get on a phone and get the 5th pick up these bodies ... they deserve more respect than being dumped here."

Allen nodded and I exited the old speakeasy. The cold air and desolate landscape of the Lower City matched the shitshow inside. The street was filthy, but there was indeed a faint blood trail leading out the door.

I was surprised it was still visible, especially considering the foot traffic in this part of town and the G-men. I supposed they had been looking for oil, not for blood. Then again, the blood trail was faint. It could have been a remnant of someone's bloody nose or someone could have gotten shot on the street a few days earlier.

The trail ran alongside the building on the sidewalk, leading into a small alley, which contained a moderately sized trash bin, along with some garbage bags and forgotten debris. The blood was far more visible here, contrasting against the dark concrete of the alley, and it led straight to the Dumpster. Judging by the garbage surrounding the Dumpster, it hadn't been moved in months. Or years.

I opened the receptacle and found a weapon. But not the one I wanted. A Foldgun was lying on top of the garbage bags inside. The large shotgun was identifiable by its straight edges, octagonal barrel, and the large handle on the top of the receiver, enabling it to fold into a large briefcase. I pulled the weapon out and cycled the pump, which yielded nothing. Even if it was loaded, these babies couldn't hold .38 rounds, and if it had been used in the shooting, those men in there would have been little more than ground beef. This wasn't the weapon I was looking for, but it was something the 5th could use. I put the Foldgun back into its suitcase configuration and carried it as nonchalantly as possible to my car. It was the smartest idea I'd had that day.

My route was interrupted by three thugs who'd no doubt seen me enter the alley and emerge with a briefcase. What a stupid set of coincidences. A suitcase meant either the Mob or big business, and both meant big money. In this district, I must have looked like Rockefeller, so they were probably hoping to rob me. One was short, white, and carried a broken bat. The weapon had either been salvaged from the garbage or broken from use. The second was black, tall, and carried a revolver in his belt. He looked like he knew how to use it. The third was white, tall, and built like he didn't need a weapon.

"All right, pretty boy, hand over the case and you get to live," the short white one said.

I considered pulling out the Foldgun to threaten them, but they might have shot me before I managed to do so. I dropped it and backed up against the Dumpster.

Though I'd started out thinking these guys were regular muggers, it occurred to me that muggers didn't often work in packs. Not unless they were being paid to keep people quiet.

The curved lid of the trash bin bounced when I backed into it. Glancing at it again, I noticed that the mouth of the bin looked sharp, with the paint scraped away by the sliding action. I tried to get a better look, but only managed to move an inch before the cocking of a hammer made me stop dead.

"No funny business or you get a bullet in your fuckin' heart."

I nodded and kicked the box to them. The taller white guy grabbed it and tried to open it. I saw the lid of the Dumpster: sharp, very sharp indeed, with old blood from past accidents. Even if it had been dull, steel bites deep.

"Do I get to go, asshats?"

"Oh, so sorry, but that disrespect just cost you your wallet, too."

I was in no mood. "Come get it, shitbirds."

"Look, old man, I will fuck you up if you play this game."

"Son, I've seen Germans hold a pencil in a more frightening way than your friend is holding that gun."

Shorty was the leader, Big Guy was the muscle, and the kid with the gun was the hit man. The gun was shaking in his hand. He had killed before, but he was hesitating. He looked older than the other two, at least in his late twenties. Still younger than me. "I'll give you to three," the kid began. "One …"

I looked at the trash bin. *Time to dispose of the garbage. Ha.*

"Two."

Big Guy was still wrestling with the Foldgun, and Hit Man was shaking like a leaf. Shorty was still mouthing off. If I took him out, the rest would fall, easy. I didn't need my Diamondback for this little encounter. Not yet.

"Three."

They weren't expecting me to move after three. Hit Man hesitated, losing his bead on me as I grabbed Shorty, pulling him with me to the garbage while Big Guy was still wrestling with the Foldgun. He was easy to move — he must have weighed ninety pounds or less — but he had some muscle on him. He swung at my ribs, the hit aggravating the bruises that the GE rent-a-cops had given me. But I was tougher than that. I made sure his back was to the group so that the bullet would hit him and not me if Hit Man got brave. I got Shorty in the cheek, but he was still fighting.

While I braced against his punches and kept a grip on his collar, with my other hand I opened the Dumpster lid. Shorty was still on his feet. After finding that the suitcase wouldn't open, Big Guy dropped the Foldgun and ran at me, hoping to catch me off guard. I threw Shorty against the Dumpster. His head and shoulders fell into the receptacle, and I had to duck to avoid Big Guy's swing. I was smaller and could move well, but if the big guy hit me once, I would lose.

I shifted right. Shorty struggled to push against the Dumpster and get his head out of it. Big Guy swung again. I dodged, shoving my back into Shorty. His legs gave out, and his chin hit the rim of the Dumpster, locking his head into place. I grabbed the top of the lid and pulled down hard. The sharp edges dug into his flesh — only his vertebrae stopped the metal from cleaving off his whole head. Blood sprayed everywhere, hitting both me and Big Guy, which made him hesitate as well.

My Diamondback was waiting in my holster, but I knew I didn't have enough time to pull it, cock it, and fire. I needed something else to use as a weapon — a bottle, a stick, a pipe, a wrench, glass, wood, anything. The only thing available was a broken whiskey bottle. Perfect. I dodged another of Big Guy's swings, then leaned down and grabbed the bottle's neck. I moved backward to the wall opposite to the garbage, where a fresh corpse now hung limply, and broke the bottle against the brick wall of the building to make sure it was sharp.

He swung, I went under, then came up, and the bottle followed my movement. The cracked glass went through his neck, cutting through his esophagus. I kicked his body back, pulling the bottle out as a fountain of blood poured from his gaping wound. He didn't struggle long. His crimson blood pooled with Shorty's around my feet.

The black guy with the gun wasn't firing. He had dropped his gun a while ago and now stared at me in disbelief, then at his old cohorts. I nodded to him, looking at the gun. He kicked it from himself, backing away, then breaking into a sprint.

I walked away from the ugly scene, wiping blood off my face, then looked up to see the metal man standing there. The adrenalin was wearing off, and part of me felt ... off. The fight had scared the shit out of me, but my hands were steady and my heart wasn't in my throat. I'd have been lying if I said the War didn't hit me hard, but all the same, some days, it was the adrenalin that kept me going. The 5th had just gotten a new set of bodies to clean up.

Speaking of which, Allen had chosen that moment to come walking out of the crime scene. It looked quite shocked seeing me coated in red. "Detective Roche, are you quite all right?"

"Yeah, I'm good."

"I heard sounds of a struggle, and I thought —"

"I'm fine, robot." *Fucking bastards.* Now I had to wash my shirt ... and I'd just had the thing pressed. "I cut myself on a dirty bottle, got worked up. Go run your errands. We'll meet up later."

"Of course, Detective …" The machine clearly didn't believe me, but with orders from Robins, it didn't have much leeway to argue. "Where?"

"Meet me in two hours at the Lower East Side Diner. You'll see my car."

I waited for Allen to put some distance between itself and the alleyway before I went to my car and started it up. First, to get home to change and look more presentable.

Then, I'd have a little meeting with the only person who saw and heard everything in this city and who might know a thing or two about our cop killer.

CHAPTER 7

I'D ALWAYS LOVED THIS DINER. It was familiar, clean, classic. Everyone called out to me when I came in, from Martha serving tables to Dean in the back washing dishes. The clock finally hit six in the morning, and the bulbs on the underside of the Plate started warming up and switching on. It was the signal for the night shifters to go home and the regular crowd to wake up, get some grub, and get to work.

The diner was rectangular, with a counter running along one of the longer walls, stools dotting the floor on one side of the counter, and booths along the opposite wall. The establishment was almost empty; most of the city was still waking up. I headed to my usual booth: the second one in, facing the door. As I sat down, I checked out the rest of the occupants. A young guy sat in the booth closest to the door reading a newspaper. Another guy, who looked like he had finished a night shift at GE, was sitting at the counter sipping coffee. The cooks were busy at their grills, preparing their own breakfasts or cleaning whatever dishes they'd missed during the night. Martha came out from behind the counter and strolled up to me. I barely caught a breath before she rolled by with that musk that followed her. Sure, I smoked, but not as much as she did.

"What can I get you, El?" Though she smelled like a smoker, she didn't sound like one. She had a nice face to match the nice voice, too, and blond hair still pure and undamaged.

"Coffee. Throw me a few eggs as well. I haven't been eating right the past few days."

"Your little cases got you on the ropes? Or are you always this high-strung in the mornings?"

"You'd know better than me. Technically, this is my lunch. I've been up far too long." I flashed a grin, took a folded ten in my fingers, and put it in her apron pocket. "And give me a kick. I need something to help me relax."

She nodded, smiled, and went to the kitchen, her shoes slapping against the linoleum floor. As she yelled my order over to the cooks, my eyes wandered over to the window. The streets were illuminated by incandescent bulbs high above. Light reflected off of a metal dome moving along the street — I recognized Allen approaching the diner.

Allen came through the door, and everyone inside the diner — except me — stared for a moment, then looked away. Not many people on the Lower East Side were fond of Automatics.

"You get anything of use?" I called out to Allen, so it wouldn't get cold feet from seeing their reaction. It hesitated, but moved toward me.

"I was able to dig through the records of several precincts, though I believe they would have been far less reluctant to give me information had you been there, Detective." It slid into the booth seat opposite to me. "They were not too keen on allowing me to enter their buildings, let alone access their records."

"We all need to make sacrifices some days. You show them your badge?"

"I did."

"And I'm guessing they were just as surprised as I was …"

Martha practically threw the coffee at me as she ran past the table. Considering the number of patrons in the place, I doubted she was actually that busy. This place didn't have a *No Automatics Allowed* sign out front, but every other shop did; the owners probably expected to be covered by association. Umbrella effect and all that. I could see Allen eyeing Martha with curiosity. It was a subtle reaction, but its servos twitched into a concerned expression.

"Any significant findings?"

"None thus far. I was able to find the addresses of the three officers in question. After informing Robins of their connection to the case, he has sent his own officers to the addresses to find them. He said he would contact you if he found anything of note. He seemed tense when I visited the precinct, perhaps due to the FBI's presence."

"Yeah, or maybe he just wasn't all there." I grabbed the coffee and sipped. *Damn, that feels better.* Martha was damn good at hiding the smell of the Irish coffees she brewed.

"All there? Is that a euphemism I am unaware of? Does he have frequent absences?"

"No, not like that. We don't know if it's depression, or exhaustion, or what. He's just never totally aware of everything going on around him — one of his quirks. Always has these blank stares. Some days I'm not sure he even hears anyone talking to him."

"The job of policing is tough on everyone." Allen sat there rigidly. It never seemed to be comfortable, even when it knew what it was talking about. I took another sip of coffee. "Especially for former Manual Corps pilots," it continued.

I choked on my coffee at the statement, drawing some attention to myself as I hacked the liquid out of my throat. "How in the hell —"

"His scars," it said in a matter-of-fact sort of way.

"What the hell are you talking about? I don't think I've spotted a single scar on him in the past decade. Except maybe the one on his forearm from a knife fight with a mobster a few years back. I didn't even know he was in the Manual Corps. What did you see that I didn't?"

"Around his collarbone he has two pronounced scars. They reach from his clavicle to the edges of his pectoralis major and —"

"I know what a Trauma Harness is, Allen. I fought in the War." I drank more of the coffee, hoping that would force my metabolism to start processing the alcohol faster. "But damn, if he had a deployed Trauma Harness, I'm surprised he's alive and well. Usually when those blades go into you, you're a dead man fighting. He's a tough bastard. Explains why he's more shaken than I am."

Allen perked up at the mention of myself. "You were in the War, Detective?"

I guessed it was story time. It might be useful for the machine to learn more about me.

"Yeah, a lifetime ago. I was in the CC — Cleanup Crew — for the Manuals. I was usually in the back repairing them, but in '17 we got mobilized for a full-scale assault against Strasbourg. Goddamn ... it was a nightmare." I leaned back, hearing Martha's shoes clacking against the floor as she brought my plate. The eggs still sizzled — fresh off the grill, all right. That was why I loved coming here.

"Would you rather return to the subject at hand, Detective?"

"Well, it was your tangent, but sure." I smiled and chuckled, and Allen responded with confused — or perhaps apathetic — silence. Not the worst response I'd ever received, but it was up there. "So, on the subject of bloody things, any leads on what model of Automatic we're looking for?"

"The data suggests that the machine is indeed a Swinger model from the early 1920s. It is well known that both the Swinger and Grifter models are favoured by the Mob, so this would seem to fit typical assumptions."

"Other than the FBI denying the shooting, the dead Automatic's empty head, and everything else we've uncovered thus far."

"Precisely." Martha passed by again. This time, Allen tried to get her attention. "Excuse me, ma'am?"

Martha kept walking by without acknowledging Allen, and a pin of empathy poked me right in the heart. Even with my own prejudices, it still hurt me to see something innocent being treated like that. I rolled my eyes and snapped my fingers, getting Martha's attention. She came back. I looked pointedly at Allen, and she reluctantly followed suit.

"Might I have the same as he is having?"

Martha turned to me, still silent. We shared the same confused look as I shrugged and she nodded, walking back to the window to the kitchen to call in the order — this time speaking more quietly than before.

I'd thought that metal men only drank — just for recreation — but this one seemed to be craving an actual meal. It was too early for weird shit to be happening already. I did my best to ignore it, though, not wanting to cause a scene. The Irish coffee was starting to hit me now, too. The more I drank and the longer I sat, the more things became floaty. Comfort in the familiar, I supposed.

"How about you?"

I was shaken from my daze. "What?"

"What did you do while I was collecting paperwork from the precincts?"

Allen began swaying as it spoke. Or maybe I was swaying, or maybe the earth had decided to move a smidge to the left. Liquor and exhaustion didn't mix well.

"I got some info from a few outsiders who owed me, and one of them was able to help me track down an apartment that one of those three cops owns."

"We already have their addresses on file —"

"I got an *unofficial* address, an apartment one Andrew Stern bought on the side."

"Ah, I see."

The conversation died down as the second meal arrived. I was suddenly aware of the fact that I hadn't touched my food, and it was beginning to get cold. I grabbed utensils and began scarfing it down, trying to get as much food down my gullet as possible before the conversation resumed. Looking up to see if Allen was about to rebut my claim, I had a shock. Allen, too, had grabbed some utensils and was working away at its own meal.

Alcohol made things foggy. I was halfway through my own breakfast, and Allen had begun its own. I was dumbfounded. It was *eating* — with its mouth and everything. It was strange, to say the least, like watching someone set water on fire. Allen hadn't yet noticed me staring.

"I suppose that is as good a lead as any, considering we have very few at the moment. Should we split up again to search the official and unofficial addresses?" Allen blinked a few times, doing everything a human might do. That was the worst part. I wasn't sure if it was imitating humanity, or actually operating that way. "Is something the matter, Detective?"

"No." I straightened up, recomposing myself as I finished the meal and waiting for it to do the same. "No, we'll go together, just in case things go pear-shaped. We find the bullets, we find the gun, and, therefore, the gunner. Easy stuff."

"I concur. Lead the way."

I threw down some change to pay for the food — both mine and Allen's. Hopefully Martha would just think I'd had two helpings. I'd rather she not worry herself over this sort of anomaly. We stood and walked toward the door, Allen moving ahead of me.

Just as Allen went through the door, the young man at the booth beside it knocked on the table ever so subtly.

Two times, twice.

He pulled the newspaper closer to his face before sliding a slip of folded paper across his table. I took it before Allen noticed. Opening it up revealed an address, the one I had mentioned to Allen several minutes ago while sitting in the booth. The font was neat, square, and legible. On the back was a message written in cursive.

Be quick.

She was as impatient as she was informative, I supposed, so I'd best not keep her waiting. I followed Allen out of the diner, stuffing the paper into my pocket before we got into my vehicle and headed out.

———

From the diner on Delancey Street, we drove to Hell's Kitchen, reaching an apartment building that was several dozen yards from the bottom of the Plate. It was a quarter to seven in the morning, and the liquor had finally kicked in, making it even harder for me to steer the Talbot. I nearly swung into oncoming traffic more than once. Allen kept its mouth shut for the ride, either scared for its life or trying not to criticize my driving while I had questions that needed to be answered.

I parked the car in the multi-level garage, which was as tall as the apartment building itself, then exited the car and crossed one of the bridges that connected the parking levels to different floors of the building. There were too many entrances to this place. It made me uncomfortable not to have control of the battlefield. For all I knew, the cop could be watching out for someone, ready to hightail it out of there the moment he heard the elevator arrive at his floor. Hell, we didn't even know whose apartment this was. It could have belonged to any of the three men whose names Jaeger had given us: Belik, Morris, or Stern.

But none of them was expecting me.

The landlady for the set of floors was a quaint old woman, at least seventy, who seemed caring and tolerant. However, the holster and the .44 by her waist told me this area had seen better days and tenants. While Allen informed her why we were here, I noticed how steady her hands were. She must have been one hell of a shot. I showed her the apartment number on the slip of paper. She smiled a gummy grin and led us to the elevator.

My mind faded in and out during the ride. I thought I saw the number thirty, or forty.

"Has he ever acted suspicious, or caused discomfort in the building?" I was glad Allen was doing the talking. It felt to me like the elevator was spinning while we rode up.

"Oh no, he's been a dear. He always pays his rent in advance, brings me flowers every birthday. He's never been a bother."

"Any shady characters ever swing around his place?" I piped up, though I felt like that was all the talking I was capable of.

"Now listen, whatever he's done, he is a good man. I'm sure this is a misunderstanding. Hopefully looking through his place will prove that to you." She thought of him like a son. Cute. She seemed convinced he was the golden child of this building. Maybe he was — but he might still have blood on his hands.

We exited the elevator and approached his apartment, the landlady taking her key out and shoving it in the lock. She remained outside as Allen entered first. I followed behind.

The apartment itself looked clean, respectable, quite polished. I hadn't seen an apartment this clean in a long time, which made me even more suspicious. I switched on a few lights and we started to search for anything incriminating.

The kitchen was pretty barren, but used enough to suggest a single occupant. The bathroom was clear — maybe a few too many blood thinners and pain relievers stood on a shelf, but that wasn't a crime. The living area contained a radio a few years older than what was currently on the market. The couch looked well used. Perhaps he often had guests or used it for sleeping as much as I did. I couldn't remember the last time I'd slept in my bed, so I could relate.

Overall, things checked out. Allen elected to check the bedroom. It was there that things got odd.

"The bedroom is locked, Detective. Do we get her to open it?"

"No need. I doubt she'd have the key." I swung myself at the door. The wood splintered as the lock tore off of the door and I fell to the floor, landing on something that felt harder than I'd expected the wood flooring to be. Getting back up, I noticed Allen staring.

I soon realized what it was looking at. The bedroom was stripped bare save for a bed, a crude dresser, and several tables. Every surface, from the tabletops to the mattress, was covered in electronics and machine parts. Automatic parts.

Arms, legs, chassis, servos, Neural-Interfaces, re-programming equipment, even a shoddy terminal no doubt stolen from some back-alley dealer auctioning off old GE hardware. Under some of the items were loose sheets of paper with signatures and wads of cash, all addressed to the tenant, Andrew Stern. It was a gold mine for a racketeering charge and evidence enough that we were on the right trail.

"This is concerning, Detective Roche. Keeping this volume of parts for the purpose of selling them illegally could be incriminating. I do not believe any-one in the police force could afford a licence to sell Automatic parts."

"Right you are, Allen," I responded, collecting all of the papers for later reading. I skimmed through some of the requisition orders, and two things jumped out at me: the price and the supply. Stern was selling these parts for pennies compared to what the Iron Hands or GE was selling them for, and he had *a lot* of parts. There were far more parts listed on these sheets than were in this room.

Racketeers never keep all their stock in one place, just like a general never keeps an army in a single camp.

I turned and went back through the apartment's main area, entered the kitchen, and tore open the cup-board. I pushed the glasses and plates aside and noticed that the back of the cupboard wasn't flush with the wall.

I grabbed my revolver, held it like a club, and hammered the wooden boards. Wires, connectors, motors, and servos fell out onto the countertop. Several hundred dollars' worth of parts, at least, were stuffed behind one of the panels. And that was just one cupboard out of at least a half dozen.

Next, the couch. I tossed the cushions aside. Built into the wooden base of the couch were larger Automatic limbs and chassis. The cushions, too, were stuffed with silica beads and oil.

In the bathroom, behind the painkillers and blood thinners, were unmarked bottles. I opened one and sniffed — the scent of heavy lubricant filled my nostrils. This entire apartment was a racketeer's den, and I'd have bet any money that this wasn't the only place he owned off the books.

I headed outside to speak to the landlady. She looked startled at my appearance. The sweat pouring from my forehead and the manic look in my eyes would have been enough to throw her. "How often does he pay rent? Do people come in to see him for repairs? Do you ever get complaints about maintenance issues?"

She stuttered as she replied. "He … he's always p-paid in advance. Never late or even on time — always early. I've seen quite a few people going to and fro on a monthly basis. I just assumed he had everything taken care of."

This was the perfect cover, the perfect location, the perfect unassuming landlady. If his other apartments were anything like this one, he was a big enough force in the market to begin to rival the Iron Hands. That was bad for everyone, not just him.

I almost slammed the door on her as I turned to see Allen sifting through the parts that had been strewn about by my ransacking. I grabbed its arm and brought it outside, pushing it in front of me to explain to the landlady what we'd found. She was shocked, and while Allen spent the next few minutes trying to calm her down, I went back inside the apartment. At the far end of the living area, I stepped out onto a small balcony, into the early morning air.

The lights hanging on the Plate were starting to brighten, though the Lower City wouldn't see their full power until around eight a.m.

This building was on 23rd Street, near the corner of 9th Avenue. The balcony offered a clear view of downtown and the heart of the Lower City. There were Packards and Fords everywhere below, clogging up a four-lane street even this early in the morning. It made you wonder how many people could really afford a car. Then again, swapping out the gasoline for Fuel Gel was cheaper than fixing a car. That also explained why they all looked half-rusted and ready to fall apart. The only upside to all the traffic was the lack of exhaust. It actually smelled half-decent up here.

The rising sun illuminated the larger buildings in front of me with a golden glow, most dramatically GE and the Empire. The street would be basked in sunlight only for another hour or so before the light ascended to the Plate. Another day in the hidden metropolis. I lit a dart, trying to calm myself. Mixing coffee, alcohol, and tobacco always made me go into a frenzy. Hell, what with the mounting stress since our discovery, it almost felt like the good old days again. It was a shame that he was gone.

That *it* was gone.

Then again, with all the evidence piling up, I wasn't so sure it really was dead.

Allen joined me on the small balcony.

"I've coordinated Stern's arrest. The landlady is willing to co-operate with us to prevent Stern from learning of our presence until we can apprehend him. She'll clean up the area, lock the door, and try to be as convincing as possible."

"Good. Glad I had you here to help. He'll notice something is up eventually, and when he's panicking, that'll give us an opportunity to grab him. He won't be very alert while he's busy packing up to skip town."

"I suppose it is a happy accident, then." Allen stood silently, watching the view with me.

Yeah, the good old days, I thought. Maybe Allen and I would have some. *If* I decided to keep it, that was.

"Stakeout, then?" I asked, dropping the cigarette butt onto the city below.

"Of course. On our drive over here, I noted several locations from which we could see him approaching the building. Our best bet for a clear view of his vehicle is across the street, three buildings to the west. It's a small restaurant that houses a speakeasy. Its windows face the street, giving us an excellent view of the entrance to both this building and the garage. I have his vehicle's make and model, as well as his licence plate number here."

Allen passed me a sheet of paper. There were notes scrawled by the woman and fine square letters and numbers where Allen had rewritten them. Both looked like gibberish to me, though in a few hours I'd surely be sober enough to decipher them.

"How do you know there's a speakeasy underneath?"

"The door has been refurbished and reinstalled multiple times, after many raids. Paint can only hide so much."

"Huh." I nodded in affirmation. "How long will Stern be?"

"Several hours at least. He returns here two or three times per week, she says, depending on circumstances. She mentioned that he has business outside the city and often comes back on Wednesdays, so we are quite fortunate things have lined up so well. We have ample time to prepare for our encounter."

"Perfect. Let's head to the joint."

Allen nodded and followed me out of the apartment into the hall, now devoid of life except for me. And maybe Allen, depending on what one considered to be life.

A stakeout waiting for the Tinkerman who had jerry-rigged the Red-eye to do the job. But who was he? Some high-ranking undercover FBI agent? Or some crazy scientist with delusions of grandeur? Throw in the racketeering charges we'd be hitting Stern with, and my partner being an Automatic who'd eaten alongside me an hour ago, and so far this had been one hell of a week. My head was spinning from everything that had happened, and yet it was still a nice change of pace from being chased by armed gunmen. Which reminded me: after this little stakeout, I had a stop to make.

"Since we're going to a speakeasy, Allen, do you play darts?"

CHAPTER 8

THE SPEAKEASY ALLEN AND I set up in was clear for most of the day. The sun shone high above the Plate while the fluorescent bulbs below tried desperately to imitate it. The sun appeared once more at the horizon just before the bulbs went out. I spent most of the day staring out the window, drifting in and out of sleep more than once due to the softness of the leather seats. I should have been revelling in this relaxation; I suspected that there wouldn't be many more chances to do so during this case.

Allen was pacing back and forth, thousands of thoughts running through that metal brain. I decided to hold off on alcohol — for now, at least — as the Irish coffee had done enough to turn me off the stuff for a while. Now all we had to do was wait — the one part of my job I hated. At least some of the grub here was tolerable. We had the place to ourselves until around six in the evening, when the day-shift crowd would begin to shuffle in.

Evening turned to night, the bulbs of the Plate shut off, and nightlife took over once more, the hustle of the day — men and women and machines working to a monotonous drumbeat — replaced by the business of the night. The city's malicious denizens began creeping up from gutters. The streets were once again alive with people whose business was to end lives or trade in them.

The speakeasy began to get packed. Thank goodness Allen had already laid claim to the dartboard. The barkeep hated taking it out during evening, as he said dartboards had been stolen more times than he could remember.

Most patrons kept quiet. Others joked and yelled, laughing at other people or maybe themselves. It all became white noise after a while. That was what most people become.

Stern was out of the city by the looks of it. No car matching the description of his yellow Duesy had shown up anywhere near the apartment building. Come to think of it, I hadn't seen a single Duesy since just after the War. Surprising that just driving that ritzy thing around hadn't tipped anyone off about his business ventures.

I let Allen take the first crack at the board, since I was sure it would show me up. Turned out the metal man was less perfect than I thought it'd be. It missed the bull's eye twice, hitting the black eighteen and white eleven. The third dart missed the board and stuck to the wooden wall it was hanging on.

"Little rusty, Allen?" I grinned and picked up three of my own darts, taking position in front of the board.

"Perhaps my parts are beginning to degrade. This may be cause for concern."

"No, no, it's an expression, Allen. You aren't really one for jokes, are you?"

"Humour is an interesting capability you have and share with other humans, and possibly some other Automatics, though I do not see much use for it."

I just shook my head. Allen would get it eventually. Maybe.

It took its darts down and threw them on the table next to the two leather chairs we had occupied for the past half day. I placed my left hand on my back and aimed with my right, bringing the dart level to my eye. I tossed it at the inner red seven, and the second landed in the green just millimeters from the bull's eye.

"Your chances of hitting the bull's eye with your skill and accuracy level are quite improbable," Allen chirped behind me as it lowered itself onto one of the leather chairs.

"With this hand, maybe." I switched and brought my right hand to my back, flexing my left as I tossed the small dart at the board, clipping my other dart as it pinned in the direct centre of the board. I turned to sit down beside Allen, smiling. It felt good to be winning. It felt good just to be playing.

"You're ambidextrous."

"Yes, thought that was obvious from just now."

"I knew several days prior, actually."

I chuckled — couldn't help it — and turned to look at it. "By all means, tell me how. We have the time. Did you maybe see me pick myself up off a chair with my left hand one time and my right the other? Or maybe I grabbed Jaeger with my right hand and then held him with my left."

"Nothing so benign as to be a matter of convenience for you. Rather, I read it in your file."

"Oh." I felt stupid after that little oversight. Allen had said it knew several days ago, and it had been around me for less than twenty-four hours. I let way too many things fly over my head to be called a competent detective. I wondered what else it might have said that I'd overlooked.

"But, if you would prefer an observation, it is apparent from the ink on your left hand, as well as the condition of your nails."

"Nails?" I had to sit and think. I had no idea how either of those things would give Allen clues.

"Yes. On your right hand."

"Okay, spit it out."

"I do not have saliva."

"Shut up and talk, Allen!" Christ, robots could patter on. It could probably deduce things about my sex life from the way I cut bread.

"The ink on your left hand shows you are more comfortable writing with that hand, smudging the ink on the paper as you write. As well, there is the staining of sealant on the bottom of your thumb. When you drive, you steer with your left hand, specifically with only your thumb, during leisurely drives. This means that one particular spot on the steering wheel is worn away faster. You often repair it with sealant."

"And the nails?"

"You're more comfortable holding a weapon in your right hand. You've chipped and filed down the nails on several of your fingers as you have the nervous habit of spinning the barrel of your Diamondback revolver — which is still illegal, I might add. You stop it with friction from the fingers of that same hand, leading to your nails being damaged from the action."

Well, it wasn't wrong.

"So, this is what my entire life will be like partnered with you? That is, *if* I agree to keep you around beyond this case. Remember that the G-men are the only reason you're still here with me."

"What would you have me do instead?"

"How about you stop talking and start conversing? That would be a great help to our little … relationship."

Allen was silent, either processing what I'd said or agreeably keeping quiet for once.

"I have a few things I'd like to *converse* about," I continued. "It'll help you seem more natural and less migraine-inducing."

"All right, Detective. By all means, lead the conversation."

It was dangerously close to getting on my nerves. It stared at me like a lost child, though — it wasn't being sarcastic. Hell, it probably didn't know how to be sarcastic.

"Okay. First question: At the diner, did you *eat*?"

"Yes. But, a question for you, Detective: Do you have a deduction or theory in regards to that fact?" Allen had stood up again and grabbed its darts from the table. Nothing about it made much sense anymore.

"Honestly, I got no fucking clue. You're a machine, an Automatic. You should be able to drink, but not eat. Automatics enjoy the bottle now and then, but you're not supposed to sleep or think or do most of what humans can."

"I am not an Automatic. I may have a mechanical exterior and interior — the latter is questionable, though — but I am far from one of the simple, mundane machines you're accustomed to."

Now things were getting interesting. That was a bold statement coming from a metal man.

"Want to run that by me again?"

"Although I am contained within a frame similar to other models, I am not an Automatic."

"I'm inclined to believe you, but — as with anything — I need proof."

"Were my actions at the diner, as well as my abductive reasoning at Jaeger's shop, not enough proof for you?"

It had me at a loss. It was indeed something to think about. But I was a skeptic. Always would be.

"Okay, fair enough. Then please, explain to me how you're able to accomplish such things."

"I can consume basic meals to regain expended energy. I have a recharging mechanism similar to that of human processes, though the energy can be stored in small batteries for later use."

"But you don't ever go to the pisser. At least, not that I've seen."

"I can expend my waste products as harmless gases. It did take some time for my designers to find a way to convert urea into a non-toxic, inert product. As well, the issue of defecation and hemoglobin removal has been remedied by the lack of hemoglobin in my system."

I scrunched up my nose, realizing that I'd been inhaling its waste ever since we met. But I decided to strike that from my memory, and fast. "For thinking and everything, most Automatics have a certain line that they can't cross. Most can't deduce a thing, even if a crook were standing in front of it, with a murder weapon in their hand and a body on the ground. 'Semiself-awareness,' they call it. So you're fully self-aware, then?"

"I do not have a Neural-Interface, as Automatics have. Instead, I have a synthetic brain similar to yours, though its structure allows it an edge in processing time, reaction speed, and learning capability. Automatics are limited by Green-eye protocols. I do not have such protocols, as I lack said Neural-Interface."

"Well, this is some interesting stuff indeed." I felt like I needed a drink to settle my mind after all this. So there weren't any Automatics in the Force after all, since Allen wasn't an Automatic. Not technically.

"Are you … concerned, Detective?"

"A smidge, but not enough to pull my gun on you. If I ever see you murder someone of your own free will, with your eyes still blue, that's when things will get scary for me." I stood and pulled my darts out of the board, then sat back down.

"I assure you, Detective Roche, I do not plan on engaging in any gunfights with humans, and I'm quite adamant that I won't be taking any lives in my career as a police officer."

"You say that now …" I trailed off, thinking back to when I had been a newbie on the Force. I'd thought my killing days were done after the War. How wrong I'd been. "Well, go ahead. Show me what you can do."

This time, Allen stood in a similar stance to mine, rather than its previous rigid pose. It held a dart between each of its fingers, its thumb curled back to give it some measure of control. With three quick flicks of the wrist, each dart escaped its grasp, flying to the board, and smacking into the green around the bull's eye, almost perfectly spaced.

"Damn, pretty good shot."

"Thank you, Detective."

"So … if you aren't an Automatic, what can I call you? What do you consider yourself? Not human, I hope."

"Of course not, Detective. The title we gave ourselves is Synthians. The synthetic men, or women, in some cases, as —"

I stopped it midsentence. "'Title that *we* gave ourselves'? *We?*" That was one hell of a bomb to drop. Hopefully no one was eavesdropping on our conversation.

"Yes, there are currently ten thousand eight hundred and twelve of us across the country."

"So, it's an invasion?" I chuckled. It didn't.

Right, humour. "Never mind. Who made you?"

"The National Academy of Sciences. The official name of the endeavour was Project Lutum, which was conducted in secret somewhere in the midwestern United States."

"Ah, yeah, no one would go looking in the Dust Bowl. Next question: Why?" Allen simply shrugged. "All right then, when did you begin to invade — or should I say *enter* — society from where you came from?"

"Our peak integration years were in 1925 and 1926, with the numbers dwindling until this year."

"You saw the crash in '29? Jesus, how'd your kind fare through that little event?"

"We took a hit to our finances, as many did, and, being lumped in with the Automatics, we found our rights stripped away. Many of us were left behind, so to speak. Some of us were employed in the construction sector to continue building the Plate. That allowed many of us to cope, at least for several months. I only know this from second-hand accounts, as I came to the city only last year."

Allen's deadpan delivery felt strange and more mechanical than if an Automatic were telling me all this. It gave me a feeling of unease, like it was separated from the real world.

"Well, shit, at least you didn't see Red August. Hopefully none of your friends did, either."

The machine finally made a face of confusion. "I'm not sure what that means."

"Really? You've read up all about the codes and the conduct and everything to be a cop, but no one bothered to tell you about Red August?"

"How important is this event, Detective?"

"Well, it's one of the big reasons Robins has presumably told you not to go north of 110th. It's also why no one likes GE." Allen was on the edge of its seat, urging me to continue.

"Your kind saw '29, but you didn't experience it how we did. When the Smoot-Hawley Act passed — because, of course, they thought hiking up trade tariffs would make them money instead of drive out business — things went from bad to worse, leaving most countries steering clear of American exports. Hoover's last nail in the coffin was the Corporate Relief Act. The bastard didn't want to help us, so he let the big faceless corporations do it for him. There was quite a lot of space down here when the mass exodus to the Upper City began, so they wanted to shuffle everyone in Harlem down south and turn everything north of 120th into a massive factory neighbourhood to put people to work. Needless to say, the people didn't take that lightly, and there were riots almost daily. Both cops and GE mercs were stationed there, trying to calm people down and keep the violence to a minimum ... unsuccessfully."

"And when was Red August?" Allen's voice was quieter now.

"A year later, in '31. Violence had been escalating, and then someone threw the first punch. Not sure if it was the cops or the civvies, but soon enough everyone in Harlem was diving in to try to kill someone on the other side. Did you know the police still had Manuals in commission for large-scale threats? I didn't. They're retired now, but back then, every precinct had a few on hand. You could hear the automatic fire and the rockets from Five Points. That little PR nightmare scared GE into never coming back, but the damage was done to that area. It's unlivable now. Only people who stay there are squatters and criminals. The Wild West all over again ..."

The mood had been severely soured by talk of the past. I tried to lighten it back up. After all, I didn't want to spend the whole night next to a depressed … whatever Allen was. "Ah, fuck it, at least we got Roosevelt last year, and he seems competent enough to keep GE at bay. So, tell me, how'd you get this gig?"

Allen seemed to shake off the melancholy of the previous topic. "My designers, or someone connected to them, called in some favours, and the 5th Precinct was described as one of the most reputable and Automatic-friendly precincts in the city. Thus, I was soon transferred and placed in the employment of Commissioner Robins."

"Yeah, the 5th is reputable, that's one way to describe it." I grinned, watching Allen grab its darts before returning to its seat. "It was the only precinct that steered clear of Red August. A mix of respect and fear does wonders for a reputation down here."

"I see."

I still had more questions. "So, you have a knack for 'seeing things.' All that stuff at Jaeger's proved that point … I mean, most people are too preoccupied by obvious tells and assumptions to pick out the little details around them. Spotting the less-than-obvious is one hell of a skill to have in this business. Can you do it with anyone?"

"I believe I could. The speed of the deductions will depend on the evidence available."

"Right." I looked around the packed speakeasy. It was filled with humans mostly, though some Blue-eyes were skulking about the place in a small group. They seemed quite segregated from the others, but I thought picking on them might be too easy for Allen. "Take the barkeep over there. Any thoughts on him?"

Allen reclined in its chair, narrowing its field of view as it scanned the barkeep what seemed like a dozen times. An odd silence fell in our little corner of the speakeasy for a good few minutes before it leaned toward me and began to spit out what it had observed.

"He's left-handed, as he uses it primarily for wiping the counter, but as a child he was repeatedly beaten for using it, which is why he hesitates when reaching for items with his left hand. He hasn't seen his wife and children in at least three years, judging by the grime and dust building on the photo of them behind some of the items on the wall behind him. And finally, he is far too trustful of his patrons, as he leaves his shotgun on the wall, rather than a more accessible location. Ordinarily, I might guess that he hides the shells underneath the counter, but that seems unlikely, considering where the weapon is. I'm betting that he has a .22 revolver under the bar in case he has to deter any vandals."

"Fascinating, Allen. I'm glad I'm not the only person who gets the raw end of your judgment." I leaned back in my chair, satisfied.

"It is not judgment, but simple observation."

I looked at Allen for a good while. It made a point without speaking: I really did take things too personally at times. It was something I should work on. "I need to piss. Watch out for the perp while I'm in there."

"Yes, Detective." It nodded, turning to keep an eye on the street through the window.

I left my darts on the table, stood up, and sauntered over to the bathroom door at the far end of the speakeasy. The small tiled room was clean, and I was sure the barkeep worked far too hard to keep it this way. I wandered over to the mirror to look at myself. The bags under my eyes were fading somewhat due to the naps I'd taken earlier today.

"He's not an Automatic," I told myself, unzipping my pants. I tried to imitate Allen's voice. "*Detective Roche, it is not judgment, but simple observation …* fucking Blue-eyes."

A wave of relief washed over me — or rather, out of me. I leaned my head back, enjoying the relative silence inside the cramped white bathroom.

I had only a few moments of enjoyment before some calamity outside grabbed my attention. Sounds of yelling and shuffling came from the other side of the door. Whatever the tension was, I shouldn't get involved in it. But then again, who would I be if I didn't? I finished halfway through my stream, zipped up my pants, and walked out the door to see four cops cornering Allen.

The chair it had been sitting in was turned over, and the darts that had been on the table were strewn around the floor. The Blue-eyes in the bar backed away, trying to put space between themselves and the cops. The other patrons watched, but with much less concern than they would have had if the boys in blue had been roughing up a human.

Allen looked tense. It was as stiff as usual, but it wasn't clenching a fist or even holding a hostile stance. It looked patient, if not perturbed.

The leader of the squad of cops — which precinct they belonged to, I couldn't tell — was pushing Allen against a wall, obviously enjoying seeing the machine in distress. He took the badge out of Allen's suit pocket, looked at it briefly, and threw it on the ground before stomping on it. I heard the metal crack from the other side of the speakeasy. "How do you feel about that, capek?"

"I am aggravated, officers. I'll have you know I'm legally allowed to enforce the law in this city."

"That so, eh?" They wouldn't have any of it.

I was curious to see how Allen would handle this, as none of the patrons was keen on helping out. The barkeep, too, was hesitant, knowing full well that even raising his voice against a dirty cop was a one-way ticket to the slammer. After all, good cops didn't exactly go around abusing random machines in public.

The cop grabbed Allen's coat lapels and hoisted the metal man up against the wall. Its servos whirred in surprise and the wall shuddered from the impact. Allen seemed to wince, like it had been hurt.

"You the 5th's new lapdog, capek? Gonna bark when we kick ya?"

"I don't believe it is wise to threaten another officer, sir. Especially not one from a reputable precinct."

"Look at that: capek thinks it's big shit being part of the 5th, thinks we can't touch it!" he shouted to everyone else in the speakeasy. The other cops laughed, while the patrons — both human and Automatic — kept their eyes off the altercation. "We got our eyes on you, hear me? You fuck up once, we'll shred you."

"I hear you officer ... though I must say, you are making a big mistake manhandling me." Allen's tone had changed from fear to concern. It could see me moving toward the cops from behind, and knew they were much too busy harassing it to spot the obvious danger I posed.

"Is that a fact?" the lead cop asked Allen.

"It is. I would suggest you release me."

"Oh yeah? The fuck you gonna do about it?"

The cops suddenly knew what would happen when I swung at the one holding Allen. He dropped like a sack, hitting the floor as the others backed up, grabbing their pieces. But mine was already out.

I pressed a small switch on the side of my Diamondback, hearing the internals snap and lock as the weapon went from a double-action to a single-action trigger.

Then they recognized me. Every cop knew me.

"All right, boys, you want to settle this the old-fashioned way?" I said, stepping forward and pressing my foot down on the neck of the cop on the ground. He grabbed at my leg. I lowered my gun to my hip while my other hand hovered over the top of it, pulling the hammer back. "You can try to beat me in a gunfight ... but you won't."

The silence was palpable. The other patrons had all begun backing up as soon as my hand had connected with the cop's face. The Blue-eyes, however, were getting brave, nodding and backing me up since I had stood up for one of their "brothers." Allen was slumped against the wall behind me, and I turned to see if it was okay.

It wore an expression of utter shock. Of course, I wasn't going to kill the cops, or even shoot at them, for that matter. But they didn't know that.

I kicked the cop on the ground and heard him cough as he breathed in. He pushed himself off the ground and returned to his companions. I kept my Diamondback levelled, not ready to let them off the hook just yet. They might want to take my head off, but they wouldn't. They couldn't.

"C'mon, boys …" The lead cop spat a glob of blood onto the hardwood floor. "Only dirty cops drink here."

"You got that right. Get the hell out!" I yelled.

The four cops lumbered out the front door, careful to not take their eyes off of me. I figured I might be seeing them later.

I pushed my revolver back into my holster, turned to the other patrons, and shrugged. "Round on me?" The crowd cheered and lifted whatever glasses they were holding. I slapped a twenty on the counter and signalled the barkeep.

Then I went over to help Allen up, brushing off its suit jacket. It walked past me back toward its seat. I picked up the largest piece of the mangled badge and scooped up the remaining shards from the floor. Allen could get a new one eventually — the last thing it needed now was to worry about that. It righted the overturned chair and took its previous seat, as did I. We sat together in a silence that went on for the better part of an hour.

"You okay, Allen?"

It turned to me, seemingly pulled out of deep thought as it took some time to formulate a response. "Yes, Detective. I believe I sustained only minor or superficial damage."

"Not what I meant. You good?"

"Yes, I suppose I am."

We sat in silence for a while longer. The group of Blue-eyes came up to me soon after, thanked me for "sticking it to the coppers," and offered us both drinks. A tonic for Allen, and for me, some of the beer the bar-keep kept in the back corner of the storeroom. It felt good being thanked — even if I had spent a hard-earned twenty on strangers, and even if my methods weren't the best way to defuse such a situation.

It was good to hear Allen's flanging voice finally pierce the silence. "There is one thing still bothering me."

"How fucking lowlifes like them got badges in the first place?"

"I meant about the case."

"Ah, right." I'd been so wrapped up in street politics that I'd almost forgotten why we were here.

"We have probable cause for this Stern, whom we are cornering at his apartment, and we have deduced that Jaeger did not have the necessary motivation or tools to enact this kind of vengeance. However, the absence of a Neural-Interface in the assailant that you reported is cause for concern, as such evidence could be dismissed as human error. While I am quite knowledge-able in Automatic functions, I believe that in order to narrow down the possibilities, we must definitely prove whether or not it is mechanically possible for them to run without a Neural-Interface."

"Agreed." I bit my lip, thinking. Not many people down here know anything about Automatics, beyond how to fry them or Red-eye them. Jaeger was one of the best, and he'd had no clue. I figured we needed to go higher. "Can you get me a warrant for GE?"

"General Electrics is accessible to the public."

"I meant the higher floors, where the bigwigs sit."

"Ah." Allen nodded. "I can ask Robins to try getting something that will keep us there long enough to get some answers. It might be tricky, though."

"Well, call it your next assignment. I have all the faith in the world in you." I sipped my drink, wetting my throat. "Also, be sure to check out some of the local speakeasies in the area. I know the Brass and Pass is the place for high-profile Automatics. Maybe someone there knows those dead boys and might be able to give us a lead. Something tells me it's bound to be tied up with the Iron Hands."

"The who?"

Shit. Forgot it doesn't know anything about them. Don't sweat, or it'll think something is up.

"They're the biggest Automatic parts cartel in America and currently the biggest crime family on the Eastern Seaboard. They're everywhere down here, and nothing gets past them. Most criminals who try to edge into the Iron Hands' business turn up face down in the dirt or in the bay after they attempt something. I don't know why those boys were shot at Prince and Greene, but I have a gut feeling the Iron Hands might be the cause."

"I'll be sure to check thoroughly, Detective. Until then, it seems we can't do much without Stern here. We are still at a loss as to his whereabouts and will remain so for a time."

"In any case, darts again." I stood up and felt my body bloat. I suddenly remembered that I hadn't finished my piss after dealing with the assholes who roughed up Allen. We could play darts afterward.

CHAPTER 9

HOURS INTO THE DRINKS, GAMES, TALKS, and even laughs, the speakeasy was at a standstill, and anyone still here was either passed out or very near to it. It was during this winding down of Tuesday night — or Wednesday morning, to be precise, as it was three in the morning — that the yellow Duesy came careering around the corner and shot into the parking tower. I tipped my head to alert my partner, then Allen and I got up, tossed some cash on the counter to pay for our most recent drinks, and left the speakeasy. We elected to walk over to Stern's apartment, as every cop and criminal knew my Talbot from a glance.

We headed into the building's ground-floor foyer, which was far dirtier than the upper floors that we'd seen previously. We gave the perp a few minutes' leeway before ascending in the elevator. If he was smart, he'd see that someone had tossed his apartment, and he'd start packing. If the landlady had secured the floor as she'd agreed to, the only way in or out was this elevator. Still, too many *if*s. I nervously fidgeted with my revolver in its holster. Allen eyed me as he heard the cylinder spin. I pulled the gun out, cracking the breech to see how many rounds I had to play with. One shot spent, another six loaded. If things went south, I'd need only one more.

"Where did you acquire the Diamondback revolver, Detective?" Allen asked as I slid it back into the holster tucked in my vest.

"Took it off a dead Kraut in the War. These things were valuable back in the day, and a lot of veterans sold them. But I kept mine. I made the calibre smaller, fitted it with a seven-shot cylinder instead of the six it came with, and made it my official police pistol."

"Those are quite curious modifications. How did you get such specific work done to it?"

"I have some contacts around the city."

With that, the doors slid open on the dingy hallway we'd first visited almost twenty-four hours earlier. Floor 37 — Allen had remembered.

Stepping out, I peered left and right. No sign of our perp. A few dozen steps away, I noticed that one of the doors was slightly ajar, with light creeping out from underneath. I gestured to Allen to stack up on the other side of the doorway.

I approached, grasping the handle. I lifted the handle — and therefore the door — as I pushed, keeping the hinges from squeaking. Inside, the place was more ransacked than when we'd left it. It was obvious Stern knew the jig was up and was doing his best to pack. All the landlady's work to tidy up had been undone. The kitchen was strewn with glassware and circuit boards, the couch was torn to pieces, and the hallway leading to the bedroom echoed with the sounds of zippering and scrabbling. Allen was on my heels as I skulked down the hall. The bathroom was also a mess, and a trail of debris led back to the bedroom. Allen edged ahead of me, peeking between the door frame and the door for several moments before coming close to whisper, "Stern is packing. Several suitcases, and judging by the displacement of the mattress, they're filled with some of the Automatic parts we observed previously."

"Good." I nodded, and Allen stepped back as I rushed ahead of him, throwing myself into the room. Stern turned, freezing when he saw me standing there, my finger half squeezing the trigger of my gun, which hung by my side. The expression on his thin, sunken face changed from surprise to horror.

He looked like he was freshly out of college, though his file said he was just shy of his midthirties. His clean, tailored suit was way out of the budget of a legitimate cop. He carried a basic .38-calibre pistol, probably loaded with heated rounds for taking out man and machine. Clean-shaven with a flat-top hairdo: standard issue for the 5th's boys. Yup, another faceless cop. If you needed to hide, you did it in plain sight.

"Oh, fuck … Roche, just wait a minu—"

Stern was interrupted by the butt of my gun striking his cheek. With my other hand, I grabbed his collar and pulled him hard, making his legs bend. Down he went on his knees. Allen grabbed the cuffs and locked them over Stern's wrists. I pulled hard to force him back to his feet, dragging him out to the kitchen. Allen grabbed a chair, and I sat Stern on it. I tossed my revolver to Allen. Didn't expect the metal man to use it, but Stern didn't know that.

"Roche —"

"Shut up." He snapped his lips shut, giving me the floor. "Give me one good reason not to blow the grey out of your fucking head for killing those two cops."

"I-I never killed anyone! Who's dead?"

"Don't play stupid. All your files pin you and them in the same boat for years after the Jaeger case, which made your careers. Ring a bell?"

He sat there with a glazed expression before speaking. "They're dead?"

"Fuck this." I needed this interrogation to go faster. I had no time to deal with his shit.

I pulled him from the chair, bringing him to the sink, grabbed some nearby towels to plug the drain, and began filling the basin with the hottest water the faucets could muster. Stern struggled and begged, but a quick connection of his forehead to the countertop silenced him for a good moment. Once steam floated up from the half-full basin of water, I shoved Stern's head into the sink. Allen began running up, but I put up a hand to keep it from interfering. Stern struggled, pushing against the countertop. Bubbles rose up through the water as he screamed.

I pulled him out and threw him onto the floor, where he coughed up water, his face red and spotty. I put my foot on his chest, and his eyes soon refocused onto mine. "Start again. Be smart."

"Travis Barton and Bill Ewing. Partners for fifteen years, through the War. I didn't kill them, I swear it. I had no idea they were dead until yesterday, when I got the message." He spat, his body shaking.

I could see him looking up at the robot, maybe hoping that it would give him an easier time than I was. I supposed I had roughed him up enough. Clearly he was afraid that he might be the next target of the unknown cop killer. "All right, Stern, where have you been these past few days? And I think the question I'll ask after that is obvious."

He took a few seconds before accepting that he was caught. His face went pale, and now he looked not so much frightened as angry at himself. "I was running a drop-off out of town, on the mainland. I have a few buyers out there, and I decided a week or so ago to move stock into a warehouse in Brooklyn that I just paid off. But the warehouse was raided days ago, so I thought it best to liquidate before the evidence caught up with me. Every place I've been over the past three days was either a diner or a buyer's location. I haven't been anywhere near the Lower City since Saturday. I have a few Automatic friends around the city who relay messages to me through the phone lines, so it didn't take long to get word that my old buds were history."

"Fine. Next question: Where'd you get parts like these? You just pick them up off up the street, or off the machines themselves?"

"These are quality goods from some of the best underground, all-American Automatic factories in the state. I've run my own business for more than five years.

Me and a few boys used to run the operation together, but I decided to leave before things got hairy, like they have now."

"Who ran it with you?"

"Other guys in my squad. Ewing and Barton, they were in on it, too. We all were. Jaeger went down back in '22, and because of him, we had a lot of assets. We hid some of the evidence and started the racketeering business. Just simple drops here and there at first. Then after a few years, it picked up. After Jaeger got out of the slammer in '26, I set up a little gig for us to send him a few parts now and then, my own way of apologizing. I never told the other guys that I gave him a discount, but I suppose they always knew. They had him in their sights for a while. I never knew why. But when they probed me for his information a few weeks ago, I knew something was up."

"How about the other two characters in your squad? Davin Morris and Cory Belik?"

"They took it upon themselves to run the show after I headed out on my own back in '27. Barton and Ewing were the foot soldiers for their smuggling ring."

"Would Belik or Morris ever decide to put bullets in their friends to keep those profits for themselves? After all, there isn't much honour among thieves."

"If I can be frank with you about this whole conundrum, I seriously doubt they had anything to do with this. They barely had the courage to pull a gun out on a hardened criminal. I can't imagine them pointing even a toy gun at me or any of their partners."

"That remains to be seen. After all, people change, don't they?" I heard water splashing onto the floor and turned to shut off the tap. I knelt down and helped Stern up, setting him onto the chair once again.

"Not a chance. Those boys can't change. It's just who they are. It was always my job to deal with the gun-toting Brunos we hired. For all we know, Barton and Ewing could've been offed by the Iron Hands."

The Iron Hands. So they were possibly a part of this. And owning a smuggling business didn't exactly increase Stern's life expectancy.

It also explained why he was so eager to assist me on this little issue.

I stood and left Stern there, giving him time to stew in his own failure as I approached Allen. "Ideas?"

"Stern couldn't have killed them, Detective Roche. He has the tools to do short work on repairing and refitting Automatic parts, but he has no way to Red-eye or repro-gram Automatics. I believe we may have gotten lucky finding him, though, as the other two would have been impossible to find. I congratulate you on your intuition."

"Yeah, intuition ... thanks, Allen. What about the others?"

"There is a possibility that the other two, Belik and Morris, might have instructed the Red-eyes to kill Ewing and Barton. On the other hand, these Iron Hands could have done it. It's impossible to deduce which scenario was the one that transpired until we can question either Belik or Morris ... like actual officers. I'd rather we not terrorize them like you did here."

"Oh, you know me so well already." I gave a grim smile as I turned. I knew I shouldn't rely on her to help me find people, but she had eyes everywhere. I pulled

Stern out of the chair and took the cuffs off, putting them away as he looked at me in shock. He seemed surprised that I'd even let him stand up. "You got any Automatics on your payroll?" I asked.

"Me? No. Morris and Belik, they have a few. Some are Blue-eyes, but we used to nab cop-bots back when they started turning them Green — give them a fresh coat of paint and use them as disposable messengers."

"They have any Swingers? Red-eyes? Picked up after '27, when you left?"

"M-maybe? I'm not sure."

He was looking startled again. I realized that I had been walking closer to him, backing him up against the wall.

"I'll ask them myself. I'm pretty damn sure that one of them dragged out an old cop-bot, reprogrammed it, and sent it to do the deed."

"H-how are you so sure?"

"I knew the Green-eye they rewired personally," I said through clenched teeth. Stern looked down, alerting me to the fact I was shoving my gun into his stomach. I composed myself, putting my piece back in the holster and backing away from him. "Anything else to help your case? I can still put you away with all the shit in here."

"Wait! Wait, okay, I might have been in contact with them." My eyebrows rose. "But not to that extent!" he hurried to add. "They contacted me a few days ago and asked for me to do some favours for them, since there ain't much heat on me. Just a few simple drop-offs near 90th — they don't like going there. I've done if before, and they pay me well to be discreet. It was just some scrap parts, is all. I can give you the address."

"Smart man."

He grabbed some paper and began scribbling an address on it.

I glanced at it, then shoved it into my pocket. "Get out of the city, Stern. If I see you, or hear any mention of you again in Manhattan, I'll pretend you were the killer, and one of these bullets will be for you."

"I understand. Thank you, Roche." Stern turned and ran through the hallway into his room. Did he say my name with gratitude or spite? Fuck it, it didn't matter now.

"Leave the Automatic parts. If you want to keep your hands, that is." I didn't need to hear a response to that — I knew he'd listen.

"You aren't planning on allowing a racketeering criminal to walk away without any repercussions, are you?" Allen stood in front of me, trying its best to be intimidating.

"I am. He gets to live outside of the Lower City. That's his punishment. He's still a cop, even if he has a … side business. And I might need a friend outside of Manhattan one day." I brushed past Allen before it could say anything else and walked out of the apartment. The machine looked around, trying to decide what to do next, but it relented and followed me, probably reminding itself that this wasn't a regular case. We headed down the hall, and I lit a cigarette, striding to the elevator as Allen followed.

"This is not what I would call proper procedure, Detective Roche. We must return to arrest him."

"I think you keep forgetting, Allen, that I'm not exactly police." I had a drag of the dart. Good, but not as good as whiskey. "You did nothing, so all you did was help in an investigation. You're not even an accessory if they try to convict you of anything that I did."

"I'm quite curious to know what you mean by that. I hope you tell me someday."

Allen stared into my eyes for a moment before turning its gaze to the elevator doors. "Despite this fact, Detective, and returning to the more pressing point of our visit with Stern, we have no other angles to this case. The city is large enough that these two men, Belik and Morris, could be hiding literally anywhere. What do you propose we do?"

"We split up. We now know they run a smuggling ring for Automatic parts, meaning our search just narrowed down substantially. You get the warrant and talk to some Blue-eyes downtown, get us an angle on where they're getting their parts. If this little operation that Belik and Morris are running is in competition with the Iron Hands, I'll bet money that a ton of metal men are buying from them, since they'll be cheaper and safer. I don't speak Bitwise, but I feel that you may, seeing as you still got the whole, uh … robot aesthetic."

"And yourself, Detective?" It looked at me queerly.

"I have friends in low places to check up on. Leave it at that."

━━━━━

Allen went off to search the speakeasy back in SoHo. I didn't know how it'd do, but hopefully it would get some leads. The Talbot purred as I slowed down, bringing it to first gear as I slid across West 108th, scanning the broken buildings. This side of the city, from 90th to 110th street, was almost completely abandoned — broken streets, demolished buildings. The few intact houses that remained were raided for squatters daily. The once musky city air had been replaced with the stench of mould, sewage, and decay, which wafted around every single building. The Upper City crowd kept saying they'd renovate the area once the Depression lifted, but I was sure I'd be in the dirt before they followed through with that.

Beyond 110th was where things got interesting. With everyone moving to the Lower City after the great wealth migration to the Upper City, most of northern Manhattan was left to rot. I remembered listening to a few people who hoped to find a way out to the Grotto to join up with some sort of squatter group that had built a new Hooverville up there. At least they'd gotten out of Central Park; they'd been starting to make the place look trashy. When I was a rookie, we were instructed not to go past 110th. The sixth borough of New York was said to be a seedy den of murder and lawless pleasure — the Old West all over again, like I'd said to Allen. At least, that's what I'd heard. But then again, no one who went there ever came back.

"Fucking hate this place." Toby was in the passenger seat, leaning back, its feet on the dash as it tried to stretch out in the cramped interior. "You really have to look for some fucking dumping ground out here?"

"Afraid so. It's the only lead we've got, and I need to know what Stern was asked to drop off. If it's nothing, we can cross it off. And if it's not nothing, our night will be more interesting."

"Huh, sure." Toby looked out the window, its eyes gleaming as they took in the broken buildings, the shadows creeping around, keeping their distance. "You think they know you from your car? The squatters skulking around out there, I mean."

"I'd hope as much."

"So … your new partner?"

"Drop it, Toby."

"Oh, come on! This is big news for you. I feel like a proud dad watching my son meet his first girl. Let me have this moment. It's a big step."

"Now you're pissing me off."

"Fine, fine. All right. I guess I'll have to talk to him myself —"

I hit the brakes. The tires squealed as Toby's head flew forward and hit the dash. It looked at me with annoyance while I grinned.

We finally pulled up to the address — a generous description for the site. To the south was a long stretch of road leading back to civilization. To the north was the wall of the Grotto: poorly welded, terribly balanced, an overall eyesore. Whatever happened behind those walls was alien to all but a few of us. And they didn't open their gate for anyone unless they planned to jump you, take your clothes and your vehicle, and leave you wandering around with nothing.

"Man, that's just plain creepy," Toby said, getting out of the car with me and staring at the wall. "You'd think they'd be more welcoming."

"Would you be? The government takes their money and runs, says it's their own fault, and sics GE on them. Then, when they make their own little city here, the government comes knocking and demanding a piece of the pie. I can see why they'd do it."

"You're defending the Grotto?"

"I'm just saying I can empathize. Doesn't mean I want to live there. Now focus. We aren't here to sightsee."

I was careful to lock the car door, so no one could sneak inside and hide, then later cut my throat as I started driving. The site had used to be a string of condos, all of which had been cannibalized for bricks and metal to build the Grotto, leaving a muddy pit with bits of metal and wood poking out. Snow had dusted over everything, though the grey skies had yet to release another wave of white. The still water, even with the lights from the car illuminating it, was almost pitch black. Garbage lily pads in the form of cardboard and cloth floated around, while concrete tress and lumber reeds poked out. The liquid hadn't frozen because of the filth within — which made my job easier. I wasn't planning on digging through ice to solve this case.

I was first to step into the swamp. I held my revolver above my waist. Cleaning it would take me half a week if it got dirty, so I preferred to save myself the work. I'd tucked my pants cuffs into my shoes, but that did nothing to help me stay clean, as the water came up to my knees.

"Fucking … disgusting." Toby eased its rusted silver into the muck gingerly. "Why on earth did you ask me, of all the machines in the city, to come with you?"

"You've got police programming. I'd rather have a gunslinger with me on this than a bureaucrat like Allen."

"Ah, you've named him, too."

I stared daggers at Toby, which only served to make it laugh.

"Too predictable, Roche."

Ignoring Toby, I focused on the task of finding what Stern had dumped here. It could be stuck in the muck below, or perhaps it had already corroded. It was my fault for not asking when he'd last dropped off a delivery here. I was running on nothing but expectations.

Suddenly, my foot caught on something hard and crooked that snapped up my shoe and locked me down under the mud. I yanked my foot out and called Toby over to reach down and pull up whatever I had stumbled on.

"Oh, Christ. You're paying for my refurbishing appointment," Toby groaned as it reached down, felt around, and pulled hard, its clogged servos working extra hard to lift whatever was down there.

It must have been heavy, because Toby struggled to drag it to the "shore" of the trash marsh. After a few minutes, it succeeded in heaving the dirt-covered device onto the incline, and its metal hands wiped away some of the muck. I took over, using my shirt to clean the object off and find out just what it was. A gleam of silver metal appeared under the dirt, and we looked at each other in surprise. A few moments later we had uncovered it, revealing an old, busted Automatic. The bullet holes in its chest and head told us why it was here. I popped open its noggin and found a hollow space — no Neural-Interface.

"It's just some poor bastard's dumping ground, El. No one cares about Automatic murders. Come on, this is a waste of time."

"There must be more, Toby."

"I'm sure there are, and I'm sure no one cares. You're the only one. Can I go home now?" Toby stared at me, but didn't take long to sigh and relax its shoulders. "How many more?"

"As many as we can find. At least one of them will offer some useful information."

The search took well over two hours, during which time we hoisted up seven Automatic carcasses. There were many different kinds — Erzly, Grifter, even a female Hoofer model, which was rare to see — but all of them shared the same features: bullet wounds, no NI, and at least several months' worth of sludge stuck in them.

I told Toby one more before we called it quits, so it picked up the pace dragging the final Automatic to the shore. As soon as the machine was dropped on the edge of the swamp, I saw that it was caked in a lot less dirt than the others had been, which meant that it was fresher. Wiping the muck away, I could see just how fresh it was.

"Son of a bitch." Toby's head spun to face me as I inspected the dead Automatic. "This is Rudi."

"You know him?"

"*It* … and no, not directly. But this is the Automatic that shot up that speakeasy and got tossed when I went back to the crime scene. I have a hunch that Agent

Masters had it dumped here. He must have contacts in the underworld, if he got a hold of Stern. But why would the FBI want to cover up a shooting they supposedly had no connection to? We're missing something here. What do you think?"

"Fuck if I know, Roche."

I remembered that it was Toby I was speaking to, not Allen, and shook my head before scrutinizing the dead machine to make sure it was the same one. After the third inspection, after I'd opened and closed its empty head over and over, I concluded it was indeed Rudi. But what was it that I was missing?

"Get this one in the trunk. And you can see that it's empty, right?"

"It's empty, Roche, I agree with you. Stop being so fucking paranoid ..." Toby kept grumbling as it pulled the shell up the incline toward my car. By now all of Toby's body up to the waist and its arms up to its elbows were caked in mud.

I looked over at the rest of the machines and guessed that there were dozens more still in the swamp. Every single one was headless, and I was willing to bet they could be traced to each Automatic incident in the past few months. Robins was going to call this a gold mine when I got it to him.

The marsh began to bubble behind me, the muck frothing as something moved below the surface. Toby was far and away, so I'd have to get my hands dirty for the first time all day. I switched my weapon to double-action, rolled up my sleeve, and reached into the liquid, feeling for the metal husk that was waiting for me.

It was waiting for me, all right. A metal arm reached out, grasped my forearm, and pulled, trying to drag me down into the mud. Its grip was strong, but I was stronger. With both feet planted on the ground, I yanked my arm from its grasp and stumbled back, readying my weapon. The shell emerged from the black water, red eyes glowing, both legs intact, but with only one and a half arms. I took no chances and pulled the trigger. A heated .38 round pierced its skull — the pill-shaped metalhead puffed out as the bullet passed through. I expected the shell to drop after that. It did not.

The now truly headless husk stumbled forward, reaching out with a metal claw, trying to pull me into its grave. I fired a second round into its chest. The bullet struck the Tesla Battery, which emitted a high-pitched shriek as the casing cracked. I began to run away from the machine through the murky water. At what I thought was a safe distance, I glanced back to see the husk incinerated in a bright flash. I felt my heart leap from my chest.

Reaching the shore helped me to calm my nerves. But my anxiety peaked once more when I heard metal clanking and servos spinning. The long-dead husks piled around me stirred and turned to face me. I turned and ran up the incline, screaming for Toby as more figures emerged from the black water.

"What do you want now?" Toby said, sauntering to the edge. Upon seeing the moving shells, it went rigid. "Roche, what the fuck!"

"Glove compartment! Spare pistol!"

An arm grasped my ankle as I tried to climb the incline. I looked back to see that I was dragging its legless body behind me. It slowed me down enough that some of the other now-mobile shells were able to pile on top of me, dragging me back down to the industrial swamp. I twisted around and put two rounds into the chest of the Hoofer on top of me, missing its Tesla Battery but damaging it enough that it went limp once more. The other machines clung to me like glue, just out of reach of my pistol. I'd risk losing the weapon if I tried to aim at them. My feet once more touched the murky water, and I told myself to take a deep breath before I got dragged under.

Thank God Toby had my back, just like in the old days. It ran down the shore with my spare pistol in hand, aiming at the machines atop me and firing a few rounds through their heads. These injuries did little to deter the husks, so Toby slid down and grabbed onto my hand before pushing more rounds into them at point-blank range.

"Good of you to help. Could have done without the dramatic timing." I grinned, though I was hyperventilating from fear and effort.

"Fuck off, Roche! This is not the time for jokes!" Toby pulled the trigger a few more times, and the machines released their grasp on me one by one, finally allowing me to claw against the muddy bank and pull myself up out of the marsh. Toby grabbed the scruff of my shirt and dragged me up the hill. Once we reached the top, I looked back down at the swamp.

I had underestimated how many machines were left in that dumping ground. At least ten more struggled and lumbered forward up the incline after us.

That legless machine was still holding on to my ankle. A quick kick sent it tumbling down to collide with another husk.

I grabbed the handle of the driver's door. Locked! *Fuck! Right, I locked it. Of all the times ...* One of the machines was quickly approaching as I pushed the key into the slot. I grabbed the barrel of my gun, swung at it, and bashed it in the chest, forcing it back so that I had the berth I needed to open the door. "Get in!" I shouted. Toby jumped through the open car door, emptying the rest of its magazine out through the window as I hit the gas pedal. Fuel Gel fired into the engine, and all ten cylinders roared as we flew forward, almost driving into a small hidden moat between the street and the Grotto's wall. A sharp U-turn and we were facing south, toward the city centre — and also toward the husks that were now climbing onto the street.

But my car could handle it.

I hit the gas, shifted to second gear, and heard paint and metal scraping as my car flattened the machines. I was going at least seventy, and I didn't stop until we were past 90th. Toby looked exasperated. Its weapon was smoking and the slide was locked back, signifying that it was out of rounds.

"Wait, the car was locked. How did you ..." My question was answered by the sound of wind whipping around the shards of broken glass that remained where my passenger-side window should have been. "Goddamn it, Toby."

"How else was I supposed to open the door of a locked car?"

"Did you have to break my window to do it?"

"I'm an Automatic. I take things literally, you know that."

"I sure do. So, interesting case, right?"

"You could say that." Toby slumped in the seat, throwing the gun on the floor. "You owe me big time after this."

"Roger that." I owed a lot of people. Toby was just another debtor in a long list. At least it was patient, unlike some other debtors I knew.

"You got a plan for the one in the trunk?" Toby turned back toward the back of the car. We could hear Rudi in there struggling to get out.

"I know a guy, and I trust him, too. He'll be happy to see it back in one piece."

I'd feel better once I'd proved to Allen and Jaeger that I wasn't crazy. However, I couldn't say for sure that the rest of the city wasn't going nuts.

CHAPTER 10

ALLEN RAPPED HIS METAL KNUCKLES on the door of the speakeasy. A small viewing window opened to reveal a pair of blue eyes that looked him up and down. After a few seconds, the door swung open, allowing him to enter the premises. The Automatic bouncer didn't say a word, but shot Allen a glance. The towering Titan model stood on its massive metal arms. It had a large square body, and disproportionately small legs hung underneath. Its red eyes scanned Allen several times more before determining he wasn't a threat.

The detective-in-training threaded his way between the tables and chairs and found an empty booth to slide into. A robot waitress ran past, asking for his order in Bitwise clicks. He passed his eyes over the menu that was stuck to the table and decided on sugar water.

Allen sat rigidly, peering around to discern the motives of the other Automatics in the speakeasy. A group of Erzly models similar to him — yet not the same — sat across from him, speaking Bitwise and calling out with flanged laughter, their blue bulbs glowing bright. They were unemployed, but seemed far happier than many others here who had occupations. Everything in here was a sharp contrast to the dark world he and Elias were working in: the smooth jazz, the laughter, even the variety of Automatic models.

Allen surveyed the bar for a while, making absolutely sure he was in the right place. When Elias had mentioned "high-profile Automatics," Allen had pictured the sort of noble Blue-eyes one might see up on the Plate, full of chrome and wit and willpower. He didn't see any Automatics like that, and he stuck out like a sore thumb, his dapper black suit clashing with the loose flannel shirts, torn jackets, and rust aesthetic of most of the patrons. He felt like more of an outsider than he ever had before, even going so far as to muse that he'd be more comfortable in a crowd of humans.

A few minutes later, a pair of Blue-eyes sat down next to him — a Grifter model who was far from sober, and an Erzly model much older than Allen. The Grifter's one eye flashed red in intoxication now and then. Their Bitwise was broken, and they switched to English to communicate with Allen. The Grifters had their original model name lost long ago, as they'd famously become the Automatic of choice for Brunos to send on easy hits when they'd rather not risk a human operative. This Grifter had marks across its shirt, walked funny to the table, and had some odd attachments on its crown. Construction worker? Most likely.

"Got a name, square? You new here? You look it," the Grifter said.

Allen recoiled from the forced English. "Allen Erzly. And I'm not box-shaped in any way, sir."

"Fuck off. Green-eyes aren't allowed in here."

Allen was discovering why so many Blue-eyes had been shut down or programmed to be more docile. But he was still exploring the extent of his own psyche and felt no irritation at their insult. "My optical nodes are quite blue, sir."

"What's this *sir* shit?" piped up the other one. "You a Humanist? Don't like Bitwise?"

The old Erzly model had a pill-shaped head and a slender base body. It was stripped down from the beefier models used for combat back in the War in an effort to make the human populace more relaxed around them.

"I apologize if I offended you," Allen said. "I'm just looking for information."

"Everyone is here for that reason — information and answers! And a fellow Blue-eye like myself knows all the answers," the Erzly replied, throwing its arms up and spilling some of its alcohol onto the floor.

A small Tapper bot skittered out from under a nearby table to wash the sticky liquid from the ground. It was spider-like, with a small bulb-shaped head, and it made a squishing sound as it ran across the spilled liquid.

"Exactly," agreed the Grifter, spouting off even louder than its friend. "We know everything that's happening. The world is creepy and dark, weird shit is dropping on people's heads, and the Automatics aren't free from the city, whether you're a Green or a Blue."

Allen worried that their level of intoxication might lead to violence, but knew that trying to get away might provoke them as well. The only thing he could do was sit and converse with them, no matter how difficult it was to parse their inebriated speech. "What do you mean?"

"The lies of our dreams, our heritage, our rights as citizens of this city. Humans may try and keep us down, but we're better than they could ever be. Our so-called 'betters' are weak in flesh, and they built us to be stronger in metal."

"Speaking of being 'strong in metal,' would either of you happen to know where one could acquire" — Allen leaned closer and lowered his voice — "inexpensive parts?"

"So, you *are* a Blue-eye, brother!" The Grifter laughed and slapped the table. The sound of steel on steel kept ringing for several seconds after the initial impact. Allen noticed the Grifter had burns on its shirt and belt lines. Construction worker, definitely. The clasps on its head were for a helmet — it was unmistakeable now. "The easiest place to get cheap parts is over in Times Square, or at a small joint near the western warehouses."

"Is there an address?"

"Just look for the people you can trust!" It laughed again, and its friend joined in as well. "Or at least, the people we would trust!"

"And whom do you trust?" Allen's sense of intrigue was stirring. Maybe they knew more than he gave them credit for.

"Why, each other! What's a Blue-eye without another Blue-eye beside him? We're all brothers, built not of flesh and binding blood, but of metal and eternal spark!"

The Grifter went on like this for several minutes before falling over, its upper functions ceasing as the alcohol began to interfere with its programming. It saved itself by powering down its Neural-Interface. The Erzly did little but laugh and drink.

"That did not sound like something even humans would say in regular conversation," Allen noted, peering down to make sure the Grifter had not harmed itself during the fall.

"No, it was, brother. Ha! He's a riot." The Erzly gave its unresponsive friend a quick kick of endearment. "He's been traipsing around a bunch of preachers down on 23rd Street. They're heralding in the new age of the machine — the Technossance, they're calling it. Like some bible verse or something. But let's be real — nothing changes. They're kidding themselves. And besides, he won't be repeating their rhetoric if they lock him up and Green-eye him."

"I'm sure the police wouldn't react so drastically to such … gibberish."

"Ha, maybe you're right." The Erzly grabbed its beer and downed the rest of the bottle, shaking its head before looking back at Allen. "So, you need parts? I know the people. They're not too active these days. Everyone's getting paranoid, which means we're suffering. I can get you in contact with them next time they pop up, but it might be a few weeks before that happens. Can you make it that long without?"

"I'm quite sure I can. I pride myself in my patience." Allen smiled, and the Erzly lifted its drink and laughed.

"The name's Tim," it said. "Model number TM-11. Don't worry 'bout the scrap metal on the floor, he can't do anything without me around. Be sure to look me up if you decide to visit here again."

"Thank you, Tim, for your assistance."

Allen stood up and made his way out of the speakeasy. He made sure to thank the Titan on the way out. This took the behemoth by surprise; its job was not a thankful one.

On foot, Allen could take the time to slow down, take in the city. He had been hidden away in back rooms and police training classrooms for long enough; he needed to know more about the city he'd been hired to protect. Although, given the state of SoHo, he didn't think there would be many people to speak to here.

He walked north toward the Central Village and Chelsea and noticed an increase of people and machines on the street, a kind of life segregated to certain sections of the city. Apparently, SoHo had been labelled an Automatic Neighbourhood in the early years before Second Prohibition. As the controversies arose, people had left in droves. He got a few glares from humans as he entered the Central Village, but otherwise he was left alone to explore the area.

Every corner of the city had a crier, it seemed, saying this and that, handing out newspapers or pamphlets, or just screaming nonsense. Allen's "ears" caught the words of street preachers speaking of the "coming of the age of the machine" and other apocalyptic prophesies. The subjects discussed in the newspaper sounded far more interesting, and Allen deposited a few coins into the crier so he could see what exactly was going on in the world. He sat on a nearby bench, machines and men passing him by without a second look as he read the news.

The world kept turning while America suffered, though not every corner of the great Land of the Free was under the iron thumb of debt and poverty. The West Coast was doing quite well, with construction of the Golden Gate Bridge nearing completion and reports of Automatics being brought into the workforce to expedite the process. The column right next to that one mentioned that the current Automatic crime rate was greater than what the Mob crime rate had been before Second Prohibition. Definitely something he had to read up on later.

"You! Abomination!"

Allen peered up from the pages of the newspaper. A dishevelled man stood before him, waving a pamphlet in his face. His beard was longer than the hair on his head, and he wore a tattered, stained jacket. He threw the pamphlet at Allen before walking off, talking to no one in particular. "You dare affront God with your hubris and spirit! May you be stricken down by the Lord and by mankind!"

Allen tried to think of an appropriate response. "Thank you …"

When he looked down at what had been thrown at him, his eyes narrowed. It was old — dated 1927 — but still in circulation for good reason. It was titled "The Iron Truth," and contained information and pictures about the Automatics used in the Great War. About how many had been built and the savagery and number of deaths they'd caused. There was an image of a legion of nearly broken machines slaughtering the enemy, some caked in blood, others crawling through the dirt to strangle and slay the opposition. Another image was a sketch of Automatics standing on a pile of corpses while burning the American flag, with the words *Who is next?* underneath.

Allen could see what had begun this new divide in society: fear-mongering with probable cause.

He leaned back on the bench, deep in thought, watching the people passing by. Automatics might be shunned and frowned upon by many, but he could see a surprising number of them still interacting closely with humans. Groups of Blue-eyes walked with friends — both human and automatic — talking, laughing, drinking. No one seemed to care, as there were far worse things happening down here than humans and Automatics getting along. The ritzier humans among the crowd wore suits or dresses, and were either businessmen or mobsters — or perhaps those were one and the same down here. Allen had been told that sleek fibreglass outfits and sharp, angular designs predominated current fashion, but that didn't seem to be the case in this area. Lower Manhattan was stuck in the late 1920s, and no "Technossance" would change that until the city cleaned itself up.

He saw something else when he looked deep into the crowds, something that defied the history books he had read. Men and women were both equal, as were black and white. All humans were equal, all valued above the machines, who were treated like dirt, just like the human slaves of old. All transgressions were forgiven in the name of progress and scapegoating. Human nature reared its ugly head, and again, one society was built upon the backs of another. Hundreds of years of racial tension, and all it had taken to heal those scars was something else for all humans to hate universally.

Allen was part of the worldwide excuse.

Looking up at the towering billboards and electronic screens that had recently been unveiled didn't deter this assumption. The billboards marketed everything from suits to drinks to the latest cars. Television was a burgeoning new technology used by businesses first and foremost to make back the money they spent on the devices. While nothing was overtly anti-Automatic, it was hard not getting that vibe from the advertisements. Ford was "Mankind's Car." The slogan for Land in Upstate New York was "The Eyes Are Always Greener Here." Even postings about jobs and welfare said in big bold letters, "Help for the Working Man."

He got up from the bench and merged into the crowd again. He felt like something inside him had sunk down a few leagues. Now, walking shoulder to shoulder with other bipedal creatures, he felt more isolated than he had before. The sight of rust and steel was easier to pick out and identify with than the men and women who surrounded him, giving him suspicious looks because of his blue eyes. The walk to the 5th Precinct was a hard one, but it gave him all the thinking time he needed.

"Who's there?"

Robins's office was a beacon for Allen in this dark, dreary underbelly of a city. It was late, but it seemed that the commissioner spent more time in his office than he did at home. It was well beyond eleven at night, and Robins was the only one left in the station. All the lights were off except for the one in his office and the one in the hallway leading to it. Allen poked his head in, and Robins relaxed, lowering the gun in his hand down. "Oh, Forty-One. Sorry, I get jumpy this late. What are you doing here?"

"Commissioner," Allen began, trying to reciprocate his boss's formal manner, "shouldn't there be people working at this hour?"

"Inspections, son. FBI wanted the floor cleared so they could see if my officers were hiding anything under the floorboards. They aren't. I'd know about it, after all. But we humour them." He sipped from a snifter on the desk that sat next to an M1911 pistol. "Can I help you?"

"I need access to the higher levels of the General Electrics building. It's for the case Detective Roche and I are following."

"I see." The commissioner didn't bat an eye. The alcohol was weighing him down. "It's hard to get juris- diction to go up there. Only when 'absolutely necessary,' they say. They allot only thirty minutes a month. But I've been saving them up in case it ever does become abso- lutely necessary. Best I can get you is about two hours above the Plate. Hell, what am I saying? Roche usually only needs five minutes to get his shit done. You probably won't even need all that time."

"So … you're giving us access?" Allen asked, puzzled at Robins's behaviour.

The commissioner reached into a drawer and grabbed a hard plastic card. He slammed it onto the desk and slid it to the far edge, then went back to his drink, turning to look out the window at the dead fountain outside. Allen approached the desk and took the card.

"You know what that fountain is?" Allen was caught off guard by the question, but Robins didn't wait for an answer. "That is a tiered fountain, built in 1862, and designed and crafted by Owen Jones, who helped make the Bethesda Fountain in Central Park. They shut off the water back in 1925, and they nearly took the fountain, too."

"Fascinating," Allen said, trying to be as supportive as possible, but unsure of how to proceed.

"I got them to leave it there. I had to pull some major bureaucratic strings, but thanks to being friends with the mayor … well, it was worth the effort." He took another sip. "I proposed to my wife in front of that fountain, you know, in 1918. I'd just got back from the War, and I told her that I couldn't make it through another one if I wasn't with her. You ever feel something like that for someone, robot?"

Allen was at a loss, almost choking as he answered, "No, sir."

"Didn't think so. Stuck here talking to a machine. Sounds like my life these days. All work and no thanks, not from no one but my officers. They do too much for this city, and for me. Roche especially. Bastard quit and still can't get away from this place. We'll be the death of him, that's for damn sure."

Even inebriated, Robins could be a wealth of information for Allen. He took the liberty of squeezing in a question. "Why did Roche ever leave, sir?"

"For the same reason I kept that goddamn fountain. You have your access, robot. Get to work."

Robins shut his mouth after that, leaving the room in silence except for the groan of the ceiling fan and the roar of passing cars outside. Allen took that as his cue to leave.

He patted the pocket where he'd stowed the access card as he turned and walked out of the building.

He headed south once more, toward SoHo. Perhaps Roche would spot him on his way back from his errands up north and pick him up. And then, as though Roche had heard Allen's mechanical thoughts from across the city, the French Talbot appeared, roaring down the street. Allen waved it down.

Roche pulled over to the side of the street, pushing the door open as he got out. He was panting and pacing around, and there was panic in his voice as he explained to Allen what had happened up north. His pants and shirt were stained with dirt and mud and other repulsive-smelling substances. An Automatic got out of the passenger seat, likewise slathered in muck, its eyes blue and its servos creaking. The mud had likely gotten into some very hard-to-clean areas.

It approached Allen, holding out a mud-covered hand. "Toby, friend of Elias. You're the new partner, huh?"

Allen didn't answer, but instead looked over at Roche, who had stretched out his back and calmed his breathing down.

Roche looked at both machines and nodded at the car. "Get in, Allen. We've got some juicy stuff to catch you up on. And we've got the evidence we need."

"A Neural-Interface?"

Allen jumped as he heard slamming and shuffling from the trunk of Roche's car. Toby snickered as it slid back into its seat.

Roche scoffed, wiping his nose before pushing his seat forward for Allen to climb into the small cab behind him. "Better — a suspect."

CHAPTER 11

MY TALBOT SCREECHED TO A HALT outside of Karl Jaeger's shop two hours later. I hopped out along with Toby and unlatched the trunk. The two of us pulled out the Automatic from the back. Rudi struggled in my arms, its flanging voice roaring with anger. A quick disconnection of its arm servos rendered its limbs useless. Allen stepped out of the car slowly and followed us.

I hammered on the door to Jaeger's shop. After a moment, we heard tentative footsteps approaching from inside. The door opened several inches to reveal Jaeger clad in pyjamas, his face pale with fear. "What the hell are you doing, Roche?" he whispered, peering behind me.

"And what the hell is *that*?"

"We got you a present. Open up."

He did as I asked, and we dragged ourselves in. Jaeger slammed the door shut behind us and locked it, then pulled the window blinds down to prevent anyone from seeing inside. Toby and I sat the Automatic down on a folding chair and bound its legs to the seat with belts. Allen stayed near the door, watching us work.

"Have you any idea what this looks like?" Jaeger said. "What would any other cop think if they saw you three idiots dragging a robot in here? I'd be thrown back in prison faster than I could say, 'Don't look!'"

"You're welcome," I retorted.

"The fucker's friends nearly corpsed Roche, here. Besides, we thought you might recognize him." Toby grabbed the Automatic's head and turned it around to reveal the faded spot where I had torn off its serial number a few days ago, along with the large identification letters that spelled out *RU-D1*.

"Rudi!" Jaeger's eyes popped wide open and he grabbed the machine's head himself to inspect the missing voice box and tampered-with electronics. "Where on earth did you find him?"

"*It*," I corrected him. "And that is a story to tell. But I've got something even better for you. He's moving, right?"

"Of course! Red-eyed as well ... how displeasing. This will take so long to reverse —"

He fell silent as I opened the back of Rudi's head, revealing that it was empty. "I was right. This was the Red-eye that shot up the Prince and Greene speakeasy. Seven other Automatic shells tried to do me in at the dumping ground where we found it."

Jaeger peered inside. As he pushed his hands into the tiny space, his eyes widened even more. "Impossible ... impossible! He's moving, acting, trying to kill you!"

"With no brain. Interesting, huh?" I smirked with self-satisfaction and walked off to lean against a nearby desk. Allen joined me. "How'd you fare?" I asked it.

"Good, Detective. I was able to get us access to the restricted areas of the General Electrics building. We have a Police Access Card, which will serve as our temporary warrant for anything above the Plate, so to speak."

"Excellent." Things were working out — that was a first.

Jaeger dragged a small table over to Rudi and set up a terminal and some wiring kits behind it. He pushed his fingers along the seams of Rudi's neck, finding what appeared to be a loose plate in the back and flipping it up to reveal a hole — about one and a quarter inch in diameter. He retreated to the back to root around before returning with the appropriate plug and jabbing it into the machine. Rudi's shell lurched once before the terminal took over.

Jaeger held a flashlight in his teeth as he peered into Rudi's empty cranium at what was left of the Neural-Interface's wiring. He clearly wasn't in an equitable mood, but we had work to do with this machine. It was Allen who took the initiative to remind him.

"I know this might be difficult, but could you run through the possible places it's been in the past four days?"

Allen had tried to sound empathetic, but Jaeger would have none of it. "Difficult? Difficult is searching a two-storey house for a single termite. Trying to narrow down locations through a Cortex is like dropping a penny from five miles above the Plate into a teacup. The amount of data Rudi has collected in the last few days will be a nightmare to sift through, and because I'm the only person who knows even a fraction of what it takes to build an Automatic, you two won't be much help."

"Good to see your humility is on point with your intellect." I sat down in a chair and put up one leg on an adjacent table as I tilted back. "You'll still do it, though."

"Of course I will. No one takes my machine without finding themselves in deep shit after. It'll take some effort, though. The Cortex isn't the easiest to interpret."

"And why's that?" I genuinely had no clue what he was talking about. But any bit of information could help.

"The Cortex detects the Automatic's location longitudinally from the magnetism of the North Pole, reading its location east and west, but it can't discern distances north or south. Instead, it cross-references with towers across the country which supplement those coordinates, allowing the Automatic to triangulate and receive accurate information as to its location from almost anywhere. But, if it's outside the range of those towers, then it's dead in the water. It would tell you it's at seventy-seven degrees west, but its location could either be Washington, DC, or some godawful city in South America."

"And which towers would it use as reference near here?"

"The one tower big enough to be picked up by every Automatic in the city is GE."

I stood up and went to the door, opening it just as the sun was appearing, illuminating the street beyond the blinds. I peered at the behemoth of a building looming in the distance.

"Thankfully the Cortex is often separate from the Neural-Interface and is stored somewhere in the carapace. Bootleggers used to think they could saw off an Automatic's head and steal the parts without being tracked. *Dummköpfe.*"

"Yeah, perps tried to do that to me back in '24. Did not go well for them." Toby chuckled to itself.

"That Cortex do anything else, Jaeger?" I might not have known much about Automatics, but since we had access to GE, I wanted to kill as many birds as I could with the stone Allen was holding.

"I've never tinkered with it, but as it's powerful enough to receive signals from and broadcast to the reference towers at GE, it must do something else."

I shut the door and walked back into the room. The workshop was silent other than the sound of Jaeger typing on the terminal. Even Toby wasn't in the mood for talking. Maybe he'd used this incident as an excuse not to go to work today.

I took it upon myself to wander around the shop. I hadn't gotten the best look a few days before. As far as I could tell, Jaeger wasn't currently repairing or servicing any other Automatics; this must be a slow season for him. He'd have to sell actual goods for cash.

Allen finally piped up. "Would it be possible to connect his Cortex with me?"

Jaeger glanced up from his work. "And why on earth would I do that?"

"Because I could work with the data faster than you could manually on a terminal. After all, I have a more complex system, which may be able to parse data faster than a terminal could."

"You seem to doubt my abilities. What would make you more adept than I?"

"I'm merely saying the idea is feasible, as it would save time decrypting and mapping out coordinate locations across the city. I could process the data myself and find out Rudi's precise movements over the past several days. No offence to you, of course, but any method to achieve our collective goal more quickly would be the best method."

Jaeger looked stunned — likely by being schooled at his own craft by an Automatic and by realizing that his own hubris was a problem in and of itself. He beckoned to Allen, who grabbed a chair and sat down next to Rudi. Jaeger strung several wires together and prepared to connect the two machines. "You could not have mentioned this idea sooner?" he asked.

"I wasn't sure whether your plug would fit into my terminal." Jaeger scanned the back of Allen's head for several moments. "I do believe it would be better if I were standing for this procedure," Allen said.

"Nonsense. Be quiet." I walked over to watch the two brainiacs at work. Jaeger popped open Allen's head and froze. He dropped the cords and gaped. My jaw nearly dropped as well. Even Toby's blue eyes seemed to open wider.

Allen wasn't lying — it had a brain. Or something very similar to one, at least.

From the back, the contraption looked quite brain-like, but instead of fleshy grey mounds, the organ inside Allen's head was luminescent and looked to be built out of brilliant crystal. The material felt as tough as steel. The crystal bumps and curves weaved through the head, electrical signals and fluids zipping through the clear tubes. It glowed like a gem, running like an engine, but moving and conforming like a living thing, learning and adapting.

Jaeger's eyes begged for answers.

"He's supposedly a Synthian, whatever those are. New robots, but ... they're different ... as you can probably tell." I backed away, leaving Jaeger and Toby to keep looking inside Allen's head.

"It's miraculous. *Mein Gott.*"

"Fucker's holding out on us, huh?" Toby added.

"I was attempting to inform Mr. Jaeger that the ports that connect me to basic Automatic devices are located on my torso and neck, but I think this has been too overwhelming an experience for him. If you could, Detective, please insert the plug into the port."

"Not the most comfortable sentence to hear ..." I took the cords from the floor and scanned Allen's neck, finding a node about the size of the plugs where its lower neck vertebrae would be. I jacked the cord in, saw Allen stiffen up, and gave it time to run through the immense volume of data coming from Rudi.

Seconds later, Allen removed the cord itself, closing its head, then stood and approached the desk with the terminal. "A map, if you don't mind, Mr. Jaeger."

Jaeger nodded. He removed a rudimentary map of the Lower City from the wall and flattened it out on the table. Allen retrieved a marker from nearby and ran the black ink over dozens of points on the map, tracing and crossing out each small segment and landmark in the blink of an eye. And then, almost as soon as it had begun, its movements ceased. It reviewed its handiwork and looked up at me in confirmation.

"It ... Rudi ... was indeed at the pickup point you mentioned to meet with whatever suppliers you deal with, Mr. Jaeger. However, afterward, it was abducted and brought to this location here" — Allen circled an area near the 5th Precinct building — "before being brought quite far north, where its signal was left for about thirty hours." *Interesting*, I thought.

"Doesn't explain why it came back from the dead to kill me," I said, "or all those other bots coming back, either."

"Yeah," Toby piped in. He had to be part of every conversation. "At least twenty of those bots were skulking around, trying to drag him to hell. It was freaky ... and *I'm* saying that."

"We're missing something," I said. "Someone abducted the damn thing, removed its Neural-Interface, gave it a gun, and told it to shoot up the speakeasy. Then, after the deed was done, they tossed it up north in some dumping ground. But why not just shoot up the place themselves and toss Rudi's shell in there to implicate Jaeger? Red-eying Rudi would take too long, and removing a Neural-Interface ..."

"Could take longer," Jaeger confirmed. "If they were being careful, that is. And God only knows how its moving without a Neural-Interface."

I grumbled for a moment, rubbing the bridge of my nose, the frustration giving me a headache. "Allen, we're heading to GE."

"Do you have any idea who we might speak to?" Allen asked.

"Head programmer for GE — Vannevar Bush — is a big name in the company. Maybe he has his office hours open. Lord knows he should if he wants this mess dealt with."

"And me?" Toby said.

"No, just me ... they weren't too interested in you, actually. Something to bring up later."

"No, I mean, where do I go after this?"

"Oh, sorry. Stay with Karl, make sure no one comes looking for Rudi. Turn that Cortex off for a while, too. We don't want any surprises."

Jaeger nodded and did as I said. Allen and I went out the front door to the Talbot. As we slumped back into the car, the machine looked down at my trousers: "Detective, are you sure you want to go to such a reputable place in your current ... state?"

It was attempting to be subtle. I'd give it points for that.

"I'm sure. After all, there's no fun in going up there if we can't fuck with them on the way."

The site where Rudi had been taken that fateful night was empty, as I'd expected. Not even a building they could have dragged the metal man into — just trash, back alleys, and a few apartment buildings filled to the brim with human garbage. I made sure to check every single door. Those who opened up for me were happy to say they hadn't seen any cops or G-men there. Those who didn't answer either swore at me to go away or cocked some sort of weapon as a warning from behind their door. After about an hour or so trying to find possible witnesses, I concluded my search and moved on to the more pressing objective.

Being in the neighbourhood near the 5th gave me a chance to head to the precinct and grab a Police Parking Tag, which allowed me to park my car anywhere I wanted to. Robins was happy to hand it out, since it required the least amount of paperwork to grant and made him look good in front of the agents in his office. An officer requesting something and following the proper channels to receive it? We must have looked like the picture-perfect face of law enforcement in their eyes.

Having the parking tag made me feel so much better about driving my car onto GE's precious lawn. I hit the emergency brake, and the car skidded across the grass, leaving tire streaks across the green expanse and no doubt ruining someone's day. The armoured security guard was powerless to move the car or argue, what with the big New York Police Department badge displayed prominently on the windshield.

Allen, of course, raised concerns about my parking, but I ignored them as usual.

Walking into the futuristic foyer immediately caused a ruckus when the secretary recognized me and reached for the phone. "Shit, he's back …"

"Sorry, sweetheart. You can't get rid of me today." I lifted my hand to show off the card, prompting her to place the receiver back on the base.

As we walked to the executive elevators, we were once again harassed by the same security guards who had given me a few noticeable bruises on my face. They moved to grab their pieces, but a flash of my card froze them in place.

That made me smile. "At ease, gentlemen."

"You're no better than a vagrant, you know that? You deserve to be out there on the streets."

"Try and put me there, then."

Allen pressed the elevator button, and we heard it roaring downward on its high-powered magnetic rail.

The guards parted as the doors did, but the sneers on their faces revealed fantasies of beating me black and blue. I waved at them once more before swiping my card. The doors whirred closed.

The elevator shot up faster than I was expecting. I reached for the wall to steady myself. The elevator was quite spacious — almost as large as my bedroom, in fact — with four lavish chairs bolted to the walls, each accompanied by a side table. The wall opposite the door had a large window that looked out onto the Lower City. The bulbs on the Plate had yet to brighten and illuminate the dusk. As we rose higher and higher, more of the cityscape became visible. Allen was on the edge of its seat with its hands up to the glass, taking in the sight like it'd never see it again.

For all I knew, it might not. Me, neither.

I could see many of the southern Control Points for the Plate: my apartment building at Bowery and Bayard, the Empire, Chrysler, Flatiron, and 60 Wall Tower, all of them balancing the world's broken economy on their shoulders.

Soon enough, the elevator passed through the Plate, and we lost sight of the Lower City, entering instead the dozens of layers of manufacturing and heavy industry that kept New York — and America itself — afloat.

The elevator slowed to a stop and the doors opened onto a dark-grey corridor that stretched out about twenty feet, with an elevator at the other end. Halfway along the corridor was a metal ring that protruded two inches from the walls, a sort of security gate. Allen looked spooked.

"Is this the right way, Detective?" it asked.

"Unfortunately."

We emerged from the executive elevator and started across the hall, our every step reverberating. Allen's steps were much lighter than mine, despite the metal frame. We were about five feet from the metal ring when the walls began to move; seamless doors built into the sides of the hall slid out of the way, and the Plate's own Underguard emerged to look us over.

They wore faceless masks and strange plated armour that hid their actual proportions, and they carried sleek Frag Rifles. These chrome weapons were designed with maximum lethality in mind; the ammunition was stacks of tungsten-iron flechettes which were fired silently — no primer or gunpowder needed, only magnets — and could punch through both Automatic casings and human flesh.

The guard closest to me held out a hand. "Identification?" Its voice sounded scrambled and electronic.

"Elias Roche." I jabbed my thumb toward my companion. "Allen Erzly. Here to do some police work."

"No Blue-eyes allowed on the Plate."

"It's a cop, same as me." The merc didn't believe me. I pulled Allen's broken badge from my pocket and handed it to him. "Fifth Precinct."

"No weapons allowed on the Plate," it continued.

I glanced down at my Diamondback in its holster, but instead handed the merc my access card. "Police business. I keep the weapon. Can't have me defenceless, now can we?"

They could have intimidated me, maybe raised their rifles and spooked us by threatening our freedom or our lives. But they didn't. Perhaps they were in a good mood today, because the excuse I gave seemed to suffice. They let us proceed through the ring. I felt an electric buzz on my skin. Elsewhere, the ring's security feed would indicate everything that I had on my person, both over and under my skin. The ring must also have served as a deterrent for Automatics, because Allen seemed erratic and a bit scrambled for a few moments after going through.

The elevator at the end of the hall opened, and we entered as quickly as possible, turning around to see that the Underguard had already pulled back and disappeared behind the walls, seamless doors returning to their original positions.

Allen looked at me questioningly.

"They can't have just anyone walking around up there," I said.

"I suppose."

The doors closed, and we shot upward again.

Before long, our eyes were assaulted by the unob-structed sun. The view beyond the glass was of a city alien to us bottom-feeders. The streets were adorned with cars of a much simpler and cleaner type than those found in the Lower City. Sleek, stylish, and designed for passengers' maximum comfort, these little automobiles were no doubt made by Ford or Chrysler. The roads were wide, with simple lines and no curbs; the pedestrian paths were flush with the roads. Quite an odd design choice, I thought. Even odder, all the drivers seemed to be Automatics. But not Blue-eyes; every machine on the Plate was Green.

The parks and natural green spaces of the Plate were hills and valleys that were integrated into the ebb and flow of the roads. Small parks were set in the centre of large rings of buildings. There were no skyscrapers up here; instead, simple buildings rose to a maximum of ten storeys, likely to limit the weight placed on the Control Points. People here looked ritzy and pompous, flaunting their clothing and influence as if no one would try take it from them. Up here, no one *could* take it from them.

"Wow." Allen finally broke the silence. Its face reflected both exasperation and fascination. Seeing these emotions made me feel better and made my part-ner seem more human.

"Yup, welcome to the home of those who escaped the collapse. Lucky bastards."

The elevator rang as we reached our floor: 150, head of research. The doors parted. Several people were standing there, waiting to head down in the elevator, and they recoiled at the sight of me. I waved my dirty left hand at them, and Allen apologized in passing as we walked out onto the sleek floor. Said people — dressed in their expensive, gaudy clothing — *tsked* as they entered the elevator and checked that I hadn't sullied their transportation.

The area we stood in was much like the foyer of GE, but maintained to a degree that no one in the Lower City would have considered feasible or ethical. Machines scrubbed the floors of dirt and dust, and the white tiles and silver walls were adorned with windows and interesting sculptures that made me feel like I had stepped into an art museum. The reception area was manned by a lone woman who was quite lovely and more amicable than her counterpart downstairs. Above her station was a painting of a Mercury train passing over the conceptualized and newly planned Golden Gate Bridge. The piece was called *Gateway to the Future*.

Cute.

The woman looked up at me, smiled, then frowned — not in disgust, but concern. "Sir … are you all right?"

"I'm good, darling." I showed her the access card, resting my clean arm on the surface of the desk. "Just checking in. Official police business. My partner and I are up here to question some bigwigs in the Automatic Department."

She nodded and took the card, examining it before handing it back. "Saved up quite a few trips to make this one, Mister …?"

"*Detective* Roche. Allen is the Blue-eye."

"Ah. Well, Detective Roche, I would suggest keeping your machine on a short leash … people up here aren't too fond of Blue-eyes. You have two hours to conduct your business, after which we must have you removed. Do you need assistance reaching anyone in particular?"

"Mr. Vannevar Bush's office does not seem to be posted here," Allen said, scanning a directory. "We are hoping to speak to him."

"*Doctor* Bush is the head of Automatic Research. I'm afraid you won't be able to see him on such short notice." Her tone had changed from pleasant to slightly annoyed.

"Tell him the fate of his creation is in the balance if news of what we know gets out," Allen said, interrupting her. "Trust me, he'll want to clear things up. I'd bet my salary on it."

The secretary bit her lip before standing up. "I'll see what I can do. Don't go anywhere."

———

As we waited for the secretary to return, we looked out the window, down at the men and women passing in and out of the building. I had the feeling that Allen was uncomfortable seeing only Green-eyes up here, being used like slave labour with no room for personality. The Plate was an impressive accomplishment of culture and engineering, but it had not occurred without sacrifices.

"All this space wasted on so few," Allen said, finally breaking the silence.

"Two million ain't exactly a few, Al."

"But why?"

"Why stay up here, or why leave us twelve million down there?"

"Why build it? Why create this little world separate from ours below? Do they feel that they're better than us? Why did people not fight this as it became a reality?"

"It didn't start out like that. Rockefeller started the project in the early '20s, way before Second Prohibition. He wanted to create a way to fit even more people into the city, to allow people from across the country and the world to flood into New York and call it home, everyone from stockbrokers to farmers to dirt-poor beggars. His dream was a city of two worlds, mingling and joining together in brotherhood. After GE and the first few places on the Plate were built, the FBI moved up there, followed by a few dozen denizens, then the Stock Exchange."

"And then?"

"And then Black Tuesday hit." I leaned my shoulder against the glass, with every Automatic on the floor looking at me as I stained the windowpane with my dirty clothing. "Rockefeller could build GE, but the rest of the Plate was going to be expensive, so he asked for assistance. Of course, the wealthy could afford to help, and the only thing he could offer them was space on the Plate when it was complete. The more people who helped, the more people he owed, so when everything was settled, everything on the Plate had been scooped up by those who could afford to invest or to pay the rent. It became its own monster, a monolith of hypocrisy. People say he lives in the Lower City now because he's disgusted by what he had to do to realize his now-perverted dream … but those are just rumours. I'd bet any money he lives at the top of the Empire … right next to Gould."

"Who?" Allen asked.

"Gould, the guy who runs the Plate. Or, well, it's complicated, but he has more shares in GE than anyone else and helped mitigate the financial problems they experienced when the Depression hit. Now he controls almost everything up here."

"So, how does one get on the Plate, then?" Allen asked, even as a Green-eye guided me away from the window so it could clean the fogged glass.

"No clue, Allen … no clue. I've been trying to find out for a while now. Most people pay through the nose to get up here. Or you're just born into it now. Lucky pricks."

"Born into what? Wealth, or living up here?"

"Both. Hopefully one day their world will be turned upside down and they'll understand what the rest of us are experiencing."

"That woman said to keep me on a 'short leash,'" Allen said self-consciously. "Do they treat us that badly up here? Are we not already victimized on the ground?"

"You're less than a second-class citizen here, Allen. You're less than a piece of meat. To them, you're the quintessence of slavery. The Green-eye is the perfect subservient creature that'll do everything they can't be bothered to. Drive, clean, walk the dog, babysit, work in the factories. Anything humans consider themselves too good for, they have you do it."

"But … why?"

"Because even in paradise, someone needs to scrub the shitters." I pulled out my package of cigarettes, preparing to light one when I heard my name.

"Detective Roche?"

Allen and I turned to the man who had addressed me. He was average-looking with a rectangular face, thin hair, round spectacles, and a soft, calculating face. He was smart, and he knew it, but he wasn't an asshole about it. His voice was gentle but stern, commanding authority but not demanding it. With hands behind his back and an upright stance, he compelled us to follow.

"We have much to discuss."

CHAPTER 12

VANNEVAR BUSH'S OFFICE WAS on the top floor of GE, and just based on its doors, it deserved to be there. They were tinted glass, which gave visitors a faint look at the clutter inside without giving away too much. A flash of his wallet near a sensor unlocked the doors, allowing Vannevar inside, with Allen and me trailing behind. The doors shut immediately after, locking as if to prevent anyone from interrupting our meeting.

The walls were covered with awards, certificates, paintings, and portraits of famous men and women. There was a central desk covered in papers, a small workbench big enough to play with an Automatic arm on, a couch, two chairs, and a sleek circular coffee table in the centre. Above the desk was a chiselled wooden Automatic arm filled with ornate shapes and imagery. The thumb was sticking up and the fingers were curled in. The inscription read *First Annual Vannevar Bush Engineering Award*.

"I haven't got all day, Mr. Roche. I'm quite a busy man. Keeping an entire race of sentient … things … alive, you know. So, please, do tell me how you plan to threaten my livelihood."

The old bastard was pretty tough. He hadn't the stature nor the commanding voice to say what he did with any sort of weight, but standing in his office was enough to make me feel like the Plate would crush me if I stepped out of line. I was at a loss for words.

"I never meant to say —"

"Oh, come now, everyone wants to threaten the Automatics. Politicians, law enforcement, thugs. You're no different. And so, I've made a little Riot Act for dealing with you people. Hopefully then you will think twice before coming back to the Upper City to brutalize me with such trivial arguments —"

"Sir," Allen interrupted.

Vannevar tilted his head to give the machine the floor.

"Detective Roche is no thug. There is an issue that requires immediate attention. He was nearly killed by a 'headless' Automatic." Allen mimed quotation marks with its fingers. I smiled. It sure was getting smart.

"Headless?"

"A term we use for Automatics without a Neural-Interface installed," I said. "Two Red-eyes recently shot up a speakeasy, killing six people. Three of those were cops either undercover or off-duty, and two of those cops were tied to a smuggling ring we're looking to expose. One Automatic was apprehended and shot, and upon popping it open, we found that it had no Neural-Interface. Moreover, when I found it again a few days later, it was moving again, still with no NI. We were hoping someone might be able to explain how this is possible."

"I see." Vannevar placed his glasses on the desk and rubbed his eyes. "Was this an isolated incident?"

"We uncovered the machine in a graveyard past 90th. There were a few more machines there, most of them headless as well, that also tried to kill me."

"How many is a few?"

"Twenty, I'd say."

The old doctor got up from his desk and grabbed his glasses before walking to the far side of the office and pressing his hands against a section of wall near his worktable. Seams appeared, allowing access to a hidden room through a nearly invisible door.

"Come. Perhaps we can work through this problem together."

We followed him through the door, and it was soon clear to us what the rest of the space on this floor was used for. A massive area resembling a factory floor sprawled out before us, filled with fabrication tools, workbenches, terminals, wiring kits likely more advanced than anything in the Lower City, and Automatic shells galore. In the centre of the room stood a fascinating display: an enlarged and exploded view of the innards of an Automatic, strung up by tough rods of steel and separated enough to view each and every part of the machine, while also being able to see how it all fit together. The surrounding frame seemed to be a Grifter model, but an old one: it had an angular head with rough edges, two small bulb eyes, a basic lockbox mouth, plated arms, and a barrel-chested frame to pad the interior wiring.

"Before I begin, I suspect you have your theories. You seem intelligent enough to connect the dots. So please, Mr. Roche, give me your proposal."

I hated being put on the spot, but it was better than being ignored and talked down to. "An engineering comrade of ours" — Allen looked at me shiftily as I referred to Jaeger — "told us that he believes it involves the Cortex, which contains a gyroscope for feeding itself information about its relative location in the world. But it needs a reference for longitudinal coordinates, so it gets information from GE's reference towers. We think it might have something to do with that."

Vannevar nodded, curling his lips in thought for a moment before speaking. "Your theory is interesting. However, the Cortex is much more complicated than just a storehouse for data. It is that, but it serves many other functions, too. Take the device in question, here." He grasped a nearby pointer, extending it and aiming into the centre of the exploded display at an octagonal piece about the size of my fist. "It contains a gyroscope, yes. But the Cortex is essential, as an Automatic is useless without it. I'm sure you understand why."

I did my best to hide my ignorance. "Maybe give us a quick refresher, Vannevar."

He scowled. "Dr. Bush."

"Sure."

"Ugh. Cretins …" Vannevar shook his head. "The Neural-Interface is the 'brain' of the machine, but it is useless without a way to move the data. It can conceive information, but without a way to transfer it, the NI would generate data like a terminal, keeping it in a singular point. To this end, just as a brain needs a spinal column, the Neural-Interface needs the Cortex. The latter contains many crucial components besides the gyroscope, such as the ABS and ACE — the Automatic Balancing System and Aspect Conversion Engine, both old technologies from the Manual days — as well as the receiver, capable of receiving wireless signals. Though not powerful enough to transmit data, it can receive simple data, such as reference commands. So, while the Neural-Interface is able to create the signal to move the Automatic's arm, the Cortex is the device that allows it to be executed through the ACE. With no Cortex, the Automatic is a vegetable trapped in its own mind. And without the Neural-Interface, the Cortex does nothing."

"Might the Cortex be able to receive signals from an alternative source in order to operate properly, Dr. Bush?" Allen asked.

"Indeed, it could," the old man said, smiling.

"Wirelessly?" I inquired.

"Perhaps … but the reference towers are not designed in such a way. They operate only on radio wavelengths in order to send a continuous signal that allows an Automatic to triangulate its position. A signal that could affect the Cortex would require a substantial amount of energy and would be much too weak to travel over long distances. Boosters would be required for the signals to be detected, as well as a specialized device to allow the reference towers to proliferate such a specific signal. We have been experimenting with a way to conduct wireless telecommunications using pylons connected to the underside of the Plate. As of recently, the pylons have been used for collecting wireless data from Automatics to alleviate the stress put on the Reference Towers. Unless someone has gone behind my back, nothing else has been done to those pylons or Towers."

As I looked over the exploded diorama, the pieces started fitting together in my mind. It might be a long shot, but I had a solid theory. "Could the reference tower's signal be modified to connect to those pylons? As from a singular point? Someone sends Automatic commands through the towers to the pylons, they go to specific locations which are then detected by Automatics attuned to that signal, and then the Automatics execute the commands?"

"Interesting theory, but as I said, it would require the pylons themselves — or at least the central Reference Towers on GE — to be attuned and modified to handle and transfer such signals. Furthermore, those Automatics in the graveyard — past 90th in the Lower City, you said — were much too far away for the pylons to have been within range."

"Someone could've set up makeshift radio towers, or piggybacked off old ones," Allen suggested. "There would be much less interference in that area, allowing them to connect to more than one or two Automatics at a time."

The theory didn't sound so crazy anymore. In fact, it sounded almost plausible.

"How old is this tech? Are these Cortexes standard in new models?" I asked.

"Almost all Automatic models have the same Cortex, just modified and updated — even the old Swinger models from after the War," Vannevar replied.

So ... it might have been him. Fuck. *It*, I meant. Some son of bitch could be using my friend's dead corpse to torment me. But why?

First things first: time to confirm whether this theory we'd put together was real.

"I need access to the engineers who work on those towers, to see if they were modified. They should be inside GE, right?"

"Of course." Vannevar put the pointer down and readjusted his glasses. "A floor below us, working on Automatic Support Projects. Do you think this was done by someone internally?"

"I think it was done by someone who knew who to talk to. Time to do some digging."

Whatever the boys in the room labelled *Tower Control* were working on, they dropped it as soon as I kicked open their door. It wasn't locked, but old habits die hard. At least thirty scientists stood up, complaining and murmuring to a man about what a nuisance I was. They weren't like the engineers we had under the Plate; they wore pressed suits whose shoulders were reinforced with silver and copper. They had triangular and rhomboid shapes pressed into the fabric of their clothing, giving the impression that they were humans contorting into metal — or maybe the other way around. If they were all rich enough to afford such clothes, they were also rich enough to know what they had to lose.

Vannevar had stayed behind in his office, sending the secretary from earlier to accompany us "for insurance reasons."

"All right, boys," I said as I walked in, Allen right behind me. The secretary stayed outside. I flaunted the holster to one side of my waist and the badge to the other. "Let's play a game. Who thinks they're smart enough to talk themselves out of being a murder suspect?"

The question travelled around the room like the latest gossip. Such words were foreign on this side of the Plate. They fell silent as soon as I began speaking again. "Now, we have a theory: someone here has access to the reference towers on GE, and therefore has an idea of how they operate. They might have had the crazy idea of modifying them to connect them to the pylons on the Plate, to radio towers on the ground, or who knows what else. Regardless, doing so has led to many, many deaths. How many, I can't tell you, but if I had to estimate, I'd say the number of corpses equals the population of this room, tripled. And that's in the last month alone."

Truth be told, I had no idea how many people had gotten corpsed in the past month, but they had no idea I was lying. The squares talked amongst themselves, and I kept talking to them while Allen looked each one up and down, doing its best to scout out who the conspirator might be. Some of them cursed at Allen, some calling it a "filthy Blue-eye," and one even tried to spit on it. When Allen stopped next to one of them, I knew there was a good chance we'd found the right man.

He was a technician with hair that was thin on top and thick at the sides. He wore a copper blazer with a brown vest underneath and had a squished-looking face. When I approached, he looked up at me, and I could feel his sense of unease.

"What made you stop, Al?"

"He didn't yell at me."

"Huh." I squatted in front of the man, and his eyes locked on to mine. "Consider yourself a smart man?" I asked.

"Yes, sir." Squeamish voice, with a faint lisp. Lucky for him he was working up here and not down there.

"Sir? I'm no sir. Detective will do. Now, what do you do here?"

"I calibrate the towers regularly, as many of us do. Record signal speeds, tune overall performance, install hardware updates and test parameters, make sure everything is running silky smooth."

"Do you work on the tower itself?"

"Everyone has access," he said, looking away from me, "in case someone needs to deal with a hardware problem directly." His expression wasn't exactly innocent as he skirted around the question.

"Can any terminal connect with and broadcast to the towers?"

"It's an automatic system. However, there is a manual terminal set up for that use."

"Do you have access?"

"No, only the directors and people with special privileges do."

"How might one get special privileges?"

"I don't know!" he exploded, making Allen back up. I didn't move an inch. "I don't know, okay? I just work here. Back off, will you!"

I stood up. "You know what prison is like?"

He kept his mouth shut, but his eyes went wide.

"Now, jail is simple," I continued. "Stay behind bars, wait for the trial, shit in your own bucket. But once the sentence goes through … then you go somewhere else. Most mobsters go to Rikers Isle. Rikers is bad, but there's another place that's much, much worse. It's called Silverveil Prison, and it's run by Automatics with a single human warden. They put the worst of the worst there and have no problem torturing, beating, sometimes even killing people. These guards don't eat, sleep, or shit. If there's a riot, they push gas in to calm everyone down. The guards are all Red-eyes — yes, Red-eyes — so they don't feel a thing. If I find out that you did something to these towers and didn't tell me, then when I get back here, I will drag you there myself and get my Blue-eye to kick the shit out of you before we push you through the gate. I'll make sure that the next time you see light is when they turn the cremation oven on."

I might have overdone it, because everyone in the room was on edge. Allen had its hand on my shoulder, and the poor bastard I was yelling at was crying, with snot pouring out of his nose. But since I couldn't pull out my gun here without causing a diplomatic incident,

I'd had to resort to words. It was weird seeing someone so affected just by words.

"He said … he said no one would know," he sobbed, barely intelligible. "He said he'd kill me if I told anyone."

"He had dirt on you. Most do when they make demands. What did you do?"

"I … I added a signal router on the towers and allowed it to bounce high-intensity signals."

"Who told you to do this?"

"H-he contacted me through my terminal … the message came from the Special Privileges Terminal. I tried to find out who it was b-but …"

"Show us."

He got up, wiping his eyes as we followed. The secretary gave me an inquisitive look when she saw the man in tears, but I shrugged and we moved on. The room wasn't too far. It was locked electronically, but one solid kick was all that was needed. The lock stood true, but the hinges popped off and the door opened the wrong way. GE really needed to update its infrastructure.

The interior was spartan, containing just a desk, a chair, and a terminal. On the walls were various sheets with operating instructions and codes. I pushed the technician into the chair and had him log in. "Directory, now. Let's see who has access."

He did as I asked, then I pushed him out of the way, sat down in the chair, and scrolled through the list. While he couldn't get into the system fully, he could at least see which users were allowed to attempt to log in. Many of the names belonged to head engineers: Vannevar, Whitehead, Baekeland, even Rockefeller. Some were neither technicians nor engineers: Greaves, head of the FBI; Bowsher, mayor of the city; and many others.

"Why does every bigwig need access to this terminal? This do some important thing I'm unaware of?"

"It … it activates the White-eye Protocol." The technician had finally stopped sobbing.

"White-eye?"

"The extermination protocol. If there's a massive Automatic uprising, or if Automatic crimes go up to a certain threshold, the White-eye Protocol is activated, causing all Automatics to enter a homicidal and suicidal state. They hunt down and destroy other Automatics, or themselves if none are around. It's a last resort that would destroy the entire line of machines countrywide if activated."

"Huh." My eyes caught on a name I'd been half expecting to see, but I was still surprised that my hunch had been correct. *E. Masters.* "Well, well, well."

Alarms suddenly sounded. The technician sprinted back to the Tower Control room, and we followed. The squares were all on autopilot, running around trying to deal with some issue. The technician returned to his desk and started typing at his terminal at a blistering pace.

"What's going on?"

"Signal surge," he said, eyes still on his terminal. "The towers and pylons receive an immense amount of data. We need to route it in real time through other pylons or it'll overload GE's communication network. These new systems are in their infancy, as you can see."

"Do you have a real-time feed of the signal? Intensities and all that? You set this up for that bastard

Masters. You think you can track the signal through the pylons?"

"You know quite a bit for a cop. Yeah, I can try ..." A flurry of keystrokes changed the screen: lines upon lines of numbers showed values for devices I couldn't even fathom as they tried to track down the cause of the flood. "Wow, yeah. Looks like something is bouncing through the towers. Pylons in Chelsea and the Lower East Side are on fire."

"Where's it coming from?"

"No idea ... they're both huge neighbourhoods. We don't have that kind of capability to track where these signals go or come from, but we know it's focusing in both those places."

"Fuck." I rubbed the back of my neck. Still, it was better than nothing. "Masters made one mistake: he brought this right to your doorstep. At least we know two places where the source might be ... time to narrow it down."

I called to Allen and we exited the room as the engineers continued troubleshooting. The secretary sighed with relief and escorted us back toward the main foyer.

Our two hours were almost up.

Chelsea and the Lower East Side were both massive locations, and the inaccuracy of the pylons didn't help much. It couldn't be a coincidence that Masters had been at the crime scene, had had access to the terminal that the technician had been blackmailed through, and was leading this year's precinct inspections. He was up to something in conjunction with this smuggling ring, but

I needed solid evidence before I went accusing an FBI agent of racketeering and murder. But why was some FBI agent running a smuggling operation that was cutting in on the Iron Hands' action? And why kill two cops and get my attention? Anyone with two brain cells to rub together would know that might cause a small turf war.

And why involve my old partner? Why use some beat-up old Swinger as a hit man? Unless Masters knew who I was. Those machines in the graveyard had targeted me, not Toby. What if all this was for me?

When we reached the foyer, the secretary scanned the access card once more and handed it back to me. "Fifteen minutes left. You don't dally, Mr. Roche."

"Detective, you mean."

Allen hit the button for the elevator. I turned to look out the window at the back of the elevator, seeing the sun shining down on the Upper City's many buildings. No one in the Lower City ever got to see this — such a waste. I knew I should be soaking it in. Who knew when I'd see the sun high in the sky over Manhattan again.

In the corner of my eye, I noticed a Green-eye staring at me. This one didn't look like it was worrying about the windows; it seemed awake. While Allen was watching the doors to the elevator, the Green-eye approached, reaching inside its janitorial jumpsuit. The hairs on the back of my neck stood up. Its eyes blinked red for a moment.

Then it pulled out a slip of paper. I breathed a sigh of relief.

"She's expecting you," the Green-eye said quietly, handing me the paper. Its voice sounded alien compared to Allen's. Then it backed up and resumed its duties.

The slip of paper bore an address. Apparently, she wanted updates and was in no mood to wait.

How would I ditch Allen so I could go and meet her? It would be suspicious to do so right after this. Then again, if I didn't, she might use Allen as an example of why I should be more prompt the next time.

"I have to go meet with Toby. Make sure Jaeger is all right," I said. Allen was still watching the elevator doors. "You good?"

"Yes. I just wanted to say I was impressed with your theorizing back there with Dr. Bush."

"Thank you, Allen."

"Might I accompany you to see Toby and Jaeger?"

"No." *Shit, I said that too quick.* "No, I have other business to attend to, and I'd rather we split up and cover more ground."

"But I have nothing to do without you, Detective."

This machine is going to be the death of me. "Fine ... fine. Let's just get out of here."

The elevator opened, and we stepped inside. Turning around, we saw that the secretary was standing there, waiting to see us off. She smiled and waved. "Please take your time coming back, Detective."

As the doors began to close, she relaxed into a scowl just a little too early. Moments later, the small box rocketed downward, trapping us under the thumb of the Plate once more.

CHAPTER 13

I WAS GOING TO SEE A BIT MORE SUN before the day was over. I parked the Talbot on the southern side of 98th street and got out, leaning against the car and craning my neck. I was so used to seeing the great steel slab of the American Dream hanging over us that I rarely ever looked up. This little trip to Harlem was much more relaxing than my previous escapade there had been, so I christened the calm moment by lighting a dart in my filthy fingers.

I could've stayed there just looking up. Harlem might have been dangerous at any time of day, but sometimes it was much more tranquil than the city I'd learned to love and hate.

"Detective, what are we waiting for?" Allen was getting impatient in the passenger seat, its eyes shifting back and forth nervously. It'd never been out from under the Plate.

"A signal. I'm choosy about how I meet my friends, so I often go out of the way to set up meetings in places I trust."

Allen fell silent, watching the street through the broken window.

My attention was suddenly drawn by the sound of someone knocking on the door of one of the buildings on this side of the street. Two knocks, twice.

Our signal.

The building in front of us looked like it had been bombed out: busted windows, holes in the roof, one entire wall torn out.

"Wait here." I threw the half-smoked cigarette on the ground and stepped on it, then walked toward the source of the sound.

I grasped the handle of the rotting wooden door and pushed. The sound of creaking hinges filled the space. Inside, it was dark; the other end of the room was almost pitch black. I closed the door behind me.

Seconds later, a blinding light pierced the darkness, causing me to recoil. I raised a hand to shield my eyes. Once my eyes had adjusted, I tried to focus. Squinting, I made out a lone figure sitting in a chair with hands folded, one leg resting on the other. The chair was a luxurious one, with dark wood and red cushions, a real antique far older than either of us. The industrial lights shining in my direction made the darkness even darker, obscuring her face and upper body, but I could see the legs of several of her people hiding behind her.

She must have been waiting for some time, or perhaps she'd had other clients earlier.

"We never have these talks anymore, Elias. I've missed you terribly." Her voice was throaty but still unmistakably feminine. She could have been a singer, but she'd had greater aspirations than that.

"Afraid I can't say the same for you, darling. I do appreciate the tip you gave me, though."

"I'm the Eye of New York for a reason. I see everything." She huffed with laughter, amused by her own name. "It was the only information we could find, unfortunately. Our reach extends far, but we have our limitations. And intelligence sometimes works against us. Our sentries are afraid to skulk by the 5th. One buzzer and they panic."

"Then get better men ... or whatever you use." I pulled out another dart and bit onto it.

A shadowy figure emerged, blue lights in its eyes shining as it raised a match to light the cigarette for me. "Thanks, bud."

"Smoking again? You only smoke when you're nervous."

I didn't answer, puffing away to prevent myself from instinctually throwing it down. "What do you want?"

"You have yet to deliver, Elias. This shouldn't be hard for you. You've done jobs far harder than this one so many times before, and far quicker. Perhaps you're getting old?" I couldn't see her face, of course, but I had a feeling she'd smirked.

"I'm fine, darling."

"Or maybe you've been emotionally compromised? I've heard that you're quite obsessed with the other Red-eye killer being a Swinger model. We both know how you take coincidences."

"Don't start." I paused when I heard her chuckle, but she allowed me to continue. "We met one of the perps, but the other two are supposedly in hiding. They'd formed another racketeering ring deeper than the one Stern was running. They split from him in '27, so as far as association goes, it's as dead an end as we can get."

"And the only reason you know that is because of me." She tapped her fingers on the arm of the chair impatiently. Her patient tone wavered a bit. She must have taken my last comment as an insult. Now I felt a cold sweat creeping over my body.

"Look, I'm not here to make excuses. I'm here to say that if you want this solved cleanly, I need more time and more information. Besides, I didn't factor *you* of all people into this case. I thought this would be easy, open and shut. Pop a few rounds and everyone goes home laughing. But when I saw the Red-eye's empty head, I got suspicious. As soon as I saw Jaeger, my gut didn't like it one bit. And then, when you decided to give me some charity finding Stern, I knew this started and ended with you and your ragtag group of Brunos."

She stood up and walked past one of the lights. Her silhouette dragged across my field of vision. Long hair worn down, sharp chin, broad forehead, lips like the best of dames'. She could kill you with looks and guns alike. In the dark she leaned over and whispered something to one of her associates, and the scurrying sound of shoes against concrete echoed as they ran out of the room. I caught the hint of a shimmer on her arm. Perhaps it was a bracelet, or maybe she'd decided to do some Aug-ing. She'd never give me the satisfaction of knowing.

She returned to her chair, resting one elbow against her knee and leaning her head in her hand. "Did you dispose of Stern?"

I hesitated. There was no hiding things from her, though, so I might as well save her the trouble of looking. "I let him go. He's out of the city by now."

A loud crack rocked the room, and I nearly jumped out of my britches. One of the arms of her chair was reduced to a misshapen twig. I stared as her hand relaxed and released the tangled mess of wood.

"You had explicit instructions," she said through clenched teeth.

"And I told you I'd take care of it. But not everyone has to die to solve a problem."

"Maybe in your line of work. Not in mine." My calm responses were beginning to make her voice rise in volume and harden in tone.

"Maybe if you stopped putting hits out on every poor bastard that gave you a mean look on the street you might see that this could be a setup. Those two dirty cops might be innocent."

"Innocent? Of the murder? Or of cutting in on my business?"

"Maybe both." I dropped the cigarette, my backbone returning. "This has the scent of G-men all over it. This Masters guy ... he knows how Automatics work, forced some poor guy to modify the towers at GE, and his name has been popping up far too often in my investigation.

He's controlling it all, I'm sure of it. But those other men don't need to die."

"Mercy is a sign of weakness, Roche. You of all people should know that. So when you find Belik and Morris, make sure they aren't breathing. The same with Masters, if he's part of this."

"You're putting a hit on a federal agent? That's dangerous, even for you." She didn't respond. "Any reason you're throwing me into the fire and not one of your lackeys?"

"I can't have his blood on my hands, unfortunately."

"Ah ... there we go." I smirked, and I could sense her blood beginning to boil once more. "There's the kicker. You're powerless to stop him, because everyone and their mother in Lower Manhattan would know that you were the one to pull the trigger, and then you'd have a war on your hands. Status quo, just like Robins. Now I remember why you keep me around."

"Yes, for that reason, and because your name still carries weight."

"Which name? Elias Roche, or the Iron Hand?"

Once again, she didn't respond.

"I'll do your dirty work, and you know I can set the price for these hits."

"Indeed, I do." She was grinding her teeth. "I'll have your payment ready when the deeds are done."

"Good." I turned to leave, but the click of a hammer made me stop dead. Always had to have the last word, didn't she? "Fuck, what is it now?" I said, turning back.

A skittering of feet was followed by faint, indecipherable whispers. I could see her head nodding before she spoke again to me. "Your partner. Has he any idea of our ... acquaintance?"

"None the wiser. I doubt he'd understand, anyway."

"Try him sometime. He's no regular Automatic, after all. I'm sure you two would do well to stay partners."

"How did you know —"

"I have ears where I cannot see, and eyes where there is nothing to hear." She lifted her arm and the shadow of a heavy revolver became visible in her grasp. "And an Iron Hand to reach everything. I'll be in contact soon to see what's become of these suspects of yours ... perhaps I'll give your friends at the 5th a ring, just so they keep an eye on you."

"We don't need to involve them any more than I already have."

"Why not? Robins knows you work for me, as does anyone there with half a brain. If I want something done by someone — anyone — I will call it in."

She reclined in the chair, relaxing her grip on the weapon. Her associate who had run from the room returned with the same haste, running up to her and whispering in her ear. "Speaking of which, there's a deal being done at the Crossroads. You have thirty minutes. Good luck, Elias."

I kept my mouth shut as I opened the door and sprinted back to the car. I slammed into the door of the Talbot, got in, and kicked the beast into gear.

Allen nearly jumped out of its seat. "Detective! What is it?"

"We have an ID on Belik and Morris in Times Square. We need to get there, pronto. Hold on to something."

"Like what?"

I hit the clutch and pulled it back as I gassed it, firing us off like a rocket, southbound once more. Once again I was speeding away from northern Manhattan, but this time I was running toward something. I almost crashed into a crumbled brick shithouse, but regained control and kept motoring.

The Crossroads of the World was where you could find anyone.

———

I punched the gas harder as I careered around SoHo to Greenwich Village, meeting one of the many avenues packed with cars heading north. The Crossroads of the World — Times Square — was just up ahead, the only place in town deserving of that kind of name. We crept forward in the Talbot and soon saw the golden pillars of Times Square come into view. I got closer to the sidewalk, hitting the gas and then cranking the handbrake, and the Talbot slid across the pavement and came to a halt, the tires colliding with the raised sidewalk. Looking ahead, I could see the scramble of civilians around the square. As soon as the intersection lights turned red, the street was fair game. There was no way my car would get through that. I grasped the handles on the roof of the car and hopped out through the open window. Allen was about to follow, but I put my hand up. "If things go pear-shaped, I'll need backup. And I'd rather you do that from here."

"How would you have me help, Detective?"

I leaned back through the window and pointed to the console with the gear shifter. "Listen to everything I say — and I'm making it quick. No repeats."

"Of course, Detective." Allen sat attentively, watching my finger like a hawk.

"If things go south, there's a pull switch on the shifter, near the grip … here. This will give the motor a kick and shoot some extra Fuel Gel into the engine to get you moving. It could be handy for saving my ass, or someone else's. Got it?"

"I'm not adept at the operation of automotive vehicles, but I believe I have everything under control," Allen said, sliding into the driver's seat.

"Make sure you're gassing it when you pull it, too. I don't need you fucking my car up."

I sprinted away from the car, heading into the crowd. Even half a block away, the lights and sounds of the square were dizzying. Huge screens and billboards nearly reached up to the bottom of the Plate, and a cacophony of people, machines, and advertisements bombarded one's ears. There was never a time these streets weren't congested — maybe around three a.m., the traffic let up for a brief moment, but the rest of the time it was bumper to bumper. Every two minutes all the traffic lights went red, and a sixty-second scramble ensued, with pedestrians climbing over cars to get from one side of 7th Avenue to the other. Almost everyone in the city filed through here at some point, and yet spotting a specific person in this mess of a city centre was near impossible.

I reached the great neon district of Lower New York, with its blinding propaganda and advertisements hitting me like a brick wall. "The newest Automatics, safe for all, built Green-eyed." "Drink Coca-Cola — all the celebrities are doing it, too." "Police took out another smuggler trying to cross the mostly frozen Hudson River." "War veterans are meeting at the Legion Hall in a week." Under the Plate, these were our sun and moon, seeing as the rich had robbed us of our true light. I'd have to check out that last one, see if any friends from the Great War had survived this long.

The Times Building was one of the infamous Control Points for the Plate — yet another reminder of how close, yet far, the Upper City was to us. Some Upper City executives liked old Manhattan, and preferred to commute to work by walking through Times Square and using an executive elevator. It was obvious their nostalgia was clouding their judgment about how dangerous this city had become; bumping into the wrong person or taking one wrong turn could end up corpsing them.

Still, because these executives lived close to the Times, the few blocks around the city centre were ritzier than the rest of the Lower City. The streets were clean, the buildings refurbished, and people carried themselves differently. Even the Automatics that came here were more diverse than just the standard Grifter model. Blue-eye female Hoofer models were abundant here, walking alongside top-heavy male Boomer models that often worked construction or maintenance. Ritzy folks down here could afford Titan models, gorilla-like Automatics that followed their every move and had the strength to crush anyone who got in their way. I even caught a glimpse of a rare Moller, one of the most human-looking Automatics. It looked uncannily female, though its porcelain-like face and small, shifty eyes made my skin crawl when I locked eyes with it. I suddenly realized how far I was from the Talbot, and how nervous I was about letting Allen into the driver's seat. It was my backup, after all, and if they ran, I needed someone faster than I was on foot.

I had to focus.

The lights in the centre of the square hit red, and the scramble began as the crosswalks opened and people and machines ran this way and that in a free-for-all. Some people, drunk and stupid, ran headlong into others. Businessmen and gangsters tried to keep to the outside, avoiding the local cops who patrolled the area on foot. Standing in the centre of it, everything was a blur, with faces changing a mile a minute, making me feel as if I were looking at the world's longest police lineup and had just one minute to make the ID.

But a lot can happen in a minute.

Like catching a glimpse of your target. A sickly, thin man was walking between five others, all of them wearing dark suits and carrying heavy briefcases. One was shorter and fatter than the rest, his face obscured by a hat and a tall collar. He leaned in to say something to the sickly one, whom I recognized as Belik, so I figured that he was Morris.

The other four men with them all wore identical suits and dark glasses and had the same erect posture that made them look like floating statues.

I carefully drew my handgun, keeping it close to my side as I weaved through the pedestrians to get closer.

Being stealthy in Times Square was easy enough, but men as jumpy as Belik and his associates had an edge when it came to spotting threats.

And luck just wasn't on my side that day.

Belik's eyes met mine for a brief second as I raised my weapon. The rest of the men instantly sensed something and turned to me as well. Now I recognized another one of them — a tall, lanky asshole in a black hat. Masters.

Morris and Masters each grabbed Belik by an arm, and the three of them took off running. The three men who had stayed back lifted their briefcases, grabbing the black boxes and pulling them apart. As I should have expected — the briefcases were Foldguns. Seconds later, the sleek, angular shotguns rested in their hands, ready to pump me full of lead. Each man loaded a shell into his Foldgun's chamber with a distinctive *crack* sound that was almost as loud as a gunshot and mistakable.

People either heard the guns or saw the Brunos, and soon the street was filled with the sounds of running and screaming. The men pushed past the screaming pedestrians toward me. I had to get out of here before I became little more than a bloody stain. I fired two rounds at the three hit men. One entered the lead man's leg, and the other flew close to another man's head, but ricocheted off a light pole beside him.

At the sound of the shots, people ran or dove for cover behind anything they could — garbage bins, light poles, statues — leaving a large pathway open in the centre of the square. A rare sight indeed. This afforded me a view of Belik and the other two jumping into a black Packard 900 parked at the edge of the square.

I soon heard the familiar crank of my Talbot's engine. Allen had apparently gotten the hint that things had gone south. The tires screeched as they caught the pavement and sped toward me. I ran to the street to meet him as the Packard peeled out.

Allen swung the Talbot in using the handbrake, sliding in front of me and allowing me to duck down as pellets from three shotgun shells smashed into the metal panels and bulletproof window of the driver's side. I pushed myself up and dove inside the broken window on the passenger side. Allen slammed his foot down on the gas, and I righted myself in the seat. I replaced the empty shells in my revolver and pulled back the hammer as we gave chase to the black Packard, which was now careering out of Times Square.

Allen kept the pedal down to keep up with Belik. A standard Packard could never match the speed of my Talbot, but they'd gotten the jump on us. *Allen must have driven before*, I thought, as the gears and levers ran like water under its metal hands, sending us down the alley the Packard had swerved into. The Packard hit trash cans and debris lining the sides of the small side street, forcing it to slow down and allowing us to gain on it inch by inch.

The Packard pulled a hard left onto 6th Avenue, where the traffic was far less dense than on 7th. But horns still blasted at us as we peeled through traffic, drifting between the lines and over lanes, forcing other drivers off the road.

After several blocks, Allen and I were right behind Belik's vehicle. I grabbed the handle on the Talbot's ceiling and hoisted myself up and out the broken window until I was sitting on the door. I levelled the Diamondback, pressing the lever forward to return it to its double-action configuration. I steadied myself as best I could and fired off a shot at the back tire. The bullet skipped off the pavement, missing its mark by mere centimeters. As I attempted to level to fire again, I heard a loud screech behind us. I looked back and saw that a second Packard had swerved into traffic behind us. And someone had the same idea as me. Except he had his gun trained on me, not on our tires. And his gun was a lot bigger.

I slipped back down into my seat as the familiar *rat-tat-tat* of a Thompson Typewriter unloaded .45 rounds into my bulletproof roof. I blessed my foresight months ago as the soft sound of Allen trying to chastise me for my actions was drowned out by gunfire and adrenalin. Allen cranked the handbrake, dropping us back behind a few other cars and almost hitting the other Packard as it swerved out of the way. The civilian cars that were now in front of us soon realized the danger and retreated from their positions on the road, opening an opportunity for the assailants to attack us again, this time from the front.

As this chaos ensued, Allen kept a firm eye on Belik's Packard, which had taken a hard right, smashing into a parked Adler and pushing it onto the sidewalk. Miraculously, the Packard kept going. As we followed it into the turn, the second Packard swerved and tried to catch us on our right side. It missed and slowed down, falling behind by several car lengths, giving me a chance to poke my head out and test my luck. The silhouette of the driver was barely visible behind the dark windshield, giving me a good idea of where he sat as I levelled and fired. The bullet entered the window and the car immediately lost speed, tires screeching, horn sounding in a constant drone until it hit a parked car and stopped.

Turning my focus back to the other car, I could see that our target was making up in manoeuvrability what it lacked in speed. We were speeding down West 53rd, the subway suspended high above us on the left, when the Packard sped up to pass across Park Avenue. I was pretty sure I had two shots left, and I knew I needed to use at least one, so I brought the weapon up and squeezed the trigger. Unfortunately, it didn't do much, as Belik's car had sped up just enough to pass through the traffic coming from the north without incident. The bullet instead slammed into the front of a Marmon Sixteen, probably killing its engine.

Allen yanked on the brakes and the Talbot slid to a stop, but not before scraping against every car parked on the right side of the street, leaving a strip of paint across the front panels of my car.

"Fuck, fuck! We lost him. We goddamn lost him!" I kicked the glovebox in frustration, holstering the revolver as I continued cursing.

We were so close. We could've ended this case right here, right now. Instead, we had one dead Bruno and another one wounded, which equated to nothing in terms of progress. The car full of gunmen was probably vacant by now, the body missing, leaving the police and me with nothing to go on. Going back for the car would be the surest way to get thrown in the slammer.

Allen said nothing, but looked at me with both sympathy and disappointment when I told it to drive to my place. The one thing I needed now was something to drown my disappointment in. At least things couldn't get any worse.

CHAPTER 14

ALLEN PARKED THE CAR in front of my building. What a goddamn night. Nothing had turned out right. Now I needed to get the car checked out; it had kept making concerning noises all the way back, now that there were a few new pellets and bullets in the frame.

Yuri was still selling his dogs, this time to the night crews that were getting ready for their shifts as the Plate lights prepared to go out.

"Good evening, Elias!" he said in his Russian accent. He flashed me that smile of his that could stop bullets, shook my hand hard, and nodded gratefully. "You come back earlier than you usually do. You might be first customer for once!"

"I ... I suppose so. I'd be honoured, Yuri." I smiled back and put a few coins on his little chrome cart — a little more than what the dog cost, but he could use the cash. We shared a little conversation, but I was all too aware of Allen, who was standing impatiently near the doors to the building. So I bid Yuri goodnight and we headed inside. I finished the street meat in the elevator as other people got in and out on our way up. At last, we reached floor 75 — so close to the Plate, yet still so far away. Allen followed me into my apartment, closing and bolting the door behind us. I went into the kitchen. "Well, Allen, shit. I suppose things could have been worse."

No response.

Suddenly I heard the various clicks and clacks of metal gears and felt steel on my wrist. Allen jerked me off my feet and handcuffed me to the fridge door. With lightning speed, it retrieved my revolver and placed it within its suit pocket. It took me a few seconds to react, then I blew my stack.

"Allen, what the fuck!"

"I apologize, Detective Roche, but after observing your actions tonight, I believe it would be beneficial to the investigation for you to remain here, under house arrest, until I can —"

"Metal man, take this shit off my hand and stop fucking with me."

"This is no joke. I must prevent you from endangering other civilians or law enforcement, including myself." It looked resolute, though I doubt it had any idea what it really was doing.

"Endangering? Shit ... Allen, you're essentially killing people right now by doing this. If you don't take this cuff of my hand in three seconds, I swear I'll kill you." But Allen didn't back down. It stayed silent, staring at me, calling my bluff. After a few seconds I lost it. "Allen! Fucking stop this!"

"I'm sorry, Detective Roche."

"No! No, you are *not* sorry. You have no idea what you're doing right now. I will *make* you sorry, you metal fuck!" I grabbed for my revolver, but Allen moved back just out of my reach.

"I've watched you engage in police brutality, discharging of a firearm without warrant, forced entry, and several other violations. I doubt that you have done one thing in this time span that even you could point to as 'good' besides sparing Stern's life. I've held my tongue until now, but seeing as we have returned to your abode, I thought this the perfect time to prevent you from committing any more infractions."

"And who's the judge of my actions, huh? You? A fucking machine?"

"As I said before, I am not a standard Automatic —"

"I couldn't give a shit! You live in a world of ones and zeros. You could just be some cleverly programmed Automatic Robins sent to fuck with me, but it doesn't seem that way, so maybe you need a hard lesson, metal man. We don't live in a world of black and white, never have. Maybe you and your brethren do, but we do not. But I will find a way to make you black and blue if you don't unlock these cuffs."

"Yes, I've heard before from multiple sources, including some prominent psychoanalysts, that we live in a world of shades of grey. However, unlocking your cuffs now would do little to impede the possibility of violence —"

"No, not a world of grey. Grey wouldn't do this world justice. We live in a world of shades of red, Allen."

At this point it let its guard down, perhaps trying to comprehend my metaphor, or thinking of a way to calm me. I grabbed its collar and brought it close to my face, speaking harshly through clenched teeth. "The question I wake up to isn't 'Will I do the right thing?' or 'What difference will I make?' That isn't what crosses my mind when the 5th phones me in. What I ask every day is 'How many people will die today?' The fewer, the better. There is not a single day that someone doesn't die. You can't save everyone, and sometimes to save some, others have to die. Welcome to the real world. Welcome to my job. You have no idea what it takes to do what I have the past three years. I am the one thing preventing the cops and the Mob from killing each other every goddamn day! You're not even half the Automatic James was, I swear to —"

In the midst of spitting out my anger at Allen, I saw something I wasn't prepared for. Allen's eyelids, or whatever they were, were closing around its blue bulbs, as if it were cringing. I had scared a machine. I let go.

Allen backed away, silent as it smoothed its crumpled collar.

"I left the Force years ago because I realized there's a thin line between law and justice. I chose justice. The law has rules. The law stops the cops from becoming the people they lock up. But justice is retribution. And sometimes morals get skewed when you're chasing justice. Sometimes you fall as far as those you chase. I act like a criminal to catch criminals, and that's what you see me doing. Though I must admit you're the first person who seems to care."

I slumped against the fridge. I'd never spat my thoughts out like that before. In fact, this was probably the most I'd spoken in the past few weeks. I used the cuff on my wrist to pull myself up and open the freezer. I pulled out a bottle of hooch and held it between my knees as I popped the top off. I raised it to my lips and downed some of the vile liquid. "Robins doesn't give a fuck as long as I get him a body or a confession ... or both ... and if it weren't for me, the Mafia would have torn up the 5th and every other precinct in Lower Manhattan."

Allen approached once more, sitting down beside me with its back against the cabinets. It looked like a child drawing its knees up to its chest. We both sat in stunned silence. My wrist was beginning to go numb as the handcuff dug into my skin.

Finally, Allen said, "You were admirable when we were in pursuit of Cory Belik. It was fortunate there weren't any civilian injuries. I also found it irresponsible of you to fire from a moving vehicle. I could go on for many hours detailing your infractions. However, I can see you are well aware of them yourself."

"I'm not saying what I did was right, Allen. I'm saying that sometimes you have to do what you need to do, not what you should do." I took another swig, thankful that I'd saved it. "Besides, I don't see you reprimanding the guy with the Typewriter in the Packard." I smirked. Allen didn't. Humour, right. "But you're right ... I could have killed someone. Someone innocent."

"You could have killed four civilians with reckless firing of your illegal firearm. Instigating the shoot-out also could have caused severe injury and property damage from those criminals firing shotguns in a civilian centre. I can see why you are no longer officially part of the police force."

That one stung. It was right, but it still hurt. I was getting reckless. Too reckless. That must have been why Robins had assigned Allen to me. It was there to keep me from blowing my lid and getting my name on the FBI's Most Wanted list. Or, maybe to ensure that I couldn't be tied back to Robins. After all, if they dug deep enough — and they wouldn't have to go far, thanks to the metal man next to me — they'd find many illicit dealings between the commissioner and me.

A few minutes of silence followed, and more hair of the dog. The hooch was good, dulling me. But why couldn't I shake this uncomfortable feeling, like I'd shaken so many others?

Because Allen was right. I'd gotten too reckless. I'd put too many people in danger, myself included. I probably would have gotten my old partners killed if they'd stuck around me after I threw their asses out. Allen sounded like a recruit, listing all his concerns straight from the book. Shit, Allen sounded like I had back when I'd joined up at the 5th almost a decade ago. I hadn't been much different from the machine when I'd first gotten my badge. Seeing it from an outside perspective, it really did look a lot worse than I'd thought. I'd been teetering on an edge I hadn't even noticed. Maybe Allen was my safety harness. But all harnesses eventually wore out. What had happened to turn me into such a piece of shit? Had the city gotten to me? Or …

No, I definitely knew what had pushed me over the edge, but of all things, I didn't need to think about *that* right now. I hoped to God, or whatever it was up there, that Allen wouldn't experience what I had. Or what any of us at the 5th had experienced. The ghost that had sent me off the deep end could very well have been the same machine that Morris and Belik had Red-eyed to shoot up the speakeasy. If it was, if I saw it again, would I even be able to pull the trigger?

Allen was different. The fact that I was able to scare Allen — not programmed scared, but *human* scared — was another point in its favour supporting the claim that it wasn't just a machine. It was also an indication that my personality was so godawful I could frighten almost any form of life, even artificial.

Allen didn't look at or acknowledge me for a long time, perhaps out of respect, allowing me to reflect on my own mistakes. Or perhaps out of fear. But finally it said, "Tell me, Detective, what engagements did you take part in during the War?"

"Excuse me?" That was a question I hadn't been prepared for.

"You mentioned at the diner that you were in an engagement during the War. I was curious about what you did."

I sat up and combed through all the memories I had hidden away. Nothing like a bloody trip down memory lane. "I was part of the Cleanup Crew, 2nd Battalion, 1st Manual Corps. My only major experience in battle was during the Siege of Strasbourg. After that, a few weeks later, the first Automatics came off the line, and we were all out of a job and headed home."

"Tell me about the War, Detective." The metal man wrapped its arms around its legs like a child. For all I knew it would analyze my every response. Or maybe it actually wanted to know. Textbooks didn't do those horrors justice. "It seems you have some built-up anger from the War, as many veterans do."

"It ain't because of the War, if that's what you're wondering about." I had to laugh. I could barely function, yet it was still grilling me for details. "On that day, the brass wanted to put tanks down on the field and try to push through the Austros' blockade. They had these big fucking things called Diesels — they were like Manuals, but they stole the Allies' tech and made these things run off of diesel fuel instead of Tesla Batteries. You know what a Manual is, I hope. Fortunately, the tanks had Manuals backing them up, to draw most of the fire. I was in a transport tank, and they let us out in a trench. I watched the metal suits walk over us, the gunfire was ..."

Fuck ... the sound. The sound was deafening, like the buzzing of bees ... bees whose sting was deadly.

"It was overwhelming. The Manuals were dropping left and right from the machine gun fire, and I was supposed to either reload them or drag the operators out of the metal carcasses. I watched one get chewed up, another get blown apart and vapourized when its Tesla Battery got penetrated. It was hell."

"Were you victorious?"

"We were. The tanks rolled in and stomped on the positions, and I got a few bullets across the stomach as a souvenir. After the battle, they carted me off to a field hospital, and we got to see the first Automatic Division get released as an offensive shortly after. I saw a lot of good men die then and there. Even the Krauts were helping us after they surrendered … they knew the only way the War would end was with a victor, and they'd already switched sides."

Allen, who seemed a bit more comfortable now, turned to face me. "What other things did you see?"

"I saw the reason I'm nervous around you metal men. It was nothing but brutal efficiency. I saw a robot snapping necks and tearing apart limbs even while it was riddled with holes. I saw one take a full belt of ammunition before it fell. The Automatics were scary then, and they still are now. That's why I don't like them too much. But I'm getting better."

"I see." Allen sat there processing what I'd told it, and I took another big swig. I hadn't expected to relive the War tonight, but then, I hadn't been prepared for any of what had happened today. The War wasn't my favourite thing to recollect …

"Detective." I felt Allen shaking me.

I tried to refocus on the kitchen and the robot. But I didn't feel like being awake, and I didn't feel well. "I'm good, metal man, just … tired …" Soon, I wasn't bothered by my thoughts any longer. As my brain burnt itself out, I slumped to the floor and shut off for the night.

"Back end opening in three. Get ready!"

Grey steel, darkness except for the muzzle flash from the machine guns mounted on the side of the tin can illuminating the small windows to the outside. I smelled the stench of sweat and gunpowder. The Lewis Gun Mark VI in my hands weighed heavily after three hours of moving into position, but I had enough strength to grab the top lever and chamber the first round of many. Sinclair to my right, a nameless body to my left. The only way I knew it was Sinclair was from his breathing; he was far calmer than any of the others.

"Hey, El, you good?"

"Yeah, y-yeah, I'm good, Paddy." My fingers were raw already, and I hadn't fired a shot. A mortar shell whizzed by us and hit the ground, sending waves through our ranks. Too close for comfort, but not close enough to do us damage. Any moment now we'd be over the Austros' trench, and then we, the Cleanup Crew, would do our job: making sure no one shot back at the Manuals.

"I'll stick by you — you lead, though. After all, your gun fires faster than mine." He chambered a round in his own Springfield and checked his 1911. "Think there'll be a lot down there, El?"

"Paddy … I can't …" It was hard to breathe. I'd never taken another person's life before. It was choking me, the thought of ending another's life. Someone's son, or father, or brother. They'd never come home. But I might not come home, either — then what use would I be? Whether we lived or died, the fight continued. We would just stop caring, because there would be nothing left to care about.

"Go, go, go!" the CO barked, and the rear cracked open. The bright sky was clogged with black smoke and gunfire.

We tumbled out into a trench. The tank continued on away from us, and some stragglers in the back were rattled with gunfire — three of us were dead before we'd even started. The mud nearly swallowed me whole, and Sinclair grabbed my arm and hoisted me up, propping me up against a wall as we scanned the area. I immediately realized that I wasn't standing in mud. The sticky substance was red, not brown, and the place where my head had been moments ago was where a human heart may have been beating.

"El!" Sinclair grounded himself. Two Austro-Hungarian soldiers rounded a corner and hesitated as they, too, tried to process the carnage.

My weapon was levelled at them, but my finger didn't pull. We stared at each another for an eternity, only snapping out of it when the *clack* of Sinclair's rifle released a bullet into one of their chests. Then I pulled the trigger indifferently, loosing half my magazine into them and seeing both fall. A Manual trudged overhead, metal legs blocking out the sun, and another tank made its way close to the trench to deposit another wave of the Cleanup Crew.

I made my way to the freshly dead. Their bodies were unmoving — I wouldn't have been able to control myself if they had still been alive after that. Past the curve of the trench, to my left, another Austro appeared, firing off a rifle in my direction as I grounded myself behind one of the bodies. The Lewis Gun fell from my hands, and I reached for my sidearm, which had slipped off of me during my initial entry into the trench.

The dead body I was hiding behind had a gleaming silver handle on it. I reached for it, levelled it, and fired off two rounds. The Diamondback kicked much more than I was prepared for, but it made two holes the size of my fist in the body of the other man. I got up from the mud and gore to retrieve my rifle, which was clogged from the filth. Sinclair was behind me, rechambering his rifle as he stacked up to the dirt wall.

"What you got there, El?"

"German pistol. Lost the other one." I twirled the revolver in my hands. It felt natural. Felt good. Then again, the adrenalin hadn't run out yet. I'd probably be sobbing at what I'd had to do after all this was over. Austros had been salvaging German weapons since the latter swapped sides, so it wasn't uncommon to find a treasure like this on a new corpse. The whine of pneumatic pressure being released filled the air, and I looked up to see the top of the Manual from earlier peeking over the dirt wall. Must have busted a support on its leg, seeing as it wasn't moving as fast as it should be. "You go forward. I'm hopping up to fix big boy over there."

"Roger dodger." Sinclair tipped his helmet and ran forward through the deserted trench, and I slung my machine gun over my shoulder and climbed up the trench wall.

The Manual came into view, as did the field of barbed wire, mortar fire, and tanks advancing toward Strasbourg. The device was well over thirty feet in height, with pneumatically driven legs as large as my body and a central cockpit in the chest of the machine where the human pilot sat. Two large arms sprouted from the top of the central body, the right one carrying a large .50-calibre machine gun, the other missing below the mechanical elbow.

The pilot inside was peering through the bulletproof glass mounted at the front of the machine, looking right at me to get my attention. Approaching him, I could see the large metal chest piece mounted on him was tightly locked around his chest, limiting his movement. I also saw some blood on said chest piece, but it wasn't enough to warrant concern.

"Hey, hey, Cleanup Crew this deep in no man's land?" the pilot laughed as I climbed his machine's back. "Check my pressure tank, see how things are going up there for me."

"For the pneumatics?"

"For the Trauma Harness."

I wrestled with the back end for a while before I found a mud-covered dial leading to a well-protected tank at the top of his Manual's back. The dial gave me both a general idea of how much pressure was going into that chest piece to keep him alive, as well as roughly how much morphine was being put into his system. "You're at thirty-five. Is that good?"

He laughed, the monstrous hands of the Manual gripping his rifle as he reloaded a fresh clip of .50 rounds from the belt connected to its shoulder. "Excellent. It means I'm coming home for Christmas. Get my leg fixed up and you can ride me to the end."

"I got you!"

I laughed and headed down, reaching the leg, which was as large as I was. I stripped the main hose, which had frayed, and fitted a new adapter on it. The hose was jutting out of a shelled piece of steel, revealing the inner workings of the left leg, and it wasn't too hard to find my way around repairing the damn thing.

I had trained for months learning how to fix these things head to toe, and this was the easiest repair I'd had to do in quite a while. I peered over at the Manual's missing arm, seeing a hole where the pilot could stick an arm out to fire his sidearm.

"What happened with the arm?" I yelled.

The operator looked through the hole to speak. "A 21 Morser hit me, nearly took out my real arm. Reloading is going to be a bitch, but I got the time to do it now. How are the trenches?"

I paused, the scene of gore rushing back. I nearly threw up in the middle of the repair. "F-fine, clear. Mostly clear."

"Good, good, Cleanup Crew doesn't have much to clean up." He laughed, gripping the main rifle in his machine's right hand tighter as he prepared to take off as soon as I finished.

Moments later, a whirring sound filled the air over the hissing pneumatics. I had little time to react, but the Manual operator twisted his machine and nearly crushed me. I was about to scream at him, but an explosion knocked the machine off of me and sent me skidding several feet across the mud. My teeth were like rubber, and I couldn't feel anything. Everything in my body was ringing and numb, like I couldn't work it properly.

The Manual stood, its back mangled by the direct hit from a Diesel. The Central Powers' war machine was almost double the width of a Manual, carrying two built-in 20mm cannons on its arms, one of which it had just used to fire a shell into the Manual's back. The hill roughly fifty feet ahead of us must have given it a chance to get closer to us, its lumbering speed picking up as gravity pulled it to more level ground.

The Allied Manual swung at it, trying to tear open its chest cavity and access the many pilots driving the Diesel, but its strikes were no match for the double-plated armour. The larger robot crushed the newly repaired Manual's leg, trapping it as the Diesel stuffed one of its cannons against the bulletproof glass, trying to get to the operator.

I didn't know what happened next — either the operator was alive and fired his pistol at the Tesla Battery, or the cannon hit the Manual's power source. A blinding light enveloped me, and the hairs of my beard and my eyebrows were singed. The explosion was less shrapnel than pure energy. The sound practically split my head in two and seared my closed eyes.

After the heat had dispersed, I stood up and gathered my bearings before approaching the carnage. The Diesel's front half no longer existed, and most of the Manual had been vapourized by the explosion, not even leaving a body to mourn. I fell back down, crawled to the trench, and rolled into it. Sinclair made his way to me moments later, and though he spoke, I couldn't hear. I felt water on my face — not mud or blood, but water. Tears. I got up and ran alongside him. It was so quiet — I couldn't hear anything. Another Manual fell and tipped into the trench, another blew up like a tin can over a stove.

I couldn't see — but it wasn't because of the explosion. It just didn't make sense. The crunching underfoot was either rocks or bones, either mud or organs. The metal falling from the sky was either Austrian, German, or American, but always covered in blood. It was all so fast, so sudden. I collapsed into the trench, and my brain didn't want to remember anymore. Sinclair shoved me to my feet, running toward a blown-apart wooden plank that served as a door. He shoved me through.

I felt myself falling down into the mud, my feet leaving the floor, darkness enveloping me as the warm dirt surrounded me …

And when my eyes opened, there was the orange glow of fire, the smell of gunpowder and alcohol, and a hard wooden floor against my body.

I got up to investigate my surroundings, but I already knew where I was. I always came here when I dreamed. I came here too often, yet I had only been here once in reality.

I had a Thompson in my hands, my Diamondback in its holster. Behind me was the door I'd come in through. It was connected to a large warehouse, which was currently being raided.

Morello was sitting in front of me. Three mechanical fingers on his right hand wrapped around his pistol, which lay on the desk. He'd been expecting me. I knew how it went down — how it always went down whenever I had this dream — but he never did. How many times had I shot him? Not on that night, but since that night, in dreams?

"What are you planning, Roche? Going to take me in?"

"No."

A bullet exited the submachine gun. Morello's gun fell from his grip, and he doubled over from the shock of the impact. I walked around the desk and stood over him. I tried shooting him differently each time, but he always clutched the same wound. I couldn't change the outcome; it always ended the same way. He knew it. I knew it better.

The expression in his eyes changed from one of confidence to fear. Mine changed from fear to anger. Luciano was dead, and soon he would be, too. Two kingpins dead, but with a cost attached. He looked up, putting up his hands to shield his face from the barrel of my revolver.

"Don't kill me, Roche. Please."

"We're beyond *please*, you coward. You took something from me, now I'm taking your life as recompense."

A door in the hallway behind me burst open. The raid was in full swing. Sinclair entered the doorway of the room, his eyes filled with concern. I turned back to Morello, my finger already squeezing the trigger. But this time, I didn't see Morello. No, I saw a pair of green eyes. And then, a moment later, they were bright-blue eyes.

"Elias, don't."

This time, like every time, no matter how hard I tried, I couldn't stop it.

My eyes snapped open. A featureless ceiling stared back at me.

I was in my own bed, lying on satin sheets with my shoes on the floor beside me. I still had my clothes on. I sat up and cupped my head in my hands. There was light coming in through my window, which meant I had slept through the night for once. I immediately felt the sting of the bruised purple flesh on my wrist and suddenly remembered what had happened the night before.

I'd fucked up bad. I had to try to fix things. I wondered if Allen was still here. I glanced at my closet and thought about changing, but I didn't have the luxury of time, so I just got up and left. I probably smelled worse than Yuri out there, but duty before beauty.

Allen was standing by the living room window staring down at the street. Had it been here all night? I supposed it didn't matter, since it didn't sleep. Or did it? Hopefully it wouldn't grill me on my little episode the night before. The last thing I needed was to relive the War two days in a row.

"Morning, Allen." I gave it a nod and walked into the kitchen, my gaze lingering on the notches on my fridge handle, as well as the empty bottle of booze on the floor. I grabbed a mug and slotted it into the coffee machine, hooking it up to the Tesla Battery in the wall. The machine whirred and spat black liquid into the cup. I downed my shot of caffeine for the day.

When I turned back to Allen, I saw that it hadn't moved an inch.

"Allen?" I called again. It seemed to jump, turning to me with a bewildered look on its face. "You okay there, bud?"

"Yes, Detective Roche, I was … pondering." It turned back to the window and the city beyond it. The fluorescent bulbs on the underside of the Plate poured light on the Lower City and through the window. They almost made me forget that it wasn't real sunlight.

"Pondering?"

"Yes."

I walked over and stood next to Allen. Snow was falling through the Plate's turbine frames. The immense hatches above the rotating blades were open to relieve pressure from the building snow on the Plate. In less than a day, what with the snow falling from the sky and the upper streets, and heat no longer coming down to buffer the temperature, the Lower City had been covered in a white blanket. It was still pouring into the streets. Most traffic had stopped, and cars were stuck in at least six inches of snow. People mostly scurried through the streets on foot or took the subway this time of year. But in the distance, I saw the great artery that was 7th Avenue gleaming, its towering billboards still shining across the city, even in daytime. The city would never stop the flow of traffic on 7th. On the contrary, they'd do anything to keep it going — but for what purpose, I wasn't sure.

"Care to elaborate?" I asked. "You seem to forget there are proper and improper times to keep quiet."

"I was pondering whether to let you leave this apartment."

"I'm surprised the handcuffs are off." I rubbed my wrist. It still ached, even after more than a dozen hours of sleep, and the flesh was purple and budding with welts. "Would you trust me if I gave you my word that you could?"

"I believe you could disprove my suspicion that you are constantly searching for violence. I'll be very astute in assessing you. If you exhibit the slightest suggestion of being violent toward another individual without reason, then I apologize, but I will bring you in as a criminal. I understand you are an invaluable asset to the 5th Precinct, which is why I'm giving you another chance before reporting you to higher authorities."

"That means a lot, Allen, thanks." I lit a dart and slapped Allen on the back, my hand ringing in pain. "Just to make things easier for both of us, we'll do things your way. I don't care if it's slow or painstakingly thorough. I'll concede and let you lead."

"Excuse me?" Allen's head turned toward me at lightning speed. I'd genuinely surprised it.

"You were right I'm a reckless mess of a human being. So to keep things, er, *manageable*, we should do things by the book for now. Your way." Both of us straightened up. "*This* time. And only this time. Let's see how effective you are as a leader, not just a partner. But remember, if things get iffy, I'm back on top."

"Well, that's an interestin' change of pace for ya, Roche."

I nearly jumped out of my skin, reaching for my empty holster as I turned. Sinclair — that rat bastard — was sitting on my couch with a smirk on his face. Allen must have asked him to come over after what happened yesterday. He lit a cigarette.

"Fuck, man …"

"Blind as a bat, even after sleeping off the drink all night. Man, you caused one hell of a ruckus yesterday. The G-men went wild and locked down Times Square after your stunt. 'Course, we covered for ya, as usual."

I looked at Allen, who was giving me a stare to remind me that this was yet more damning proof of my recklessness. "What are you doing here, Paddy?"

"Whoa, it's Patrick to you in front of the recruit there." He jammed a finger at Allen before sucking on his dart. "Toby came to me lookin' for you, and almost immediately after that the metal man over there called to tell me about last night. We heard about what ya found up on the Plate — about the Automatic signals. Toby did some scoutin'. Says he used to buy parts from a bunch of racketeers at Chelsea Docks. And since there was a crime in the Lower East End early yesterday, that has to be the place."

"It, not he," I reminded him. Habit.

"El, just drop it for —"

"You know which warehouse on the docks?" I asked.

"I mean, they're all connected. There's three, right? If we don't find the stuff in one, I'm sure the other two got something."

"And how did you hear about what I found at GE?"

Sinclair's face went white, and he struggled to keep from looking at Allen. "Y-you rang, don't you remember? Yesterday, before noon."

"Right … I did." We couldn't talk about *her* around Allen. I did feel a bit hurt that she'd told Sinclair about my findings before I got a chance. She must have been awfully anxious to break my trust and tell him. Of all people.

Sinclair continued. "We've been thinking about looking for smugglers or racketeers in Chelsea, maybe organizing a raid, but that's the 7th's jurisdiction, so we didn't want to step on any toes. And while *we* can't go up there, you don't exactly have the same limitations."

"Right. We'll head to the 5th, get Robins in the loop, and organize a raid on the docks, hopefully a discreet one. Get a couple of the 5th's boys pulling their weight for once."

"You'd think smugglers would try to be discreet, but it seems they're trying to draw as much attention to themselves as possible with that business at GE. And they're still selling crap after the stunt they pulled at the speakeasy," Sinclair said. "Maybe they want to be caught?"

"Like someone on the inside got cold feet and wants out? I wouldn't complain. Case closed, smuggling operation toppled. Two birds, one bullet — right, Allen?"

"Of course, Detective. I believe you'll be needing this, for now." For a moment I thought I saw it smirk as it handed my revolver back to me. A quick check revealed that it had removed the rounds from the cylinder. I supposed it thought I could use it as a deterrent. Or maybe it could tell what this hunk of steel meant to me.

"No bullets, huh?"

"When we arrive at a juncture that requires you to be armed, I'll happily give them back to you."

"How many did I have on me?"

"Fourteen total."

"You've done more damage with less, Roche." Sinclair threw his dart into my ashtray and grabbed his coat. "Toby is waiting in the car downstairs. You planning on riding with us?"

"Nah … I'll take my car. Let's get this done tonight."

"Prick … I don't drive that slow," Sinclair said, laughing.

It was two in the afternoon. Not much time today to pull this off. We had to hurry. If she'd spoken to Sinclair, it meant she was flexing her muscles, telling me that if I didn't get this job done, he'd become a target, along with Toby.

Not on my watch.

CHAPTER 15

IT HAD BEEN A FEW DAYS SINCE I'd shown my face around the 5th, but that had been for the best, as Robins didn't need my presence making the G-men more suspicious. I wasn't one for wasting time during an investigation, but letting things calm down after my little stunt in Times Square hadn't been a bad idea.

We rolled up to the station as the afternoon faded away far above the Plate. This deep in the city, the only way you could tell it was getting late was the dimming of the bulbs on the Plate as the control room workers prepared for the six o'clock shutdown.

Sinclair hung back with Toby as Allen and I entered the station. Where I had expected the bustle of nighttime patrols, I instead saw every single seat occupied by a constable sifting through what looked like enough paperwork to crush a horse. To call this an inspection was an understatement; considering all the stress everyone seemed to be under, it felt more like a goddamn tax collection.

Robins's office wasn't much better. Files and papers were strewn across his desk, the floor, even taped to the walls. Robins was reclining in his chair, pinching the bridge of his nose with his fingers. Beside him, a man wearing a dark overcoat was scanning some of the files. The whole place felt ready to go off at the slightest inconvenience.

Robins shot me a glance that indicated that I should have called ahead. The other man glanced up before croaking out what sounded like a cross between a sneeze and a cough. "We aren't expecting any callers. You've been out for a while, haven't you?" Posh, well spoken with a hint of condescension ... and yet I sensed some nervousness. Definitely a G-man.

Robins would appreciate me playing it up. I needed an inside look at what they knew and to see if I couldn't get paid sooner. "I've, uh, been on a stakeout for a few days, near a speakeasy. Anything the matter?"

"The matter is, I have dozens of constables who need a careful watch, and I haven't the time or manpower to carry out that order. We — and by *we*, I mean me and my associates in the FBI — need to be one hundred percent certain that you're still here to serve and protect the right people. This simply isn't efficient in the slightest, and we've been racking our brains trying to solve an unsolvable problem. Have you got a name, Constable?"

I couldn't be sure that he hadn't been sifting through the files and found something saying that I was retired.

"Stern," I said. "Detective Andrew Stern. These are my partners, Allen and Toby — the Automatics — and Paddy ... er, Patrick Sinclair."

"Agent Ewalt, acting on behalf of Agent Masters for this inspection."

My eyebrows popped up at the mention of the name.

"I had the pleasure of meeting Detective Sinclair a while ago, back in Rotorbird training. Ace pilot, he is. Surprised you're stuck here, though. You should be flying paramilitary, or even executives up on the Plate," the Black Hat said, grinning.

Sinclair's expression was equally jolly. "My heart is in the city, sir, born and raised. Sometimes the grass is only greener 'cause of paint," he said, half kidding, half sincere. "How's your little operation been rollin'?"

"No progress. We've been here for hours, and nothing. There was some shooting down near Times Square that riled up all my bosses, in case you hadn't heard, Stern — and now the bigwigs want me planted here until we can better assess the threats rooted around the city and see whether the 5th is doing its job. Problem is that Masters has gone AWOL, and I've got no way to raise him. If he doesn't get back in a few hours, we'll need to pull out and reorganize this venture ... and think of a fitting punishment for Masters for his vanishing act."

"But he's your superior — do you have that right?" I asked.

"This is the FBI, son. We can do much more than you can, especially concerning our superiors. Now, if you'll excuse me ... and get those Blue-eyes out of here unless you plan on Greening them!"

I snapped my fingers and Allen and Toby silently retreated. The former was proper and well-mannered about it, while the latter, I could tell, wanted to spit on the floor.

Robins was unnaturally silent — eerily so, actually. I'd never seen him like that. Sinclair offered to help the G-man find whatever he was searching for, while Robins stumbled from his chair and followed me and Allen out of his office, out of earshot of the Fed. He seemed more stressed than usual — due to the piles of paperwork, no doubt. And my sudden appearance at the precinct would have made things worse.

"What the hell is this, Roche? I know you popped those bullets last night, and you hanging around here ain't exactly *lying low.*"

"Robins, I think we have our man." Relief appeared on his face. "It's a racketeer group. They've been cutting loose ends, and the two dead badges were supposedly in on it somehow. Belik is leading them — he used to run with the 5th, I think."

"Belik left the Force five years ago," Robins said. "Said some 'business venture' picked up and led him to be filthy rich. I didn't expect him to run down that road, though." He leaned his big frame against the wall for a moment before straightening back up. "So, do you have evidence? I can't put together much of a court case without any damning proof."

"I have some unofficial statements and a smuggling presence in Chelsea Docks that Toby scouted out. You can confirm everything with Allen if you —"

"Allen?"

"Forty-One. Whatever. I gave it a better name. It looks like an Allen. You gotta admit that, at least." Robins peered at my partner and chuckled. "Allen has everything you need," I continued. "It's been on my heels since you put me in charge of it. Toby was an immense help as well ... there's a lot of evidence that it's helped me retrieve."

"Toby, that funny tin can." We both grinned. At least Toby wasn't easily forgotten. "What happened to him — *it*, sorry — when it left the Force after Second Prohibition?"

"It works construction for GE now, apparently. The job pays so well it turned to bootleggers to get quality parts, so that should tell you about its situation."

"I'd have Toby back on the Force in an instant if the FBI would let me. Bless that metal soul. But I'm glad its situation led us straight to the perps responsible for putting my boys down. I really couldn't care less if they were part of some side op that wasn't totally legal. They're still my men. I'll have Belik put down just as brutally as he put them down." He peered over at Allen, who, as usual, was too busy observing us to talk. "How is Elias doing, Allen? How's it been in the field?"

The metal man looked at me queerly before turning back and replying. "Detective Roche has been admirable, and though he is somewhat *passionate* in his approach, he understands the intricacies of the police work, as well as the concept of subtlety."

Robins nodded, biting his lip before turning back to me. "Not too many dead bodies this time?"

"Just one — the boy in the Packard 900," I answered. I wouldn't mention the stiffs in the alley behind Prince and Greene.

"Good. Can we absolutely confirm that it was Belik who rewired that Red-eye?"

I glanced at Allen.

Robins got the hint and turned to the machine. "Allen, do you mind assisting Sinclair and Agent Ewalt in my office? I feel like you'd be an invaluable resource. And be sure to keep things under wraps. He doesn't need to know anything about your past few days with Elias."

"Will do, Commissioner." Allen attempted a smile — a good step toward its integration into this shitty little city — and walked through the door, taking care to close it behind him.

Robins put an arm around me and walked me down the hall a little farther away from his office. "Roche, what's off about all this? I've seen that face and heard that tone enough to know that you're bothered by the situation."

"I can tell something about this is rubbing the Eye the wrong way; seeing as she wants everyone connected to this dead. I doubt Belik was the one behind all this. I think that, just like Jaeger, he's a meat shield. Think about it: Has the Eye ever been this jumpy dealing with other racketeering gigs?"

"She's a paranoid person. But she's dealt with rivals before, and she can handle it. Status quo."

Of course Robins wanted the Iron Hands to be unhindered. They were far more of an asset some days, rooting out the wrong kind of criminal and keeping the right kind. Even the commissioner knew that, as he was an avid believer in risk assessment.

"I know she has," I said, "and she's been fine before with any number of rivals. But these guys are giving her the willies. And one reason she'd have to be afraid is if they have serious backing. Like, above what *we* believe to be serious backing."

"Police? Paramilitary? Some big top-hatter up on the Plate?"

"Worse." My eyes darted back to his door several times before he caught my drift.

"What, the fucking G-men? You can't be serious, Roche. This is one hell of a claim, even for you."

"Well, it fits, doesn't it? Everywhere I've gone, this Masters guy has popped up. He denied the shooting me and Sinclair saw first-hand. His name was on the computer used to blackmail that technician into rigging the towers at GE. Hell, just the fact that he hid the scene and then dumped the Automatic shell in that graveyard past 90th is damning enough, since he's probably hijacked shells to do his bidding before."

"Wait. What graveyard?"

I brushed aside his question and continued. "Paddy said there was a shooting in the Lower East End. Have there been any official statements from the FBI or anyone from down there?"

Robins rubbed his neck. "There were rumours that the Red-eye that raised hell didn't have an NI ... but the FBI aren't saying anything."

"Masters is running the inspection! Don't you see? The Iron Hands have been a heavy presence, and no one can root them out, not even the 5th, not even several dozen companies trying to buy them out. The only thing that would scare them is someone with the full force of the country's government behind them. And if this really is an undercover organization wrapped around Uncle Sam's finger, we both know the FBI would send tanks down Broadway before they let business be ruined by some bootleggers that have only been around for a decade or so."

Robins nodded again, deep in thought. "No matter how much I believe you and want to help you, I can't exactly subtly organize a raid team without that posh prince in there noticing ten badges are missing from the station. That would lead to them being followed, and if this *is* being run by the G-man leading this inspection, it's your ass and mine. So … I'm sorry to say it, so I don't think I will say it."

Of course he wouldn't say it. I was on my own. He knew I'd object, that there would be some speech about justice and law — like the discussion between Allen and me — and then I'd reluctantly agree. This time, I'd call the shots for a two-man raid.

"Double," I said.

"Double? You're kidding me. How much are the Iron Hands paying you? Her pockets are deep enough to cover the cost. You're making me quadruple your already insane rates."

"If you want a massacre and some evidence to support that you weren't involved, I can ring the Eye up. If you want Belik alive, standing trial and rooting out the G-man who organized this little venture, you'll pay me double."

That face he gave was like a slap sometimes. He hated me for extorting him, but he agreed.

I went to get Allen, but before we left, Robins called it over. He pulled a weapon from the holster that lay snugly under his arm and placed the handle in Allen's outstretched palm with a metallic clang. "Forty-five-calibre pistol, heavy frame, eight rounds, sticks on reload if the mag is empty. Rules of Engagement are: shoot anything that moves, but bring Belik and whoever else is running the show back alive. Take Sinclair and the bird upstairs ... but it ain't ours, you hear?"

"And Toby?"

"Tin man is good with a Thompson ... grab one from the armoury and head upstairs."

Allen was shocked, to say the least, but had no time to react as I grabbed its metal arm and pulled it along with me. I went by the office door to get Sinclair's attention before we made ourselves scarce. An off-the-books raid meant we needed some serious firepower for four people.

———

"Is the bird good to go?" I asked.

Sinclair descended the stairs after heading up to run diagnostics on the machine resting on the 5th's helipad. Toby had also joined the gathering group, carrying a large steel case over its shoulder, fresh from the the armoury.

"It's out for some reason or other, I can't keep track anymore," Sinclair said. "However, that doesn't mean the helipad is empty." My eyebrows went up at this. "We both know these agents didn't drive here, right?"

"Right," I confirmed. "But won't that cause more issues if they go upstairs and see their own executive

Rotorbird missing?"

Robins put his hands on his hips. "What's that motto you follow again? 'Fuck it,' right?"

I grinned and grabbed Allen's shoulder, gesturing to it to follow me and get ready for our little escapade. This time, Robins would get his money's worth.

And so would she.

———

We soon found ourselves strapped into the back of a Rotorbird — specifically, the executive Rotorbird belonging to the FBI. I doubted the G-man down there would hear the turbines spinning from more than a dozen floors down, but we were quick to take off, regardless. To avoid being conspicuous, we'd taken the stairs, staying away from the constables and interns stuck in the building during the FBI's inspections. Whoever was pulling the strings must be powerful and be dead set on keeping their assets from falling into the hands of the 5th's best. Or anyone's hands but their own.

The dark-grey aircraft we were riding in had a wide carriage that tapered at the ends, with sliding doors on either side of the front half of the compartment. Allen and I sat buckled into two of the four retractable wire seats in the centre of the craft. The seats could be folded up and stored on the ceiling to accommodate heavy equipment if necessary. The back half of the aircraft, behind a set of doors, had another eight seats for a rapid deployment of anything from a heavily armoured squad of commandos to backup police officers. Another small doorway separated our compartment from the cramped cockpit, which held a single seat for the pilot and just enough room for another person to lean on the wall behind them.

Sinclair was already in there, pulling levers and opening valves to allow the fuel cells to release their energized liquid into the beast. The oozing was audible, but was soon drowned out by the sparking and whining of the twin rotors on each side of the bird. Large rings on either side held three-bladed rotors, the engines spinning them in their sockets. Seconds later, the craft lifted off the roof, and the carriage dipped as we pivoted forward. I felt the lurch — my stomach felt it as well — of the craft dropping from the rooftop. The rotors caught us moments later, propelling the aircraft upward.

I always hated that first drop. It always aggravated my stomach, and the alcohol still stuck in me did little to help the situation. Though, compared to Allen, I must have seemed the picture of comfort.

"You okay there, bud?"

"I'm not a fan of this experience, Detective Roche."

"You afraid of heights?"

It looked back at me with widened eyes, its shaking hands grasping for the small handles located near the butt of each seat. I couldn't help it — I laughed my ass off. I really didn't care if Allen hated me for laughing; a robot afraid of heights was the highlight of my month.

"Don't sweat it, Allen," Sinclair said over the loud-speaker. "We'll only be in the air for a few minutes, just until we get close to the docks. Then you're going to have to jump out. Not from high in the air — maybe a few inches from the ground."

"How's she doing?" I called out, hopeful my voice was being caught by the carriage microphones. "Sounds rough around the edges, though I have a lot less experience in the air than you do."

"She's an older model," he responded, "but the blades spin, which is all we really need, eh? At least the Black Hat topped the fuel cell up beforehand, else we'd be in a jam."

"Well, if we do need to find a place to refuel, we can always get the metal man to do it, right, Al?"

I gave Allen a quick knock on the shoulder, which led to a ringing hand that would probably bruise quite badly in the coming days. Allen continued to sit in a silent panic, unaware of its grip strength on the seat's handles.

Toby was in the back of the Rotorbird setting up the Thompson from the steel case it had lugged up the stairs. It had put these weapons together so often that it was second nature, which unfortunately meant that it was going to talk to us while it prepared for the raid.

"So, boys, how goes your little ragtag partnership? Can't be too bad, seeing as Elias hasn't dumped you past 90th yet for 'insubordination.'"

"Does he do that frequently, Toby?" Allen asked, momentarily forgetting about its discomfort.

"Toby, don't you dare —"

"Shit, yeah, he does!"

There was a hint of laughter being repressed in the little wire voice box hanging where Toby's mouth should be.

"Past three partners he's had — human and Automatic — have been sent on a fool's errand up there while he disappeared without a trace, leaving them to wander around. Then he wrote them up and demanded they be removed from his watch."

"I suspect that this hasn't occurred to me due to the high calibre of my assistance. Or possibly because I could find my way back to his abode if he attempted to dispose of me."

Was that a hint of worry in Allen's voice? No, I must have be imagining it.

"Either way, that's how he does it, regardless of who you are. People who know him know he doesn't like 90th, and that's why he leaves them there — because someone else will pick them up."

"I'm right here, you two." I had to butt in, lest I hear about this all night. What a rat bastard Toby was. But I couldn't help but smile.

"You see, Allen?" Toby continued. "That's the smug face he makes whenever he has a bluff and people are falling for it. He's a terrible poker player. Too bad the other humans at the table are just as garbage as he is, which is why they never call the bluff."

"Sinclair ain't too bad, but his bluffs are more obvious than mine," I said. "How many times have we heard the silver gun story from '28?"

Toby knew exactly what I meant and chuckled to itself at the remark. "Shit, don't mention that story." It tried sitting back, its metal plates scraping against the carriage's interior. "Next time I hear about that time he led an investigation, I'll toss myself off the top of the new Control Point ... after I get paid, of course."

"Of course," I said.

We banked right and were able to get a glimpse of Lower Manhattan out of the window in front of us. The bulbs on the Plate shone down on the city streets below.

"So, Toby, how's GE been treating you? You're working on a Control Point, right? I never thought you'd be there; figured you'd be in Jersey or somewhere else."

"So did I. Those goddamn politicians pushing Second Prohibition made everyone outside of Manhattan a nervous wreck when it comes to machines, so it's 'get the Green-eye' or you're out of a job. Thinking is an ability I enjoy having. The only place that takes Blue-eyes is GE, and they needed a crew to build the Control Point for their Plate expansion. And hell, if it keeps up, I'll have enough cash to buy a bigger place than any white-collar Green-eye ever could. Maybe it'll even be enough to keep me from falling apart, Automatic parts ain't cheap, after all."

"Sounds lucrative. For now, at least. But, you've got to miss the Force a little? Something about the garbage pay, terrible hours, and smell of death in this city made it so appealing."

"I guess. I did run a few ops on my own, and it was exhilarating having a squad of rookies shooting up a speakeasy with me during a raid. 'Course, I went in first, since bullets need more *oomph* to hurt me. But, hey, we got the memories, and mine aren't going nowhere." Toby sat back as it clipped the barrel into the base of the gun. Though it couldn't smile, a look very close to satisfaction spread over its metal face.

A silence rested in the cab of the Rotorbird as we all thought about the good times. Mine were crazy: drug busts, raids, heists. Hell, all of it had been exciting.

But Allen had to break the silence with its insatiable hunger for information. "Did you lead operations, Detective Roche?"

At this comment, Toby moved forward, its solid metallic eyebrows shooting up in surprise as it turned to face me. "You didn't tell him? What the shit, man? That's classic New York history and you didn't tell him?"

"*It*, Toby. Like you. *It*. Not *he*."

Ignoring my comment, Toby continued, half jumping in his excitement to fill in my partner. "Good ol' Elias here ran more than a *few* ops — he ran the big one!"

"Toby …"

"You must've seen how the cops, and maybe some criminals, look at him. Haven't you wondered why he's such a big deal to people in these parts?"

"Well, I've been curious, but I couldn't find any reliable sources on the matter. Though I would prefer to be told by the detective personally."

I guessed I was stuck. Toby looked at me, eyebrows jumping up and down as if to say, *Tell him!*

I reclined more into my seat. "A few years ago, back in 1928, I ran the Morello raid, which aimed to prevent Murder, Inc.'s expansion out of New York onto the mainland. Our best bet was to hit a shop in Hell's Kitchen that was experiencing a large volume of cargo truck traffic. We got in, mopped up, and it didn't do a lick of good. Morello and Luciano were both down. A new boss came into power and did something worse than expanding. He doubled the Mob's efforts in New York, leading to the fucked little city we all live in. That's the big one. Happy, Toby?"

"You're saying that you led the Morello case, Detective, and in doing so, caused the city to be in the state it currently is?"

Allen seemed confused, but Toby wouldn't let it slide and piped up before I could respond.

"Hell, no! He *is* the Morello case. And it wasn't just him that caused shit to spiral. Let's be honest, he single-handedly stopped one of the biggest Mob wars in history and broke the Mob in two. He made it impossible for them to even think about expanding past the Hudson."

Silence again, and this one wasn't at all nostalgic or comfortable. I looked out the window and saw the line of warehouses. Sinclair was skirting the edge of the bay to stay away from FBI-patrolled airspace. He was awful quiet up there, no doubt smart enough not to comment on this subject.

"I killed Morello. My gun, his head. I ended it. That's that. Ancient history. Drop it."

"That was outside the duties expected of you, Detective, and you would have been reprimanded."

Didn't skip a beat, did it? Allen was all over the bureaucracy of any situation.

"I would have been, if I'd stayed."

No one moved. Allen was obviously thinking of more questions to prod me with.

"And the Mafia has yet to exact vengeance on you for killing their benefactor?" he finally asked.

Too far, Allen. "They already did," I said.

Don't. Don't tell it. Just move on, I thought. "Toby, shut up and finish what you're doing," I said pre-emptively.

There was silence in the aircraft once again, this one tenser than the last. I was not in the mood for any more questions from Allen. That didn't stop it, however.

"How many partners have you had before me, Detective?"

Allen had just had to pipe up again. He couldn't keep his fucking mouth shut for ten goddamn seconds.

It. Not *he.*

Damn, now I was slipping. Probably because of that slip, I didn't immediately chew Allen apart. I supposed it gave me a moment to compose myself. Allen had probably seen the look of rage on my face and had second thoughts.

"Several," I said

"Is there an approximate number?"

"Are you asking how many I've had, or how many were around enough for me to consider them a partner?"

It hesitated before responding. "Both, I suppose."

"Ten, give or take, have tried accompanying me. Two were actual partners."

"When was the last time you had a legitimate accompaniment whom you considered your partner?"

"Back in '28, a little before Morello." I had to give something like an actual answer, or else it would keep asking. "There's a few things that … well, we don't speak of much. *We* being the people I'm close to or who know me well. I suppose you don't know any better, but some subjects are touchy. I don't blame you — you'll learn. I just want to give you a heads-up."

"Detective, are you quite all right?"

Change the subject — don't let it get under your skin. "Paddy! ETA?"

"Five minutes before we're in position to wreak some havoc. Get ready, everyone!"

"Your friend Toby is taking an unusual amount of time preparing his weapon," Allen commented.

Toby looked up and gave us both a cold stare. "It's called being thorough, and people who've worked with me know what that means."

"In what way?" Allen asked.

"He's been doing this for as long as I have." *It.* Damn it. "Now lay off and get your head in the game. This won't be a walk in the park."

CHAPTER 16

THE ROTORBIRD BANKED to the right once more, our heading now the western docks as we skimmed over the bay. We had a picturesque view of Lower Manhattan's skyline and the underside of the Upper City. The small staircases and catwalks of the Plate were more noticeable from here, with tiny people moving about on them, inspecting the area before the nighttime cycle began and the fluorescent bulbs were shut down. I checked my watch and saw that it was almost four.

"Shit," I said to myself. "We gotta hurry, not much time until the bulbs go out."

"What's the hurry, Detective?" Allen asked.

Toby butted in to answer the question. "Chelsea is Maranzano's neighbourhood ... old bastard. Of all the places we gotta go to find this Black Hat, we had to wind up in the Mob's territory."

"Maranzano?"

"Salvatore Maranzano, last big-name Italian mobster in the city," I responded. "He's old school, which means there ain't much leeway for negotiating if we get found on his turf when night hits. But, at the same time, he respects the rules enough to wait until six before blowing our brains out."

Two hours wasn't much time to clear a warehouse of illegal assets and crooked cops.

Looking around the cabin, I wondered if we needed a more capable group than two men and two Automatics wielding a modified German pistol, an M1911, a standard .38 police pistol, and an outdated Tommy gun. Just as that thought passed through my head, I noticed a strange contraption hooked onto the wall of the cabin. Attached to a small pivoting arm was a triple-barrelled Suppression Rifle — or, as we called it, the Suppressor. To be honest, that name was one of the greatest euphemisms in the Force. It was really a vehicle-mounted rail gun and did little to "suppress" perps. Most Suppression Rifles had been built during the last years of the Great War, after scientists realized that Tesla Batteries could power more than just Manuals and Automatics.

The weapon was hooked up to the fuel cells in the Rotorbird via several thick hoses connecting the bottom of the gun's base to the wall of the Rotorbird. This posed a minor issue in using the weapon: any power bump it caused when firing could force the entire aircraft to plummet downward, jerk forward into a building, or any number of terrible manoeuvres that could kill us all if we weren't in a stable position.

"Paddy, you know there's a Suppression Rifle in the back here?"

"No shit, eh? Well, I have a feelin' Allen would be sternly advisin' you against using it, if it wasn't shitting itself. So, when you use it, try and … miss."

"I wasn't even thinking of aiming this at anyone. At least not intentionally." I unhooked myself from the seat, grabbed the bulkhead, and reached for the rifle. The Rotorbird wasn't the most stable platform for me to be standing up on. Upon inspection, I noticed foot hooks in the floor, which helped me keep my balance after I jammed my shoes into them. The aircraft banked once again, heading downward. We were closing on Chelsea Docks, and the tension was tangible.

Grabbing a small rope on the top of the bulkhead, I lifted one foot from the floor and kicked a small pedal in the corner between the wall of the pilot's cabin and the sliding door. The device released the lugs holding the door in place, the springs pulling the metal back quickly. With the door open and my feet anchored, I yanked the Suppression Rifle from its mounting. The swivelling arm bore the weapon's weight as I pushed the barrel outside the aircraft. I grasped the two handles at the Rifle's base, feeling the size of its triggers.

"This fucker is big. You think you can keep us from dying if I use this?"

"Depends on how patient you are. I'll radio over and tell ya when we're good to fire. I've been through too much for you, of all people, to kill me, El!"

"The War and the Force … seems to me we've been cheating death for far too long."

I got a laugh from Sinclair at that last comment. We dipped down again. The sinking feeling lurched through me once more. Anticipation and excitement kept my feet pinned and my knuckles white as I gripped the rifle with sweaty palms.

"This would be considered excessive force, Elias. Is it really necessary for us to use a weapon of this calibre? No pun intended."

I could barely pick up its rattling voice through the howls of the wind and the engines, but I'd heard it call me Elias, not Detective Roche. I smiled. Either it had been a slip of the tongue, or Allen was growing more confident.

"Firstly: we were given free ROE from Robins, and I plan on exercising those rules however I choose. Secondly: I'm glad you're finally learning some humour. Trust me when I say that it helps to cope with a job like this." I laughed, and Allen looked more uncomfortable than usual.

"Detective, this could be extremely dangerous for your well-being. The percentage of your body that is exposed while you operate the weapon carries a high risk of fatality, or at least injury."

"High risk, high reward, Allen. Keep your head down until we need to disembark." It planted itself back into the seat, gripping the handles tighter. "And I promise I won't try to kill anyone. I really will try." I meant it, but if anyone got in the way of a blind shot, it was their own fault. "Fly me over to the side of the warehouse, Paddy! No reason to use the front door."

"Detective!" Allen nearly stood in its little seat. "You can't possibly be thinking about firing a rifle of this size for the arbitrary reason of making an entrance."

I gestured to the weapon. "You expect me not to use the big goddamn gun? What other suggestions do you have?"

"We can have Sergeant Sinclair bring us near the docks, then disembark and use the front door."

Toby and I looked at each other, letting a silence hang in the air. "Load the gun, Roche," Toby said.

I pulled back the bolt and loaded three 30mm solid rods into the rifle's breech. A *thunk* followed, along with the sharp whine of electric energy.

"Mark to fire in thirty seconds, El," Sinclair barked over the amplifier.

"And what if we fire at the wrong warehouse, Detective?" Allen asked again.

"I guess we'll pop the top off every one until we get it right," I said with a smirk.

"Now I remember why I never went on raids with you," Sinclair said.

"I mean, they're all connected," I said, quoting him. "If this one doesn't have what we need, the others will!"

The Rotorbird's propellers caused water to splash up across the bottom of the open door, soaking my shoes and slacks. Mist covered the floor by the door, and my shoes lost some traction, but thankfully the anchors kept me from falling into the bay.

The aircraft hung in the air outside the edge of the southernmost warehouse, adjacent to the river. To the right was 11th Avenue, full of cars minding their own business. The last thing those drivers would want to trouble themselves with was why a Rotorbird was aiming an onboard weapon at a supposedly abandoned warehouse. We were so close that I could see through the dirty glass panes of the building. I spotted at least a dozen people moving about inside. The faces turned toward the window, indicating that they'd either seen or heard us.

Sinclair called to me on the loudspeaker, "Don't kill us, Roche. Fire!"

I leaned into the weapon as I placed both index fingers on the red triggers. The Rotorbird jerked as the rifle shot shells at the glass panes.

Normal rifle rounds would have passed through glass, cracking the surface but leaving the glass mostly intact. Not these rounds. Three solid cylinders of metal flew forward with barely a whisper. The brick wall and attached windows shattered and flew into the warehouse. The rods went through the concrete floor, burying themselves deep into the earth.

No doubt Allen had been appalled that I was willing to fire such a weapon without being 100 percent sure there were criminals on the other side of the wall. But now that the inside of the warehouse was visible, the sight of wooden crates and metal bits strewn about gave weight to my decision, no matter how reckless it was. I couldn't imagine how the metal man would have reacted to all the other shit I'd done over the past four years. At least there were no civilians in the way this time. I had enough time to load another triplet of rounds in preparation to fire.

Inside, dozens of bodies began to stir and recover from the sudden attack. Many were Automatics, Blue-eyes probably stacking and moving boxes for some extra cash. They all ran the moment they recovered from having their wires scrambled. Dealing with fewer attackers certainly made my life a lot easier. One of the bodies, however, was a Red-eye who drew a pistol to fire in my direction. Toby stepped up beside me, holding the Thompson by its waist, and pulled the trigger, emptying the magazine of heated thermite rounds and thus turning the Red-eye into swiss cheese. The husk flopped over before it had even pulled the trigger of its own weapon.

"After you." I gestured to the hole in the wall. Toby leaped across and landed on the splintered wooden planks.

I pushed the Suppression Rifle to the side, pulling my feet from the hooks on the floor, backed up, and made the leap myself. I felt my left foot catch the edge of the floor, but it wasn't enough to make me tumble into the sea. I recomposed myself and yanked my Diamondback out of its holster.

"Just like the old days, huh?" Toby laughed, releasing its first straight magazine and loading in a second one, charging it with a *crack*.

"Yeah, but these places used to have more competent guards around ..."

"Elias!" The loudspeaker in the cargo bay of the Rotorbird was loud enough to be heard in the warehouse. "I got movement farther up — something's coming toward you. Might be a Titan model. I'll get in position to —"

Boom!

The crates behind me exploded into shrapnel, flooring me as something massive sprinted past. The aircraft lurched and swerved. I glimpsed Allen spewing clear liquid from its mouth into the sea below. The aircraft successfully dodged whatever was trying to grab it, flying out of sight for the moment. The massive figure turned around to face Toby and me as I pushed myself from the ground.

He was about seven feet tall, dressed in ragged clothes like mine, and he had so many metal attachments on him that a war vet might confuse him with a Manual. His hands were stripped and retrofitted with mechanical augmentations. Everything below the knuckles was probably bolted onto his bones. The tubes which ran from the massive backpack attached to his shoulders powered his mechanical bits and pumped chemical mixtures into his blood to keep him from feeling pain. His face was thick and greyish with bloodshot eyes, and he wore a retracting mask that pulled to either side of his head.

"Of course they have a fucking Auger." I put two bullets into his chest, only to see them get squashed against the dermal plating he had under his clothing. "Goddamn it!"

As the thing ran toward me, Toby put half a magazine into him. The .45 rounds could get through the dermal plating, but it wasn't enough to stop this beast, especially with all the medical equipment in and on it pumping away. I made a run for it, heading for the bramble of crates ahead of me with the intention of going straight through and continuing northward toward the other adjacent warehouses. I looked back but couldn't tell whether Toby had bit it or the Auger had just ignored it.

He'd probably been too crazed to process the difference between a worker bot and a brand new one.

I found a spot in the labyrinth where I could rest, feeling my heart running at a mile a minute. The Auger was losing its shit, smashing things to try and find me. Meanwhile, the sound of the Rotorbird's propellers moved from the west side of the warehouse to right above me. Looking up through a ceiling window, I could see the bird scouting for another way inside. Unluckily for me, it wouldn't be much of a distraction to the Auger all the way up there.

The click of a drawn hammer made my head snap back down to see a gun barrel pressed to the side of my head, held by a Red-eye. Despite the rust and patchwork of parts keeping it operational, I could see that it was a Swinger bot. No doubt a Swinger with police programming that I myself had put in. To my surprise, it didn't fire, though the trigger was half-pulled.

Was it him?

I wanted to level my own weapon and protect myself, but I was frozen in place. I couldn't pull the trigger.

I'm going to die here, I thought.

My brain went fuzzy as a loud crash and several gunshots sounded.

I blinked a few times and looked around, realizing that I was unharmed. The Automatic in front of me was crushed under the weight of another metallic body and had a few more holes in its chest than before. The body lying atop the Red-eyed Swinger was Allen, who held a smoking 1911 and was groaning and pulling itself to its feet.

"Where the hell did you come from?" I finally said. Feeling glass in my hair, I looked up at the broken window.

"I jumped," it said, nursing fresh wounds that were hidden under its suit.

I looked down at the motionless Automatic. James. There it was … dead again. Or was it? My brain was whirling. Was it really James? Was it really trying to kill me? Had Allen killed the right Automatic?

"Detective!" Allen yelled to get my attention. "I think we should move."

I knew the monster of a man had heard the crash and the gunshots, because I could hear everything that lay between him and me being crushed or thrown out of the way as he approached. Instinct took over as I ran, and Allen followed close behind.

We neared the northern wall of the warehouse, where a large metal door between this building and the next was thankfully open. We ran through, Allen grabbing the sliding door and throwing it closed with inhuman strength. This gave us a few seconds to look around and note that this building, which was much larger than the previous one, was even more full of crates and containers. Some held Automatic parts, others alcohol, weapons, even car parts.

The Auger began bashing against the closed metal door, leaving several impressive dents. Rather than waiting to see what other damage it could do, we ran, putting several feet between us and the entrance, and hid behind some boxes.

"Detective, what is that?" Allen asked, panic in its voice.

"We call them Augers. Mean, nasty assholes who trade out flesh for metal. The tech isn't good enough to completely replace limbs, so they just bolt the metal bits onto bone, which I've heard is pretty painful. It also means he has to carry a Tesla Battery on his back, which is our best bet to beat him."

"I'm sorry to ask redundant questions, Elias, but aren't Augers mechanical devices used for digging into dirt for the implementation of supports?" Allen looked very worried, even if it didn't mean to. I figured it wasn't always in control of its expressions.

The metal door finally flew open, slamming into a nearby pillar. The Auger hadn't spotted us yet, so I lowered my voice.

"That explain it, Allen?"

"Yes, Detective. What is your plan?"

"I never have one. But, maybe I can try to lure him through the crates, slow him down, find a way to get outside and into the Rotorbird and use the Suppression Rifle on him. Or, while I'm distracting him, you can take Robins's gun and shoot him in the back."

"Will that endanger his life?"

"Probably not, but just be sure, for your conscience's sake, to aim for the battery. As soon as that goes down, so will he — like a brick. And be quick with your shots when you get the chance. I'd rather not get turned into paste."

"Roger that, Detective."

I snapped my head to the left, spotting the large glass-topped entrance on the east side of the building, about fifty feet ahead of me. I could get outside from there, but that door led right out to 11th Avenue, and the last thing I wanted was civilian casualties. Maybe I could run north and get out onto the Pier 62 park, where the Rotorbird could actually manoeuvre. I guessed we would see.

"Hey!" I yelled, standing up.

I started running as the Auger made a beeline for me. Allen remained where it was, and I soon lost sight of it while I ran between the shipping containers and small loading vehicles littering the warehouse floor. I wasn't expecting any more adversaries, but more Red-eyes came out of the woodwork as I ran northward. They'd probably been preparing for an ambush after hearing my entrance. The sporadic fire of a Thompson deafened me. My eyes searched for the source as I held up my weapon parallel to my vision. Another Red-eye stepped out from behind me, and a moment later a thermite bullet pushed into its chest, flooring it and giving me room to breathe.

Throwing myself behind a crate, I opened the breech of my revolver, replacing the spent casings and waiting for my hearing to return. I could faintly make out the sound of automatic fire, possibly from the Red-eyes, or maybe even from Toby. It seemed the Auger's attention was directed toward the robots, giving me a moment of respite. I pulled my leg up and grimaced as the skin burned and I felt a moist sensation along my leg. It seemed the Red-eye I'd taken down had gotten lucky and clipped me. Bastard.

I had no alcohol on me to numb the pain, but luckily for me, these racketeers were transporting more than parts. One of the boxes hit by the machine's .45 rounds had spilled onto the ground, revealing the whiskey within. I yanked a bottle out, removed the cork with my teeth, and swallowed some of the liquor.

"Thank God …" I said to myself, moments before another Red-eye appeared. Its bullets missed me, but hit the glass bottle, causing it to crash onto the floor. I levelled my Diamondback and fired a round at the machine. "Goddamn it, come on!"

My journey north continued, and before long I had reached the doors leading to the northernmost and final warehouse along the docks. There was another set of massive metal doors ahead of me, with a smaller, man-sized door nearby. Behind me, the area between this door and the eastern doors leading to 11th Avenue was filled with Automatic parts and still-smoking guns. I wasn't sure where Allen was, but I hoped it was okay. Toby came out from the labyrinth of boxes, walking backward at a brisk pace, putting sustained fire on the approaching Auger.

"Good job, Toby, keep it up!" I yelled.

"Not the time, Roche! I swear —"

Toby didn't finish its sentence as the Auger grabbed it and tossed it south. Toby's body slammed through many more boxes and landed somewhere unseen. The Auger then turned to me, his chest piece riddled with holes, his mechanically reinforced organs still functioning, and his dinner plate–sized pupils staring me down.

"Shit," I whispered to myself.

He let out a guttural roar and sprinted toward me. I kicked open the door leading into the last warehouse, jumped inside, and slammed the door closed behind me.

I looked around. The building was empty.

I figured it must have been designed for aerial shipments, but the retractable roof had been left unfinished, leaving a large hole open to the elements. Through the opening I could see the tops of buildings and the Plate's bulbs gleaming down at me. The sight reminded me that I was on a strict schedule.

Suddenly the Rotorbird appeared in the opening, and Sinclair skillfully lowered the aircraft through the hole until it was hovering just a few feet above the floor. High-calibre rounds might not stop the monstrosity hunting me down, but I doubted he could survive rail gun shells.

I was about halfway to the aircraft when the Auger pounded his way through the doorway, which was just a bit smaller than his massive frame. My burning thigh slowed me down a bit, but I had just enough time to crawl into the bird and grab the handles of the Suppression Rifle before the Auger reached us. He was running toward us, bellowing loudly. I eased open the breech of the gun, making sure there were three shells loaded, and then centred the rifle.

"Goodnight, asshole."

I fired. The shells hit the floor just ahead of the Auger. The explosion hardly fazed him. He jumped through the mess of rubble and concrete, arms outstretched, and grasped the bulkhead of the Rotorbird, attempting to drag it down. Sinclair was still trying to maintain control of the bird after the recoil from the Suppressor shot, and now he had to contend with the added difficulty of the Auger trying to pile-drive the entire aircraft.

He gunned the engine as the steel underbelly of the aircraft was forced down, just centimetres from the floor. I could hear the engine revving as it struggled against the Auger's strength. The bulkhead began to creak, the rotors spun faster and faster, and the metal wavered as the Auger's steel fingers dug into it. I pulled out my Diamondback, aiming to put a round in the Auger's head. But the retracting mask slid down over its face, protecting its cranium; three bullets bounced off and ricocheted around the empty warehouse.

With all other options exhausted, I grasped the Suppression Rifle again and tried to charge it up.

"Paddy, load it!" I yelled.

"You will fucking kill us, Elias!"

"We got a better chance of surviving if we use the damn thing!"

Sinclair slammed his hand into the dash of the cockpit in anger, but still, he flipped the switch that charged the rifle. Static whines sounded from the barrel of the weapon.

As I prepared to fire again, I heard a single gunshot. I watched as the Auger, still masked, released its hold on the bulkhead and began to pivot forward. The Rotorbird almost flipped before Sinclair wrestled control at the last second. He swung the bird back several feet as the giant man fell forward and lay stone still on the concrete floor. Behind the corpse of the Auger stood Allen, the M1911 in its hand still smoking. Allen seemed stunned, almost as rigid as the dead man. It didn't lower the gun from its firing position, but just stood there, its mouth hanging open, an expression of utter surprise on its face. I hopped out of the Rotorbird, and Sinclair pulled the aircraft up and away from us, taking out the landing gear and setting it down safely.

I walked over and peered down at a large hole in the back of the Auger's head. Blood was leaking out from the edges of the mask, still covering the corpse's face.

I placed a hand on the pistol in Allen's hands, lowering it as the robot released its grip on the weapon. Allen's fingers curled, appearing to still be holding an invisible firearm, even when I pushed its arms down.

"Allen, you okay?"

It didn't answer.

"Allen?"

CHAPTER 17

"MAKE SURE ALLEN'S OKAY, then get Toby and get the hell out of here!" I yelled to Sinclair, who had just stepped out of the Rotorbird's cockpit.

Peering up, I saw movement in the window of a small office up on the catwalk that surrounded the room. I snagged a pair of cuffs from Allen before Sinclair grabbed the robot and led it over to sit in the Rotorbird. I'd check on the metal man myself in a bit, but first things first.

I ran over to a stairway that led up to the catwalk, grabbed the railing, and started up. The bullet wound on my leg was giving me some trouble, especially now that the adrenalin rush was fading.

As I reached the top, two people came out of the office. I instinctively lifted the 1911 and fired two shots at them. One hit the wall inches from their heads and the other passed by their feet. "Get back in there now! Back the fuck up!"

They followed my orders as I ran forward, weapon outstretched. Adrenalin kicked in again. Both had their hands up, smart enough to leave their pieces where they were. I manhandled the one in front, grabbing his pistol and tossing it down from the catwalk before grabbing the cuffs from my back pocket. I hadn't put cuffs on a man since '28, so I fumbled a bit locking the first suspect to the railing of the catwalk.

The second man was lanky, taller than me, though he looked older. A square head and shallow jawline contrasted with the shaggy hair, and his rigid stance made me think that he'd once been military or police. He'd been there at Times Square, I was almost positive, but I needed to be absolutely sure that I had the right man. I grabbed him and threw him into the office, where a terminal sat on a wooden desk flanked by three chairs and a locker rack. A small telephone hung on the wall. I forced him into one of the chairs and used my foot to push both him and the seat against the lockers. The wooden chair legs creaked and squealed against the floor, and the lockers rang out from the collision of the chair against the metal. I levelled the 1911 at the man's forehead as his chapped, drooling lips spit out some sort of excuse.

"Y-y-you don't understand, l-look, it was simple business. All's good now. You need money, I can get you a ton. A literal ton! Sixty percent of my profits, we call this square, and I'll get out of town. Right, Roche?"

He knew who I was. He knew how deep in he was.

"Cory Belik?" I asked.

"Yeah?"

I kicked him in the chest, knocking the wind out of him before hitting him in the jaw. Blood sprayed across the steel locker doors.

He looked back at me with a level of fear that I'd only ever seen once before, long ago. It was pathetic. He was frailer than my grandmother, with the shaking voice and teary eyes of someone who'd rather not be threatened, no matter what they'd been through. He was weak, physically and emotionally. He looked like Allen for just a second ...

Revenge and duty might have been my driving forces, but I wanted the right person to pay. Until then, there didn't have to be any more bloodshed. Allen would be talking my ear off about that, and while it wasn't here now, I was thinking about what it might say. Why would I kill someone if the evidence suggested that he'd little or nothing to do with what occurred at that speakeasy? I sat on the desk and did my best to make the atmosphere more comfortable for Belik. Making him hysterical wouldn't help me get the truth out of him.

"You apparently killed two men from the 5th. But listen to me. I don't care that you were in on something with them. I don't care that all of you were breaking multiple laws. I couldn't give a fuck what kind of pay-roll you had them on, or that you were on with them. They died, and a lot of people think you pulled the trigger. As much as I'd love to do the same to shoot you and blindly follow my orders, I don't like ignoring my gut feelings."

I tucked Allen's 1911 in my waistband and placed Belik's weapon on the desk, then showed him that my own revolver was empty. "You know who I am, which tells me that you weren't aware of the severity of your situation. But let's make a deal, because I'm sure you'll be more useful alive than dead."

"This isn't my fault! Well, it kinda is, but not really. I didn't want this fiasco to happen, but he told me it would."

"Who is *he*? Are you talking about your partner over there, Davin Morris?"

"Morris?" Belik wiped the blood pooling under his nose and chin and peered over at the man cuffed to the railing. He looked back at me, apparently insulted. "Morris got taken out in '27 in a raid on a speakeasy in Hell's Kitchen. *That* is just some lackey who does the heavy lifting. I'm the only one left from the original group."

"So Morris and almost everyone else are dead? Then who is *he*?"

"A Black Hat, G-man, whatever. He never gave me a name or a handle, but he was the one who planned on taking out my old friends in a bid to give me control over the little empire we had. I just rolled with the plan. But I had no intention of dragging *you* into this. You're a death sentence in this business, and I'd prefer to keep living until my hair goes grey."

"Glad you know what you've got yourself into. But tell me, was he worth all this trouble?"

"The G-man? Fuck him, seriously. If it gets me less time, I'll rat him out. There may be honour among thieves, but not people like him. But then if none of this had happened, he'd still be running around without anyone chasing him."

"So then, explain how he fits in with you and everything else that's happened. Start at the beginning ... but be quick. More cops, maybe even the Mafia, might be stopping by after the lights go out, so you have less than an hour."

Belik shifted in his seat and wiped his bloody face before beginning his tale.

"It started back in '22, after the War, when the Automatics were welcome on every street corner and the Iron Hands had just begun peeping out of the shadows. The five of us — by now you must know who we were — were running a few ops, scouting a lot of heavy traffic at this speakeasy. We thought it was alcohol from up north. Little did we know that we'd walked into one of the Iron Hands' biggest outposts for racketeering, with our old friend Karl Jaeger at its head. Smart bastard, he was, but he was still surprised when three cops in street clothes pulled .38s on him. Still, I felt bad about that fiasco, so after he got out of the slammer, both me and Stern decided to give him a deal on parts."

I stopped him with a raised hand and leaned forward. "Jaeger worked for the Iron Hands? You can't be fucking serious. I thought he was a freelancer."

"Freelancer? With those resources? Hell, no, man. He was loaded to the neck with money and parts, so the bust was easy when there was evidence up the wazoo. We took him down and locked things up, but that's as far as it went. As I said, he was a smart bastard: he burned his paper trail, so we couldn't get a single lead that truly connected him with the Iron Hands. After the trial and our formal promotions, we thought maybe it was more than just a fluke, maybe it was even a blessing after all the shit we went through during the War. We brought a ton of parts in as evidence, and they were all detained and catalogued, but we hid some in our personal vehicles. Not a lot, just a crate or two. We planned to make some money on the side, divvied up the parts and ran a few small deals. We got good coin. Eventually it led to us finding dealers, suppliers, running trade routes, making deals out of state, and it boomed from there. After we all met back up and none of us had been caught during those few months, we pooled our cash and graduated to a full smuggling ring and split the money five ways. We funded a ton of things over about five years, from weapons deals to information on rival smuggling companies that we funnelled to other cops. Things took a dip when Morris took a bullet at that speakeasy a few years back.

"Because of that and the Iron Hands putting more eyes on us, Stern decided to stem off on his own again, run smaller ops for his own stuff and keep his money away from ours. We kept in contact, but he was way too paranoid for his own good, or ours. Things went okay for us for about three years, until our old supplier got canned a few months ago and we got a new one: the Black Hat, who offered us better parts but wanted forty percent of the cut. One hell of a cut to take, but after we saw what our stock sold for, that sixty percent the three of us shared was more than double what we used to make.

"Then, apparently, the other two found out that the Black Hat's forty percent was funding some shady government projects and told me about it. This included a little pet project he had going downstairs in the attached office. The G-man came down a few days later, asked me if the others had told me anything. I denied it all, of course, but he wasn't one for taking chances. Maybe it was his way of tying up loose ends, but he didn't expect it to attract the attention of … well, you. He said if I crossed him, I'd get two bullets of my own. But fuck, man … what he can do with Automatics — it's scary."

"At Prince and Greene he had one shell and one regular Red-eye doing the shooting. You know where that Swinger model is?"

"It should've been outside … the same bot that shot them up is the one that was guarding me, making sure I didn't try anything."

"I suspect the agent's plan was to let things play out. The evidence and the identity of your two friends made it look like Jaeger was getting his revenge. You also grabbed Jaeger's Automatic during a pickup and used it as your shell to draw attention away from your associate. The G-man saw that I'd ripped off the serial number and would use it to track down Jaeger. Seeing as it served its purpose, he dumped the shell up north. After all, he wouldn't want any other cops spotting a brainless Automatic with a missing serial number at the scene of a crime, now would he? Too bad I didn't pull the trigger."

"You got it. The G-man said it'd work out well and I'd be swimming in three times as much money as before. But I was uneasy knowing you were still out there. I thought this would get pinned on me if you dug deeper. Then again, knowing your reputation, I was more afraid of getting shot on sight, especially at Times Square a day ago. That's why he placed the Auger and the Red-eye here, for my 'protection.' Still, big guy didn't last a week before you blew his brains out."

"The original plan was to put a bullet in you and be done with it; you have that metal man down there to thank for my letting you live this long."

I hoped Allen was all right, now that I thought about it.

"An Automatic for a partner? During Prohibition? Bah! Still, give it my regards. Anyway, back to the story: I knew you'd eventually find me, so I planned to liquidate my stock fast. I told the G-man I was moving to a more secure location. He wasn't a fan, but he couldn't stop me from getting rid of everything and pocketing the money. My runners are loyal, something his shells aren't. It was only a matter of time before you found me — you have that knack — so I just waited for you to find this place, hoping I'd live long enough to explain everything. Today was going to be the day I moved the bricks to my bank box to grab later — if there was a later."

"Bricks?" I popped up an eyebrow and Belik nodded toward the corner.

Looking around, I found a large briefcase standing on edge. I gripped the handle and yanked it up, bringing it back to my chair. Fuck, it was heavy enough that I had to use both hands. I sat down, placed the cumbersome suitcase on the desk, and opened it. I was not at all prepared for what was inside.

"Holy shit."

The briefcase was filled with enough solid gold to make any miser swoon with lustful greed. I counted thirty-two small gold bars lined up neatly in the case.

I'd never seen anything that shiny and pristine. Heavy, though.

"You move your cash in gold? I never thought of that. Untraceable, unchangeable, and easier to hide than stacks of cash. You're a smart man, Belik."

"It took me years to get a gig with some local banks and factories that let me run pure gold shipments, but it was worth it in the long run. I used fifty-ounce bars, less traceable than the standard two-hundred-ouncers. This, and another three suitcases I have stowed elsewhere, are the payout from liquidating just this portion of the warehouse stock, and it's valued at about a hundred and twenty-five grand. Less than what I was hoping for, but it'll do, especially just from selling the less valuable stuff. If I'd sold everything in the other two warehouses, I'd have had around one million in gold, maybe more."

"What was the less valuable stuff?"

"Silica gel and lubricant. They took up a lot of space and were too fragile to move discreetly, so we sold it off first. The rest would've been much easier."

I stood up, leaving the briefcase on the desk, and walked over to the window. The warehouse was immense, around eighty feet by ninety, with enough space to store a huge amount of silica gel. The shipments that had come through here should have been easy to spot, but we hadn't been accounting for the G-men to be distracting the 5th. All of it had been a ploy to move this shit out and make a quick buck before the operation was compromised. And after they moved it, all they'd have to do was sell off the gold and buy more parts. Belik said the Black Hat had wanted a 40 percent cut of all profits, which meant that if all this was sold, four hundred thousand dollars would be funnelled into some shady government dealings. And that was far too much unaccountable money, especially in that business.

"Take the gold. I don't need it." I spun around to face him. He couldn't mean it. But he repeated himself. "Take it. I know how you run, Roche. This little excursion must be costing Robins one hell of a chunk of pocket change. Take the gold and call yourself paid. Hell, I'll even tell you the location of the other three suitcases. But first, I need a favour."

"Depends on what you need." I sat down again, leaning in.

He took a minute to collect his thoughts. "I'll give you his address, that's all. He planned this entire shitshow — the deaths of my old friends, nearly destabilizing police activities across southern Manhattan. Just make him pay and give me a sentence I can work with."

"That won't make up for you being an accomplice to a cop killing."

"No, but I feel like shit enough for that. I let my friends die, and I can't bear to run from it any longer. There's a reason you found me, Roche. Because I needed and wanted to be found. Put me away, take the gold, and take him down. For them and for me."

I looked at his face and saw that he was serious. Those wary eyes were also the eyes of a man with regrets he could no longer bury. He needed this case wrapped up as badly as Robins and I did.

"All right, I'll take the gold, and get you put away for … accessory to racketeering and smuggling. Ten years, tops."

"Sounds good. Great, even." He stood up and followed me down the stairs, leaving his friend chained to the railing.

———

Belik hopped into the Rotorbird and sat down beside Allen.

"How did the talk go, boys? You good, metal man?" I asked.

"Yes, Elias." It nodded at me. It was still odd, hearing it use my first name. I'd have to get used to that."

"Take Belik here to the 5th for lock-up. Charge him as an accessory to racketeering. He didn't set up the murder of our boys. Oh, and the guy up there — the 5th's boys will get him later."

Out of the corner of my eye I noticed Sinclair's look of resentment diminish into one of mild irritation. Sinclair had been sure that Belik was the one who'd gunned down his fellow officers. But one glance at the man — along with my word — reassured him that Belik wasn't a cop killer. Sinclair got into the cockpit and started the rotors.

Belik gave me the location of the Black Hat as he got belted in. The address was a few blocks south, on the border to the Meatpacking District, which gave me a bit of time to do some searching.

"Dismantle his little project and then get there. He'll be waiting on the helipad for his ride up," Belik said.

"When does he usually get picked up?" I asked.

"He'd often leave this place at six, so I guess around seven."

"Roger." I looked inside at Sinclair, who was preparing to lift off. "Send some squad cars from the 5th to set up a perimeter, keep Maranzano's people from investigating."

"Got a plan for this place?" Paddy asked.

"Yeah, it'll be our tribute to her, a show of good faith." Paddy nodded in response. "Also: Belik will give you an address. Be there at seven."

He gave me a thumbs-up, and I stepped out onto the warehouse floor once again. Allen made a motion to follow me, but I put my hand up. "No need, Allen. I'll handle this one. Did you find Toby?"

"Toby left the premises some time ago, with several useable parts."

He's a slippery bastard, all right. Good ol' Toby, I thought.

"You just keep Belik safe and get him processed."

"But, Detective, surely you need assistance in the investigation."

"There's no investigation this time," I yelled over the noise of the rotors as they began to pick up.

Allen pulled the sliding door closed, and the Rotorbird ascended through the skylight into the dimming sky. My watch read five thirty. Looked as if things were going well for once — quite the opposite to how it had all started.

As I wandered through the carnage inflicted by the Auger, I was able to trace my path back to where Allen had fallen through the roof, and where the Swinger model had collapsed. Tracking the machine down took little effort; I had but to listen for the grunts of effort reverberating through the quiet building. I found it heavily damaged. There was a thick trail of green fluid oozing from the Automatic's chem system, and its legs were barely functional. One arm hung useless, and there was a long gash in the metal on the side of its head where the bullet had grazed it.

I approached the Swinger bot and pushed it onto its front to inspect the back of its head. I'd been expecting to see the characters *J4-35* engraved there, but instead saw *TH-30*.

"Fuck."

It wasn't him. Wasn't *it*. It wasn't James. James wasn't the killer. I'd been so sure of it …

Or maybe I'd just been chasing a ghost again.

Good thing the capek was awake, though. I turned it over and pulled it up by the collar. Its red eyes were shimmering and blinking from the damage it had sustained.

"You pull the trigger, metal man?"

"Sure did." Its eyes contorted to give a look of self-satisfaction. "Almost did it for free, too."

"Bastard. How many cops have you killed for Masters?"

"Oh, I've killed many, trust me. Not for Masters, though. I'm no slave to a fucking Black Hat." It struggled to grab my arm and laughed in my face. "It's all for the greater good, right?"

Its eyes flickered from red to blue, making me panic and release it as its laugh echoed through the complex. The laugh was cut short by the sound of glass breaking and the shockwave of a rifle shot echoing through the building. The Red-eye's Neural-Interface was strewn about the floor.

That answered that question: it had definitely not been a shell.

I raised the 1911 and pivoted around, but I had no idea where the bullet had come from. Whoever had killed the machine could easily have killed me, too.

One thing at a time, Roche, I told myself. *First the Automatic, now the project.*

─────

The office portion of the warehouse was connected to the main complex by a door located on the main floor directly under the upstairs office where I had apprehended Belik. Like the warehouse itself, it was mostly empty. In contrast, though, there were myriad machines and computer parts jerry-rigged together.

There were ten or so Neural-Interfaces hooked in to one another in the office, with a central terminal controlling them all as coolant regulators and devices kept the processors from failing. Most of the maintenance equipment necessary for keeping an NI running was contained within an Automatic, and so it was more like a human brain than I gave it credit for.

Never before had I inspected a Neural-Interface. It was a work of art in its own right: various spark plugs, alternating dynamos, vacuum tubes, and dozens of other small devices circled a central metal core where the plug was attached. Miniature pumps began to oscillate faster as the "brain" warmed up, sparking as it began to transfer data to the terminal. It was an engineering marvel, an analog computer stuffed into a small space. While I might have some animosity toward shut-off coppertops, I could still appreciate their complexity.

The centre of the office held a large server-like block of hardware. The Neural-Interfaces were all connected to it, with several wires coming off it from the top, probably connected to antennas which broadcasted right to the Plate. Had I been riding up in the Rotorbird with Sinclair, I would have seen whatever antenna array they had for this thing. It had to be massive for all the data that must be running through this little space.

Thankfully, the connected Neural-Interfaces had their Automatics' serial numbers attached. They were from a variety of machines — E1-1S, R0-GR, among others. One NI that was much less rusted than the others had the code RU-D1 on it.

Rudi. Jaeger's Automatic.

I pulled that Neural-Interface from the contraption, hearing the coolant devices slowing down as the strain on them was lessened by one.

But even with one less Neural-Interface, this machine was still dangerous. The 1911 in my possession did the rest, destroying whatever processors were active and springing a leak in the coolant system. If any NIs were still intact now, they wouldn't be in about ten minutes, after they overheated.

Six o'clock was when the lights went off. I assumed both cops and mobsters would be sprinting over here after hearing all the noise we'd made. That gave me thirty minutes to clear out before things got ugly, which they definitely would, seeing as this warehouse was situated smack dab in the heart of Maranzano's territory. The less I interacted with that old school Mob, the better. I stumbled outside, suddenly reminded that a chunk of my thigh was still missing. My grey slacks were soaked through with blood. I'd try not to get any on the seat of my car when I got back to the 5th. For now, unfortunately, I had to lug a case of gold and a Neural-Interface across town on foot. At least no one would fuck with me when I looked like this.

Especially not Masters. He was my next stop.

CHAPTER 18

"ALLEN, LOOK AT ME. YA GOOD?"

Allen sat in the same folding seat in the Rotorbird that he'd begun the journey in, the steely blue lights of his eyes bouncing across the metal of the bird. His hands shook, and the metal plates of his palms clicked against each other. Looking outside, he could see the vast ocean of buildings in the Anchor, a nice change of scenery compared to the warehouse. Sinclair had just come back from booking Belik and had felt it appropriate to keep Allen from going downstairs just yet.

"Allen, look at me. I need ya to focus now. Roche will handle the case, but right now you need to keep yourself from goin' belly-up … if you can. If you had skin, you'd be positively green right now."

Allen's eyes shot up to meet Sinclair's. The cop had a look of understanding on his face, clearly empathetic to the anguish Allen was experiencing.

"Patrick, I killed a man. He's dead because of me."

"Yeah, I saw. You killed him, but you had to. Try not to think about it anymore."

"Police doctrine states that no perpetrator should be fired upon without instigation, and —"

"Allen, he provoked you, since he was tryin' to kill *us*. I need ya to focus on somethin', okay? You may have killed him, sure, but you saved my life, and Roche's as well. If Elias had fired the Suppression Rifle in that situation, the electrical discharge would have destabilized the Rotorbird, and we would have ended up in the ceiling, or flipped, or worse. *You* saved the lives of two officers today — well, an officer and a vigilante. I think that's fair, eh?"

"I attempted to render him inoperable by aiming at the Tesla Battery. However, I found the armour to be too tough to puncture using a regular firearm. The only possibility to prevent more mortality was …"

"I know, bud. I do." Sinclair sat in the seat beside Allen, putting a hand on his shoulder. "You need to calm down before ya hurt yourself. I need you to take a breath … if you can breathe."

Allen stopped shaking momentarily, sucking air into his synthetic lungs and holding it for some time before expelling it violently. He began shaking again, his jaw quivering as he continued to try to calm down. Sinclair kept a close eye on him.

Suddenly Allen jumped out of his seat, threw himself from the aircraft down onto the helipad, and spewed a clear liquid from his mouth onto the floor. Sinclair jumped down to help him up, but Allen yelled at him to stay back. "Don't touch it. Highly concentrated hydrochloric acid. I don't want you losing any skin."

"Didn't think you metal men had any fluids in ya, to be honest. Other than alcohol, that is."

"Most of us don't. We have no saliva for initial digestion, though we contain acid in our stomach-like compartment for breakdown and absorption of organic molecules for our metabolism. We operate similarly to you, though with exceptions."

"Yeah, like the whole replacin' of your limbs … thing," Sinclair said. "Sometimes I wish we could do that. Be easier than having to get a broken arm worked and pulled for three months before it even rotates properly, eh?" He rotated his stiff left arm.

Allen picked himself up, shaking the fluid from his hands before climbing back into the aircraft to take a seat again.

"Look, Allen, just breathe, that's all ya need to do," Sinclair continued. "Just … let's get your mind off of it. Tell me somethin', anything."

"Like what, Detective Sinclair?"

"Tell me about … tell me about where ya came from. Usually that helps normal people — humans, I mean — try to get their mind to a more relaxed state. Maybe you work the same, Allen. Somethin' about your 'childhood' … or the equivalent."

"I was made exactly seven years ago in a secret location known as Camp Theta in midwestern America, but I was born far earlier than that."

"What do you mean *born*? You're a machine. Right?"

"In the early 1920s, China was conducting advanced research in human biology. This was feasible only with the increase of accessible technology

due to the Tesla Battery's widespread availability —
America transported Manuals through China during
the Great War, and proprietary technology had been
'lost' time after time. With that in mind, after China's
major breakthroughs in researching the human brain,
most of their data was stolen through espionage by the
Allied countries of America and France after rumours
had begun to spread of such experimentation. These
developments enabled further Automatic advancement with minimal effort and prevented China from
getting an economic edge in either the Automatic or
medical industry. American scientists endeavoured to
enable true synthetic intelligence, and so a project was
founded to create me. Or, rather, us — the Synthians.
This was the briefing they gave to us after we developed
true consciousness."

"Really? And how do you feel about being 'born'?"

"What do you mean?" Allen asked curiously.

"Well, a lot of people — me included — often look
back and ask ourselves if our lives are any good, or wonder if we were born at the right time. For example, if I'd
been born a few years later, I'd never have joined the
military and learned to pilot Rotorbirds. If Elias had
been born earlier, he might not have met ..." Sinclair's
voice trailed off. "You got any thoughts on that?"

Allen stared at him for a while, pondering the question. "I suppose I believe I was born too early. As of now,
we Synthians are still herded in with the common traffic
of simple Automatics and are regarded as nothing more
than programmed machines. The few humans who
do learn of our true nature either fear us as imposters

trying to replace humanity, or revere us as engineering marvels rather than seeing us as equals. I believe in a way that we were created by scientists just to prove they could play God. Maybe in several years — perhaps even decades — we will be accepted, but as for myself, I feel stuck here, attempting to set precedents that I will never be able to take for granted."

"Allen, there's no reason to say that." Sinclair put his arm around him. "Maybe you will enjoy those precedents and rights, eventually. Everything takes work and time. Look at humanity itself: before you — I mean, before Automatics came along — there was a lot of inequality between races, sexes, ideologies. A lot of it has been swept under the rug. Overall, things have improved … marginally."

Allen raised an eyebrow. "Marginally?"

"Look I'm just saying that things will get better. Maybe not now, while things are on edge, but it'll happen, eventually you'll be accepted …"

"Perhaps, but at whose expense? Another machine, far more advanced than I, might have to suffer as I do now, while I sit there powerless to help. I believe the cycle of scapegoating must end here, with us."

"Yeah, good luck with that, Allen. Human nature — so your nature as well, I suppose — dictates otherwise."

Sinclair leaned back in the chair, pulled out a cigarette, and lit it. He offered one to Allen, who shook his head. "Speakin' of which, you seem more knowledgeable about human nature than most humans. What did you do while you were stuck in that camp out west for seven years?"

"I was educated through academic study, mostly. New areas of study emerged after the War in the fields of physics and psychoanalysis, which intrigued me, so instead of going out like many other Synthians, who attempted to integrate along with the Automatics, I decided to further my knowledge in hopes of using it to better human- and machine-kind."

Sinclair nodded. "Why are ya trustin' me with all this, by the way? This whole Camp Theta thing sounds shadier than mustard gas. Why do you trust me with all these secrets?"

"In our limited contact with each other thus far, I have observed you to be a trustworthy individual."

"Right, you have that 'seein' things' knack. I hope you're right, Allen. But while we're on the topic of honesty, we should really talk about your bedside manner."

"You mean my lack thereof?"

"Yes, that." Sinclair leaned against the sliding door frame. "Police work isn't usually like this, Allen. Ya can't go around telling everyone they're wrong and you're right. People have far too much pride to roll over and accept what you say, and some might even put a bullet in ya for disagreeing with them. Real police work is gut feelings, knee-jerk responses, and sometimes puttin' a sock in your mouth if someone starts gettin' hysterical. I just need ya to realize you can't play the detective all the time. That sometimes other people have to be right, eh? Today you did somethin' any sane officer would have in the situation, and you resorted to violence only when it was *absolutely* necessary. But as y'know, not everyone follows doctrine like me or you."

"Like Detective Roche."

"Like Elias, yes. Roche is risky and reckless, but I give him the benefit of the doubt in some areas. If there's ever a case that needs solvin', no matter how incredibly illegal it is to investigate or how insanely dangerous, I'd trust him with my life to get it done. No matter what the cost. And sometimes that's what it boils down to. Ya don't have to go in guns blazing, killin' people, but you can't sit by and expect everythin' to clean itself up if things go south. Ya get me?"

"I do, truly. I suppose I've been looking at his methods as an outsider. To look at him as an insider — such as yourself — might lead me to understand why he operates the way he does, and why you and Robins continually trust him with such delicate cases. Regardless, however, I still cannot condone the liberal use of lethal force."

"I agree with ya there, but that's a conversation for another day. The last thing we need to do is set him over the edge when he's this close to finishin' the case. First, we end this fiasco, and then we get ya a cozy little cubicle where you can spend your slow days at the station. After that, you and Roche can have a long talk about his 'methods.' You can even talk to him at your little desk. Now, let's get the hell off of this bird before any G-men wander up and see us. They might think we're planning on stealing it."

Allen snickered at the comment before disembarking. Just then, the precinct's own Rotorbird appeared in the sky, beginning its descent to the large helipad. Sinclair turned back to Allen with an anxious look, checking his watch to see it was nearly seven o'clock.

"Actually, you head downstairs. Tell the agent in Robins's office that Belik was booked … I have somewhere to be."

Allen knew better than to question him. He nodded and headed for the stairs.

Agent Ewalt seemed relieved to hear that an arrest had been made without the need for guns — at least, that was what Allen told him. Ewalt phoned the Plate, trying to find out where Masters had gone, but eventually gave up and decided to reschedule the inspection for a less tumultuous time. The agent contacted his Rotorbird pilot and flew back to the Plate, and soon enough, everything started to go back to normal. The stress of the past few days had earned most of the officers a night off, told that the 7th would pick up their slack. When ten struck, the station was deserted save for Allen and Robins.

According to Robins, if there were any issues tonight, the 7th would deal with it. Allen, however, couldn't relax like everyone else until he'd settled a few things. When he knocked on the door, Robins yelled gruffly, "Yeah? Get in here."

At the sight of Allen, the commissioner's hassled demeanour shifted to a welcoming one. "Forty-One! Good evening, come in. Sorry about that."

"It is quite all right, Commissioner Robins. And if you don't mind, I believe it'd be easier for you to call me Allen."

"Right, right, of course. Take a seat, Allen."

Robins waved a hand toward a chair. As Allen sat down, Robins walked over to a small table that held a few confiscated alcohols and picked up a bottle of brandy. His desk was still covered in loose pieces of paper, files, and other sorts of information, but whatever forms or figures the FBI agents had pinned to the walls had since been torn off and scattered on the floor at the edges of the room.

Robins filled a snifter and looked at Allen. "Care for one? I only break it out for special occasions. And it's legal ... well, mostly."

"I ... I believe I would like some, Commissioner."

Robins chuckled as he poured a second glass and brought both over. He sat down and met Allen's gaze. The robot wrapped his metal fingers around the glass. The feel of the cool material was somewhat alien to him. He thought for a moment that drinking might be irresponsible, but his qualms went away after several drops passed his lips.

"What brings you to see me?"

"It's ... it's about an incident that occurred three hours ago, at about five thirty in the evening, at the western docks, during Belik's apprehension." The robot looked at his glass for a few silent seconds before electing to pour more brandy down his metal throat. The liquid passed though him and hit his stomach. The sudden influx of alcohol into his synthetic circulatory system sent jolts through him and produced a ringing sensation in his head. "I don't believe I'm fit for active duty, sir."

"Fit for duty? What makes you say that? Sure, it was a rough patch taking care of that raid, but from Paddy's description, you did phenomenal for a rookie."

"Yes, I understand that. The problem is ..." Allen realized that the alcohol in his system was making this both harder and easier. His silicon organs worked harder than their human equivalents, giving him a buzz faster than any lightweight. Robins got up, retrieved the bottle, and poured another inch into the robot's glass. "Under the circumstances, I had to take a life in order to rescue Detectives Roche and Sinclair from the augmented human who was assaulting them. If the job calls for me to have other people's lives in my hands, I don't believe I can continue."

Robins nodded, an expression of empathy on his face. "Allen, it's not always like this. Your investigative skills are magnificent, and I wish I had twenty of you. But I hate to break it to you — you can't always play the nice guy. You gotta switch between good and bad cop. Good cop gets the perps to talk and tries to understand why criminals do what they do. Bad cop keeps those people from hurting others — including officers, if they become unreasonable. What you're experiencing is something every cop in every city in every country has gone through. It's just something that sometimes happens. You have someone's life in your hands, and you need to decide whether that life can be redeemed, or will only continue to cause destruction and pain. And if you decide the latter, then sometimes you have to make an even tougher call ... which you already have done. Honestly, I didn't think you'd have this experience until far later, but I also believe it's best to have the experience as early as possible. The earlier you learn to deal with this kind of guilt, the more prepared you'll be the next time a life is in your hands.

"This is not to say that a life you have to take is worth nothing. Every life is worth something. But we follow a code: that we will never kill anyone who has not taken the life of another. Someone who has taken the life of another is no longer a man or a woman, but a monster. And we do more than just hunt monsters: we see if they can become human again. Or we prevent them from causing more pain if they cannot be brought back."

"That seems like an extreme perspective to have, commissioner, especially in your position."

"Yeah, well, you develop some interesting perspectives if you stay in the lower city long enough …"

Thousands of thoughts were running through Allen's brain. The alcohol made it easier to sort through which ones were worth listening to. "I just find it odd that we are sanctioned to kill in order to prevent others from killing. It feels oddly backward and self-destructive. What discerns us from the 'monsters,' as you call them, if we do what they do? Is there a guarantee that we will always be good and they will always be evil?"

Robins stood up and looked out the window at the fountain outside his office. He let out a long sigh. "There's no guarantee, Allen. We can't know for sure that no one will switch sides, as you've seen from this case. But I suppose the best thing I can say is that police work isn't shades of grey."

"It is shades of red. Though death is an inevitability, we kill only when absolutely necessary. Spilling blood to save lives."

Robins grinned, his shoulders relaxing as he returned to the chair. "I'm glad Elias has taught you as much as you've tried to teach him."

"It was a difficult situation when we first became partners, but we've worked past our immediate differences. At least for the moment."

"Excellent, excellent." Robins sat back in his chair and sipped his brandy.

"But to my original point, I do understand the reasoning behind the methods. There is no doubt in my mind as to why killing may be necessary. But the fact is, I just cannot accept these methods. I'm not built for this work. I can't see myself becoming accustomed to this sickly feeling of —"

"Allen, stop." Robins didn't let him finish. "This is the way to look at it: you're now at a crossroads. You can either move on and fight like hell to never let it happen again. Or you can let it haunt you, and become a nervous wreck of a man ... er, machine. Sorry. You killed a man, and that's hard for anyone, even me. I've been doing this for more than thirty years — first in the War, now down here — and I still hate the feeling of having to pull the trigger. So, use this as a way to remind yourself to be the good cop. But know that if push comes to shove, you can handle the aftermath of having to play bad cop. Now, I swear, if you mention quitting again, I'll slap you myself."

"I ... I understand, Commissioner." Allen grabbed the glass and sipped again, letting the liquid churn inside him. He reclined into the chair.

Robins was the first to break the silence. "What else is on your mind, Allen?"

"There is something, though I feel it is more difficult to express than my own issues. I'm curious about Roche's past, specifically his past career as a police officer."

"That's quite a big topic. Anything more specific?"

"He told me briefly that he'd had more than ten 'partners' since he left the Force in 1928. That is quite a few. I suspect you gave him these so-called partners to try to keep him in check, but I was hoping to learn the reason for the large turnover rate and why I seem to have succeeded where others have failed in remaining his partner. He also mentioned someone named James …"

Robins sighed, cradling his head in his hands for a moment before getting up and closing his office door. He sat back down and dropped his voice to a low whisper. "James was Elias's partner between '27 and '28. They ran nearly every op together, regardless if it was a hit-and-run investigation or a full-blown raid. He was Elias's second partner, after Sinclair went solo to finish his advanced Rotorbird training. James and Elias ran together for almost two years, until they looked into the botched investigation of a missing business magnate.

"They found the kidnappers and tried to subdue them, but … well, James was killed in the crossfire. It devastated Elias. Put him out of commission for a while. He did some digging and found out that the kidnappers were working for Murder, Inc., which at the time was run by Morello and Luciano. I'm not sure which one coordinated the kidnapping, but Roche didn't really care. In his mind, both of them were responsible, and so he took the lead on the investigation, coordinated the raid on Morello's personal compound in one of SoHo's speakeasies, and the rest is history."

"I can't imagine the pain he must have gone through, losing a friend like that."

"James was one of the only things Elias gave a shit about — more than his own reputation or his life, even. What was done to James before it was killed was far worse than being shot, but Morello finishing it off was the nail in the coffin."

"Before it was killed?" Allen looked confused.

The commissioner didn't seem keen to explain, but he continued, nonetheless. "James was an Automatic. In 1928, he was Green-eyed, and then weeks later, he — it, I mean — was killed. Elias thought of James, or rather, J4-35, as his best friend. Seeing its mind and soul watered down, turned into a mindless machine before his eyes, just so it could stay in the Force — it destroyed Elias. You probably haven't seen him around Green-eyes, as he does his best to avoid them. He's fine with Automatics in general — at least, he tries to be — which might explain why he thought that it was a terribly cruel joke for me to set you up as his partner at first. Maybe he thought I was replacing James, but I wasn't trying to. Surprisingly, however, it seems you two have done quite well together, all things considered. And maybe you've even helped him move past the Morello incident a little. The fact that he hasn't stranded you on 90th Street is progress in and of itself."

"But I thought he'd had Automatic partners before."

"I gave him Automatics to tag along. I never said they were official partners, just ride-along buddies. He wasn't too pleased with me those times. He wouldn't take my calls for weeks afterward. The important point is that this isn't a widely talked about subject. Everyone in the 5th knows: you don't talk about Roche's past. Not to him. Not behind his back. It's a no-go. You wouldn't have known that, but now you do. Just … keep it on the DL, you know?"

"Yes, thank you, Commissioner. Though it was concerning when he became obsessed about the killer in this case being an Automatic — specifically, a Swinger model that had been Red-eyed."

"Oh, Jesus." Robins rubbed the bridge of his nose again. "This is the fifth time this has happened. He's chasing a ghost, Allen. He imagines James is alive and well somewhere, or maybe that it was salvaged and Red-eyed and used by the Mob. He's confident almost any Swinger model in the city is his old partner."

"He did hesitate to kill one such Red-eye during the raid this evening …" Allen thought back to firing down at the Automatic that would have killed Roche, had Allen not screwed up the courage to jump from the Rotorbird. "Has Roche ever investigated the location where his old partner was killed? At least to see if it was taken?"

Robins hesitated and thought. "I have mentioned it to him a few times, but he was always adamant that James wasn't there any longer. I doubt he even checked …"

After a while, Allen stood up, leaving his half-full snifter on the desk. "Thank you again for the information, Commissioner. You've helped me very much."

"It's no problem."

He stood, wobbling a bit from intoxication. But he felt a weight lifted from his shoulders, now that he knew more about Roche's past. He would never understand the detective's pain, but he could do his best to fill the void Elias had endured for almost five years. He turned to leave, feeling what might be a smile forming on his metallic face. Maybe he *could* stay on here. Maybe Robins was right.

As he opened the door, he turned to bid Robins farewell. The commissioner smiled ... then his face paled in an instant. Allen turned to see Roche standing in the doorway, his face and clothing covered with blood. He was panting for breath, and in one hand he held a briefcase that looked like it weighed a ton.

He walked past Allen, nodding at him, then slammed the briefcase onto Robins's desk. He unlatched the case to reveal it was full of gold bars. Pocketing five of the bars, he piled the rest of them on the desk. Finally, he slammed a bloodstained note onto the table, grabbed Allen's glass, and chugged the rest of the brandy.

"You don't need to pay me. You were bought out. Keep that ten grand you owe me for a rainy day. And keep the gold, too. You'll need it. Oh, the addresses listed are for three other gold drops. Keep them or send them to me, I don't give a fuck."

Both Allen and Robins looked at Roche with a combination of curiosity and horror. After a long pause, Roche said, "I'm going home for a shower. Be back tomorrow to see how things are. I need sleep, and maybe some bandages."

With that, Roche walked out, leaving Allen and Robins staring at the empty doorway, the trail of blood, and the pile of gold bars on the desk.

"What happened to him?" Allen asked.

Robins finally spoke. "I don't ... I haven't seen him like that in a long time. But, as you can see, Allen, that's why we hire Elias Roche: you get results. You get justice."

CHAPTER 19

THE ROOFTOP THAT MASTERS was using as a heli-pad belonged to an old apartment complex in the Meatpacking District that had recently been condemned. The floorboards inside the building were cracked, there was mould and garbage strewn everywhere, and I was fairly certain that I'd caught the smell of a decomposing body. I stashed the Neural-Interface and the briefcase under the concrete stairs and headed up at a quick pace, determined to reach the top before Masters's Rotorbird appeared.

My watch read ten to seven. Sinclair had better be here.

The door to the roof was ajar, the wind swinging it on its creaky hinges. I pushed it open to reveal the flat surface of the roof. Agent Masters — still dressed in black — stood looking at his watch, watching the Plate in anticipation. I approached, pulling out my Diamondback and pushing the mechanism back to single-action. He must have heard the click of the hammer; he turned around slowly, a gun of his own pointed at me.

"Detective, you've been busy. I saw you coming from a mile away." Even with his back against the wall, he was acting smug. *Lanky fuck*, I thought.

"I wasn't trying to hide. I've got a score to settle with you, Masters."

"Oh, do you now? What are you basing your 'score' on? After all, what possible evidence could you have? Other than me being a bit tardy for our inspection at your precinct."

"You killed those cops at Prince and Greene and others with your shells and your broadcast system. Not only that, but racketeering is still a federal offence, as is the extortion of an Upper City resident. Each of those alone is worth a hefty sentence. You won't be getting out of prison until you're a corpse."

Masters chuckled, his gun still trained on me. "Who would believe you? Show me tangible proof that I did any of what you said. Sure, I might have covered up a crime scene that was under FBI jurisdiction, but I won't answer to you for that. You're barking up the wrong tree, Detective. What was your name again? Ronald? Ross?"

"It's Roche, you fuck."

He flinched, and I stepped forward, calling his bluff. He didn't fire, which gave me confidence.

"Killing two cops —"

"Two *dirty* cops. You forgot that part, didn't you? I'm sure you also forgot that there were *three* dead cops there. One who, unfortunately, got in the way. Convenient for you to forget about that third one and focus on your contrived faithfulness to the 5th. Then again, maybe that third cop from the 11th wasn't there undercover. I dare you to point to a single cop in this city who isn't a fucking rat. So, who bought you, huh? Gould? Maranzano?"

"The Eye of New York sees everything."

He spat, his face twisting in disgust. "You … you're her Iron Hand, huh? I've heard stories about you, but I didn't take them seriously. If they're true, then you're a monster, plain and simple."

"And you aren't?" My raised voice spooked him, making him back up a bit. My gun was pointed downward, but my stance was intimidating enough. "You're a sick fuck who hides behind bodies and shells. You don't deserve to judge me."

"I have every reason to judge you, Roche. You're a criminal, plain and simple, stringing Robins along, making him think you're loyal. I'll be sure to relay this tidbit of information to my superiors as soon as I get back Plateside. Speak of the devil …" He looked up. A black Rotorbird was approaching, and it was definitely an FBI aircraft. Masters's smug grin brought my blood to a boil. "You can't touch me, and neither can she. I'm a federal agent. Even looking at me wrong is an offence. But I'll keep your sentence light if you walk away right now. If you don't, I promise nothing."

"You won't get very far."

"Excuse me?" He cupped a hand around his ear, mocking me. "Say that a bit louder."

"You won't get very far, *asshole*."

The beating of the air alerted us to a second Rotorbird approaching: Sinclair, prompt as always. His

Rotorbird, loaded for bear, flew in front of the FBI aircraft. The speaker on the front of the machine blared out his words. "THIS IS A RESTRICTED AIRSPACE! WILL OPEN FIRE IF YOU DON'T PULL AWAY NOW."

I knew he wasn't bluffing.

The FBI craft circled, testing the waters, but quickly realized it was too dangerous to land. The Black Hats might oversee everything from up top, but they were bound by regulations. Namely, that any crime scene under investigation was under the direct jurisdiction of the nearest Lower City precinct, and only legitimate agents could supersede that. And we knew for a fact that there were no FBI agents who could fly a Rotorbird. Outside hires flew the brass around.

The pilot spun the bird around and headed back the way it had come. They might be planning to return, but there wouldn't be anyone to pick up.

Masters turned to me, finally showing an emotion I was glad to see: nervousness. His gun wasn't trained on me anymore, giving me a clear opening to fire a bullet of my own. A quick flick of my wrist put a round in his thigh, making him scream in agony and drop to the ground, gasping for breath. He released his hold on the gun and I kicked it away as soon as I got close, my barrel now held parallel to his gaze.

"You … fucker!"

"You're scum, you know that?" I ground my teeth. "You won't leave here alive. I'm here to maintain justice, no matter what. Those boys were dirty, but they were part of the 5th. And I don't take kindly to cop killers."

"I thought you of all people would understand the concept of the greater good. That's why you work for Robins, isn't it? You work both sides, and keep the peace. She worms out the smaller fish for the sharks, and the sharks leave her be. You're keeping a dangerous balance. The longer she's around, the more prepared she'll be to take this city for herself. You're fuelling a future war."

"Better than what you were doing by starting one."

"I was ending one!" He was surprisingly well spoken for a man with a bullet in his leg. "She can't touch me unless she wants the entire Plate on her ass. I needed those smugglers to start fighting against her influence, knocking her down a few pegs, giving her a reason to worry. I was untouchable, and so were my people. If Belik ever bit it, I'd just find another, help them along, do what I could to get them into fighting shape. I'd cut her out of the market, drain her dry, and then we'd find a way to make her bleed. I was doing more to combat the Iron Hands than you ever did as a cop, and especially as a fucking lapdog!" He yelped in pain, clutching his leg.

"She'd find a way. She always does …"

"No excuses, Roche! You say you're here for justice. Fine! I killed those two assholes because they would have ruined everything! If the Bureau ever found out, I'd be finished, and if the crime lords found out, there would be a turf war. I was keeping things under wraps. Only gangsters got killed by the shells I stole and programmed. No one will miss them. And yet you, the one who keeps the balance, can't even choose a side. You do the Eye's dirty work, and yet you try to put criminals down? Do you really think keeping her in power saves lives? Or is that just what you tell yourself?"

I lowered my gun. He was right. If anything, he and I were the same. We both were looking to accomplish the same thing. He was just far more productive than I was.

"You're living a lie, telling yourself whatever it takes to make you feel like the hero in all this," he went on. "How many people does she kill every day? How many cops are put in the line of fire because of raids against the Iron Hands or whomever they point out to you? If I'd had another few months, I would have had the financial backing to ruin her, or at least to threaten her and save this city from the crime wave we've been in the midst of since '29. *My* ends justify my means, but for you it's the other way around. You're delusional, Roche. You think every problem can be beaten to death and buried."

I couldn't think straight. I just stared at him. Sinclair was gone by now, leaving us alone on the darkening rooftop. Looking to the west, I could see the sun finally disappearing. The cold wrapped around me like a glove as the twinkling reds and greens above us shone down. He may have been a dirty bastard, but his plan for the city was far better than mine. What was my role in all this? Was I even a man anymore, or just some story to scare children and Brunos with a conscience?

The hammer on my gun was forward, requiring another pull. My thumb went to it automatically, lining up another .38 round with the barrel.

"Killing me will be the beginning of the end. You kill me ... you die. Your friends, your benefactors, this entire city will go up in flames. Do you want that to happen?"

"Better to sift through the ashes than search a broken house," I said, speaking for the first time since he'd begun his tirade.

And then he started laughing. Laughing at me. "The famous Iron Hand, speechless at his own hypocrisy. Just keep living the lie, then. Thinking must be too much for you." He looked into my eyes. "At least James isn't around to see this."

My brain seemed to snap with those words. Things turned black, and my body went on automatic. I dropped my gun, jumped on top of him, grabbed his chin, and pulled his head up. "You're going to see why they call me the Iron Hand."

Masters was still laughing. He may have won the battle, but he had lost the war. He didn't care, though. He'd done the damage he needed to.

I was just getting warmed up to do my own.

"Welcome to Manhattan, asshole."

CHAPTER 20

THE EYE NEVER USED THE SAME apartments for meetings; she was always shifting and moving around the city. She even used other people's apartments while they weren't home, fixing the places up so well afterward that they looked almost too clean to the returning residents.

After dropping off the case of money and gifting Rudi's Neural-Interface to Jaeger, I went home. I knew all too well that she would want to see me after what had transpired. Just before I turned the tumblers of my door lock, I heard the knocking behind me. It came from behind the door of my neighbour's apartment. Two knocks, twice.

I sighed, pulled my key back out, then turned and grabbed the handle of my neighbour's door. The dark apartment was lit by a small light that faced me from behind a chair. The Eye was sitting there, her hands folded, elbows propped up on the arms of the chair, and one leg resting on the other. Once again, I could see her silhouette, but not her face.

The place looked empty besides her, but I knew there were others lurking in the other rooms, maybe even in the hallway, waiting for me to slip up. She pointed to a folding chair leaning against the wall. I unfolded it and sat down. The blood and filth on my clothes was beginning to stink up the place.

"Really, Elias? Now I have to clean that up, too, along with every other piece of refuse this woman hoards in here." Her voice was far less stern that it had been the last time I'd seen her. She almost seemed relieved.

"I was on my way home to change. But, knowing how impatient you can be, I decided to humour you."

"Well, I thank you for your respect, as well as your word. I doubt it was easy to solve this case, given the limitations you were under, but I'm impressed, as always."

"The only limitation I had was not to kill the wrong man. Honestly, you shouldn't be too impressed that I decided to use more brain power than your cronies usually do."

She took the insult without comment. "Then tell me, who was the person who threatened my entire operation? Cory Belik or Andrew Stern?" She actually seemed interested to hear my explanation. There was a first for everything, I supposed.

"Belik, Stern, and even Jaeger were played for fools, scapegoats to a Black Hat named Masters who decided to take the operation to the next level. He was planning on fighting you bit by bit, pulling the rug out from under you and building up his smuggling ring until he could dominate and take out the Iron Hands. It didn't work, but … he had a plan."

"A poor plan, seeing as he failed to see what would do him in. Nevertheless, I wasn't worried. No one will be removing us — not even you, my trusty Iron Hand."

Something about her saying that stung. Masters was dead, but his words were very much alive in my head. And the worst thing about them was that he was right. Without a doubt, he was right about everything.

"The job is done. I expect my payment by next week."

"Ah, but one moment." She stood, letting her hair fall forward to cover her face before she began pacing. "You retrieved a case of gold bars used by Belik for his payments to the FBI contact. I believe I am entitled to that gold as compensation for lost profits."

Shit, I thought, *one of her cronies must have seen me when I went back to the 5th*. Well, she wasn't getting any of that gold, not on my watch.

"It's already in the hands of someone who deserves it." I saw her hands clench as I finished my thought. "But that warehouse where our raid went down on the western docks — it isn't guarded by anyone but some stragglers from the 5th. Hundreds, maybe thousands of parts are in there, and though quite a lot was destroyed in the crossfire, what's left could probably fund your operation for a few months. It would keep you from relying on outside sources too heavily and would mean a hell of a lot of money in your pocket and no one else's."

She seemed to relax, and I soon heard movement inside and outside the apartment. Her cronies didn't need prompting, it seemed. After the footsteps outside stopped, she spoke again. "I suppose all is in order, then. Fine job, Elias. Your payment will be in your account within the week."

"Fantastic." I pulled out one of the gold bars I had pocketed, throwing it toward her. "Catch."

With lightning reflexes, she snatched it from the air effortlessly and put it down beside her on the ground. I did it partly to keep her happy, but also to see her arm. I'd noticed it earlier. The augments she had were quite compact and looked very human, despite having a metallic sheen. She had the money and the means to build a custom arm, which probably meant that it was even more advanced than anything Allen had. Still, she'd need a Tesla Battery to operate it properly, but I didn't see one lying around.

"A bonus for your helpful hints early on in the investigation."

"Much appreciated, Elias."

"We good?"

"We're good. All favours paid." She gave a whistle as the front door was opened by someone from the other side. As I passed by, I glanced over at him and recognized his face. He'd nearly broken my arm a few days back at GE. He still had his security uniform on, with the wireless radio attached to his vest. That explained why I hadn't ended up in the slammer of some other precinct after getting Jaeger's information.

I turned back to her. "It seems you have your hand in everything."

"As I've told you, we have ears where we cannot see, and eyes where there is nothing to hear."

"Fine. One last question. The Red-eye at the speakeasy, the one that got domed when I tried to question it at the warehouse. Who was that? Did it work for you?"

"I have no idea what you're talking about." I couldn't tell whether she was bluffing or telling the truth — but then again, when could I?

"Goodnight, Elias. And give my regards to Allen. I feel that he will be invaluable in the future, for both you and me."

"*It*, you mean."

Back in my own apartment, I could hear the sounds of shuffling and moving as the Eye's cronies began to pack up and evacuate the borrowed apartment. I dropped my bloody coat on the floor. The gold bricks in the pockets most likely dented the wooden floor beneath the carpet. This was the first time I'd finished a case without feeling like I needed a drink. I figured it was getting better. At least, I hoped it was. I needed a shower, and maybe some dinner. I could always get someone to bring me something. I was in no mood to leave tonight.

Then the phone rang.

Please don't let this be another Night Call. I approached the table and lifted the receiver. "Talk."

"Good evening, Detective Roche."

Speak of the devil. Hard to mistake that voice and tone, even through these goddamn wires.

"Allen, yeah. What's going on?"

"I was just curious about what to do now, seeing as

our case is closed. Should I stay at the precinct and file paperwork?"

The damn machine was perky, I'd give it that. Didn't skip a beat. It had pulled a lot of its own weight, and most of mine at times. I couldn't be ungrateful, not after tonight. "No, get home and get some rest, Allen. Everything we did was off the record. There isn't any paperwork for us to fill out. I'll grab you tomorrow."

"Tomorrow? For what?"

"I have some business to attend to around the city, prepping for Night Calls and visiting some old friends. If you'd like to tag along, I think you could help."

There was silence for several seconds. "Detective, does this mean we'll be working together on more cases?"

"Yeah, Allen. I'll get you at seven, partner."

"Thank you, Detective."

A click followed its last words as the phone line went dead. I dropped the receiver onto the phone base, walked to the bathroom, and began to strip for the shower. Something about saying *partner* had felt like a weight off my chest. Why? Maybe because of James. Allen couldn't ever replace James, but neither could dwelling on James bring him back.

It back.

But we'd see how the new duo would work out. Allen and me. Partners.

Yeah, I think I could get used to that.

For now at least.

CHAPTER 21

THE STATION WAS BUZZING. Two weeks after the impromptu FBI inspections had finished, there was a happy, colourful atmosphere around the Lower City. The murder rate was at an all-time low for the 5th. I couldn't say the same for midtown Manhattan, though; their murder rates might have doubled or tripled to even us out. Sinclair was reclining in his little chair, feet on his desk and a cigarette in his fingers. Allen had its own desk, too. Unlike everyone else, though, it was actually doing work. It probably went through more paperwork in one day than the whole precinct had in the past year. Maybe that was why Robins had recruited it. Who knew? Keeping me in check couldn't have been the only reason.

Rain was falling outside, and the heaters on the Plate spooled up enough to keep the winter chill away from the heart of the Upper City, melting the frozen water into a torrential downpour. Sure, it was unusual to see rain in late November, but it beat shovelling snow, or having the Upper City dump it on us.

"You coming to the next poker night, Roche? Pot is twenty bucks this time, meaning whoever wins has one hell of a good week ahead of them." Sinclair was enjoying the lull in work, catching up on some rest in his free time.

"Maybe. Depends how much work I got. For all I know, Allen and I could get a surprise Night Call."

"If I remember correctly, Detective Roche, you receive more than one dozen Night Calls per week, though why you answer the select few is beyond my comprehension."

To my disdain, Allen was capable of multitasking. Its criticism of me never seemed to end.

"Not the time, Allen."

Did I really get that many? How many times had the phone rung while I was passed out? At least Allen was there now to pick up the phone now and then. I turned back to Sinclair and continued.

"Besides, I shouldn't be drinking. That bullet wound is still healing. It took out a piece of my leg that I was quite fond of."

"I'm surprised you're even standing, let alone coming into the office. You got some good stuff, eh?"

"Sure is. No clue *what* it is, though. Spray-on skin, for all I know."

"Actually, Detectives, the Syneal substance is a latticework of polymer fibres that form a synthetic layer of silicon-based platelets and fibrin threads, decreasing healing time tenfold," Allen said smugly. Maybe it was showing me up, or maybe it was just informing me. I hoped it was the latter.

"Thanks, Allen."

"Anytime, Detective Roche." Allen turned its head and returned to the paperwork without skipping a beat.

"Anyway, Paddy, things have been relatively quiet, but it's like a tsunami. It all comes back eventually."

"Don't worry about it too much. You may be an anxious bastard, but sometimes you shouldn't question a good thing." Sinclair laughed.

I leaned against Allen's desk, folding my arms and trying to relax, if even for a moment. I deserved some relaxation after this past case. It might do me some good.

"It's almost Christmas," Sinclair mentioned. "Just over a month left. You got anything planned? Any resolutions for the big three-four?"

"Same as every year. Maybe get a nice imported bottle of Scotch and drink it in front of my window. Maybe get out of the city for the first time in two years. Or splurge and trick out the Talbot. She's been making some concerning noises."

Then the tsunami hit with a crash as the doors of the precinct were thrown open.

Three figures entered, their features obscured by heavy coats and rain hats. They brushed past us, the wind from outside swinging the doors open again, rain soaking the floor near the entrance. Robins must have felt some strange vibe, because although it was impossible to hear the front doors from his office, he appeared in the main area before any one of us could blink. I could have sworn I saw his face turn white.

"What did you do, Jeffrey Robins?" asked the figure in the lead. The voice was feminine, but gravelly.

"W-what?" Robins looked surprised, to the say the least.

"You know damn well what! I have no clue what this little conglomerate of idiots has been doing recently, but as soon as your business starts branching into the Upper City, it becomes *my* business."

She removed her coat and hat, and finally I got a good look at who we were dealing with. The grey streaks in her dark-brown hair reflected the light from the dim overhead bulbs. She could've been in her early fifties, or maybe she was older, and all the fieldwork kept her going instead of sitting and rotting like most other desk jockeys.

Yup … we were in for one hell of a time, with her here.

"Well, first of all, what did I supposedly do?" Robins said, trying to reclaim dominance in the argument without success.

"Well, Jeffrey, I received a report that Agent Ewalt had returned to the Bureau with the team of agents, but his superior, Agent Masters, was missing. We prepared a formal reprimand for our senior agent's negligence, but then, a Rotorbird pilot mentioned that he'd been instructed to pick up Agent Masters at a specified location two weeks before. However, upon arriving, the area was locked down by a police Rotorbird securing a crime scene."

Sinclair's face went white, and he sucked harder on his cigarette.

She continued: "So, we went down there to check out the area and see if there was indeed a crime scene. But no such crime scene existed, nor had one existed within the last six months. We even questioned some civilians, who confirmed that there hadn't been a police presence in that area on that specific day. We questioned the pilot, and found out the exact location where he was supposed to meet Masters. Lo and behold, in the very building Agent Masters was supposed to be picked up from, we found this."

One of the Black Hats accompanying her in passed her a folder; she in turn handed it to Robins.

I knew right away that there were pictures in it, and soon got a confirmation when Robins went green. For a split second, his eyes darted to me, then they spun around so the Black Hats wouldn't get any ideas about who he suspected.

I knew what he was probably thinking: *What the actual fuck did you do, Roche?*

"Not used to seeing blood, Jeffrey?"

"N-no." He stood erect, trying to avoid her eyes. "Christ, who would do this?"

"I thought you might know."

"Of course I don't. I would never condone something like this!"

"Perhaps I was wrong. Old habits, you know." She grabbed the folder and handed it back to her associate. "The body was about two weeks old when we found it, which puts time of death at about the same time those inspections were being conducted and Masters supposedly went AWOL. We're still trying to figure out which police Rotorbird was the one that prevented the other pilot from landing, so I wanted to come down here and inspect yours personally. I hope that's all right with you, Jeffrey."

"Yeah, okay, of course. Jesus."

I'd never seen Robins so shocked before. He'd seen his buddies die in the Great War, and he barely blinked when talking about his own service. He'd seen cop killings, perps torn apart by machine gun fire, and Suppression Rifle shots. That meant that what I'd done was worse than all that, which was hard to believe.

Had I gone too far this time?

She looked Robins up and down for several moments. An uneasy silence followed as he regained his composure, only to be crushed by her gaze.

"You look like you've been under a lot of stress. You look older than usual …"

Robins didn't respond. Was he subdued by her, or by what he'd seen in those pictures?

She was turning to leave when she caught sight of me. I doubted it was a pleasant surprise. Her eyes narrowed, and she walked over. I hadn't believed there was anyone out there scarier than the Eye, but it seemed I was wrong. "Sergeant Roche, I thought you left the Force back in '28. I'm surprised to see you here."

"A lot of surprises have been happening recently. What's one more?"

"This is one too many. And maybe not so much a surprise as an ill-timed coincidence." She looked me over.

My legs were trembling, and I felt my heart racing. She had a soul-crushing presence, a stare that could burn through steel. She grabbed my vest with her left hand and peeled it back to reveal the silver handle of my revolver. "A Diamondback. I'd ask you for a permit, but we both know it's illegal, don't we, *Mister* Roche?"

"To be completely accurate, it is illegal, but in the hands of a registered police officer," Allen said, coming over to join us. "The guidelines state that an officer may carry and use any handheld firearm as long as its calibre does not exceed a .45-inch diameter." Had it been monitoring the situation the entire time? Whatever it was doing, it had better tread carefully.

The woman raised an eyebrow, surprised. "Well, well, well," she said, "a Blue-eye in the 5th. Well done, robot. But I'm afraid that guideline was removed from the police handbook in 1929, after he *left*. I don't suppose that the handbook also covers officers in possession of powerful war relics?"

Allen remained quiet, looking at me as if asking for assistance. I shook my head. It turned back to her and said confidently, "No, ma'am, though I can vouch for Detective Roche's efficacy and restraint. I believe your argument is based upon surface concepts alone, not evidence and circumstantial observation."

"*Detective* Roche, is it?" She turned to me, cocking an eyebrow. "High praise for one lower than a gun for hire. And *you*." She turned back to Allen. "Do *not* counter-argue me, machine. You've got some balls."

"I believe I am allowed to make a valid point to refute your claims and support my partner against your accusations —"

"Allen!" I barked.

It stopped talking.

Her eyes had narrowed upon Allen's referring to me as its "partner." Maybe I could still surprise people.

She turned back to the commissioner. "Where is your bird, Jeffrey?"

"It's out. Patrolling," he stammered.

"Uh-huh. We'll be back later, then. Have a good evening, gentlemen. If anything else comes up, do inform me. I'll be in touch. You can be sure of that."

Allen and I walked over to the door to watch as she and her cronies hopped into a Bugatti Type 41 Royale and roared off. How she'd gotten her hands on that kind of vehicle was beyond me.

The general hubbub of the station began to return to normal, but the three of us — Robins, Sinclair, and I — just stood there silently, staring at Allen. I doubted it had any idea to whom it had been speaking

Sinclair was the only one of us who'd kept his lips sealed from the moment she'd entered the station. If only the rest of us had followed his lead.

Suddenly Robins let out a sort of growl, and before I knew it, he had me up against the wall, his hand grasping my collar. "Jesus H. Fuck, Roche! You did *that* to the perp? No, not just a perp, an agent! He looked like a cracked egg! How did you think this would go down? Did you not think that *she* might show up?"

"Well …" I fumbled for words and looked around, feeling caught in a corner yet again. "I had to set an example, right? No mercy for cop killers, no matter who they are."

"But an agent? This time it really does matter who

you killed, and how. Fuck, Roche, I knew you were reckless, but *this* ..."

"At least you didn't know about it, which made it that much more convincing when you denied any involvement."

"Do you feel *nothing* about this?" he shouted. "Not just for putting us in danger, but for this kind of violence? Nothing?"

It was the first time in a long time that I wasn't able to answer a question. On the one hand, sure, I had gone overboard by splitting him open with a pipe. These days, the smell of blood made my stomach churn more than it had used to. But on the other hand: no cop killer could go unpunished, period.

Masters's question kept creeping back: *You think keeping her in power saves lives?* That was what I kept telling myself.

Robins released his hold on me and turned on Allen, pushing it back, though less violently than he had me. "And *you*!"

"Yes, Commissioner?"

"Don't you *ever* use that tone with her again, not unless the next thing you want to see is the inside of a recycler. And she won't be the one to put you in there. Do you understand me?"

I could tell Allen was attempting to figure out what specifically he had done to make Robins so angry. Poor thing — it really had no idea.

"I understand," Allen said, "and I will not attempt any more insinuating or otherwise aggravating dialogues with her."

"You've got no clue who she is, do you?"

"No, Commissioner, I am quite ignorant as to the weight of my actions."

Robins seemed to calm down on hearing that. He let go of Allen, backed up, and leaned against Sinclair's desk. "Right," he sighed. "I should have explained this to you in training. But I figured everyone knew. Guess you skipped that history lesson."

"I am up-to-date with most Lower City officials, though her face is unfamiliar to me."

"She ain't a Lower City official, Allen. She's head of the FBI, and the second most powerful person in this city after Mayor Bowsher. She's been heading the departments since '25 and was one of the first people to put her feet on the metal of the Plate when it was opened for business. Our motto here is 'the less Greaves knows, the better,' and for good reason."

"Greaves?"

"Eva Greaves, if you need an actual name to search. Hard to miss her, what with her being the first female director — and the most ruthless — in the history of the organization."

"I suspect Greaves is her maiden name, before and after she was married?"

Everyone's eyebrows popped up at that comment, and Robins stumbled for words. "Do you ever *think* about what you're about to say, or even *hear* yourself? You can't say shit like that!"

"I was simply noting the faded, pale spot on the fourth finger of her left hand, indicating the presence of an object that prevented melanin from being produced in that area. This would have been caused by an object obscuring the sun's rays for a significant length of time — most likely a wedding ring. The current absence of the object would suggest that she is divorced. I cannot safely assume who her spouse was …" Allen looked around at us, coming to realize what it might be implying. "But I believe it is best that I do not know as of this moment."

"Great. Fantastic. Just get out there and do something, anything. I need a drink."

Robins lumbered into his office, leaving us three to our own devices. Sinclair was still too shocked to even speak, and waved goodbye to us as he drew a bottle out from the recesses of his desk.

———

Going for a drive seemed like the best thing to do after that little stunt, and Allen was only too happy to slide into the passenger seat beside me. Despite those unblinking blue lights not giving anything away, I figured I knew what it was thinking.

"You knew exactly what was up, and you caught yourself for the first time, didn't you?"

"Correct, Detective. It seems you are more observant than I initially thought."

I decide to let that insult slide.

"To answer your question, yes, she was married to Robins. It's not the best thing to parse through, though. Lord knows he'd have an aneurysm if people found out about their past. And, before you ask: no, they don't hate each other. It's just that … well, Robins takes his job very seriously, more seriously than he took her. But I'm glad you were able to keep it to yourself for once. Just don't mention it again. Ever."

"I understand, Detective Roche. And I believe that getting far away from the station for the time being would be an intelligent move on both our parts."

I had to laugh at that. It was learning *very* fast.

"Exactly, Allen. But before we go, I have to thank you." It turned to me with a look of what appeared to be surprise. "I know it's a sensitive subject to bring up, but it's been a few weeks, and I feel like this would be a safe time to mention it again. You saved both Paddy and me back at the warehouse. I'm not good with being open to anyone, really — especially not metal men — but had you not done what you did ... I'd be fucking dead. And even before that, if I had never stumbled into the office after seeing Prince and Greene, if you'd never come with us on the raid, and if you'd never talked me down after that chase in Times Square, I probably wouldn't be here.

"Even if I had survived the Rotorbird crashing after firing the Suppression Rifle, I would have shot Belik on sight without realizing that he wasn't the one who shot those cops. Hell, I might have killed Jaeger on sight just for the implication that his Automatic was at the speakeasy during the killing. There were too many factors going on at the time. But it was you — a weird-ass 'not-robot' — that kept things from going from bad to totally fucked up. So, thank you, Allen, for being a restless, unrelenting, irritating, and persistent wannabe police officer, and for keeping me from flying too far off the handle. Thank you for doing ... what a partner should do."

Allen looked at me in stunned silence. It seemed awkward silence would be another hurdle for us to overcome ... or perhaps it was another way we could really communicate.

"You are quite welcome, Detective," it finally said. "I will do my utmost to become more acclimated to your expectations."

"Well, don't get too hard-nosed on me. I need some-one who looks at things in a different way. Without you being yourself, I doubt we would have come into pos-session of half the evidence we did. So, don't stray too much from how you are. Just maybe learn that there's a time and a place for everything, all right?"

"Of course, Detective.... I did have one last question about that case. When Masters was supposedly broad-casting that signal to control those Automatic shells, how did he specifically target those Automatics and not all others in the vicinity?"

"No clue, Allen. At this point, the machine is busted, so I can confidently say that it doesn't matter in the slightest."

Allen nodded, not completely satisfied with the answer. "What is our plan now?"

"Head home, wait for a decent Night Call, then do our jobs. And by Night Call, I mean one that *isn't* from some dame with a missing puppy. It is pretty late, though. Dinner?"

"There is a restaurant on the border of SoHo and Manhattan's Anchor that serves fine Italian dishes, and it is quite good in my opinion."

"Then let's get dinner. I'll treat. After all, I just got one hell of a paycheck."

The Eye was ever so good with timing, and an additional five figures in the bank was the perfect excuse to celebrate.

"And after we eat, should we get back to work?"

"Of course, Allen. Back to being the saviours of this city. It never changes, and neither should we."

EPILOGUE

THIS PLACE WAS SYNONYMOUS with death. It oozed death from every recess. It had sat vacant for years, with no one daring to enter. I'd had to come back, though.

Most of the roof had collapsed, allowing the lights from the top of the Plate to seep in to illuminate the normally pitch-black corners. The corpses had long ago been devoured by rats. Now clothes hung loosely on bone. It didn't even smell of rot anymore, just the earthiness of dust and ashes.

In the centre of the room lay the rusted remains of a single Automatic, riddled with enough bullets to cleave it nearly in half across its midsection. His eyes were cracked and broken, with evidence that another clean round had passed through the head. It was here that I decided to sit, dragging over an old rotting barrel for a seat.

"Hey, James, it's been a while ... too long. I had a feeling you might still be here."

I pulled out my pack of darts and offered it to the old corpse. I nodded after a second and withdrew them. "I'm still trying to quit.... So is Paddy — Patrick, sorry. You don't like it when I call him Paddy. I only smoke when I'm nervous now ... which is more often than you'd think these days."

He wasn't much of a talker anymore. Not a problem. He was a good listener.

"I got a new partner. Allen, I call him — 41-EN is his serial number. *Its*. Its serial number, sorry." I pulled out a cigarette and lit it. "Had a case where a G-man was pulling the strings on a racketeering group trying to go up against the Iron Hands. He ... well, he didn't make it. This wasn't just another victim, though. This one got in my head, made me think about what I've been doing. He was trying to take them down and crossed paths with me. You think I've gone off the deep end? You think Robins is the formality preventing me from going all the way down the rabbit hole?"

No response.

I got off the barrel and knelt beside him, putting my hand on his metal back. "I went to the Plate ... first time in ages. Saw a diagram made by the guy who's head of GE. See ... the FBI guy was controlling machines using their Cortexes, some little bit of tech near where your shoulder blades would meet. Controls how you move and whatever. Turns out the Neural-Interface doesn't do much without it."

I pulled some of the metal off his carapace, lifted a section of his metal exterior, and searched the circuitry. I found the small device that I thought was the

Cortex — octagonal, sleek, and shimmering gold in colour. It was rusted and had pockmarks all over, seeing as it had been sitting here for almost five years. I ripped it from the wires and dropped it on the ground, then ground it down with my heel. He didn't seem to mind.

"There ... now I know you're really dead."

I dropped my dart and crushed it along with the remains of James's Cortex, mixing the ashes with the bits of silicon and steel. "I'll see you later, James. Maybe ... I don't know. Hold down the fort for me, will ya?"

I walked to the open door of the factory, turned back for one final glimpse of his shell, then pulled the door shut behind me.